THE SUBMISSION GALLERY

It was as if he was punishing her for being desirable and yet unobtainable through her absolute compliance. She could not be tamed, or made his own, and dreams of her beauty and pain would haunt his sleep for the rest of his life. This self-imposed vulnerability at the hands of a stranger seemed tantamount to insanity, but the pain and humiliation did nothing but thrill her. With each successive blow, she was giving everything to the barbaric – relinquishing independence for a moment of primal hunger. From this, her next piece of art would come.

A NEXUS CLASSIC

THE SUBMISSION GALLERY

Lindsay Gordon

This book is a work of fiction.
In real life, make sure you practise safe, sane
and consensual sex.

This Nexus Classic edition published in 2006

First published in 1999 by
Nexus
Thames Wharf Studios
Rainville Road
London W6 9HA

www.nexus-books.co.uk

Typeset by TW Typesetting, Plymouth, Devon

Printed and bound by
Clays Ltd, St Ives PLC

ISBN 0 352 34026 6
ISBN 9 780352 340269

Prologue

Exclusive lingerie producer requires guinea pig to test luxurious garment range. Opportunity to wear the world's most expensive boudoir attire. Generous gratuity on completion of contract. Send CV, recent photograph, sizes and short biography to:

Sheen Couture
PO Box 966
Agrippa Building
Darkling Town
DKY 7PG

Dark Chic: The Magazine for Modern Women,
October 2020

One

November 1 2020
Sheen Couture
PO Box 966
Agrippa Building
Darkling Town
DKY 7PG

Ms Poppy Stanton
Flat 20
Crowley Tower
Darkling Town
DKY R18

Dear Ms Stanton,

Congratulations on your selection to test Sheen Couture's latest range of exclusive, tailor-made garments. Your instructions are simple:

1) Wear all of the garments as part of your normal life.

2) Do not launder them. This is very important. Our own dermatological department will carry out tests on the lingerie.

3) Once each item has been worn, seal and return them in the package provided to the above address (postage is enclosed).

Providing you follow the instructions to the full, your gratuity on completion of the contract will be 10,000 credits. An advance of 2,000 is enclosed.

Please sign and return the paperwork. We hope you enjoy the first instalment.

Yours sincerely,

Eleanor Ruperts
(Head of Fabric Development)

Two

'Magnificent.'

'Yes. It's depraved, though sensual.'

'The face is masked, but I can sense the anguish.'

'And the pleasure.'

'The pleasure?'

'Yes, the pleasure. See how the back arches and the toes curl. If it could speak, I am sure the gagged mouth would be trying to scream in both defiance and ecstasy.'

From a distance, Poppy watched the two art critics with amusement. On the marble floor, under soft white lighting, they circled her sculpture, bending down to squint at certain details before straightening to make sweeping gestures with their arms. An audience gathered around the critics to stare at her exhibit as if never having seen anything so obscene, and curiously pleasing, in a respectable art gallery.

The Frenchman, who had declared her work 'magnificent', began to play with his bow tie. Impulsively, he stretched out his hand to stroke the sculpture. The fingers paused, an inch from the latex-wrapped figure, and his face reddened. Suddenly, he retracted the arm and glanced about to see if anyone had seen his loss of control. No one cared. They were all ready to do the same thing – to touch Poppy's shining figurine.

Art students, members of the public and several journalists added themselves to the growing throng of

4

admirers, all staying silent save for the occasional whisper drifting across to Poppy in the cool air of the Daemonic Gallery.

'Who is the artist?' someone muttered to their neighbour.

'No one knows. They prefer to remain anonymous, which is no surprise,' the French critic said.

His colleague nodded. 'The skin is so lifelike. If the limbs weren't so static, I could swear a real woman hides under the rubber.'

Poppy watched a woman in the audience trace her painted nails around her left breast. Another man knotted his fingers together and muttered something to himself as if in the middle of a prayer.

Alone on a wooden bench, near the crowd, Poppy sat smiling. Draped in black with her pretty face veiled, she closed her eyes and relished the moment. I've waited my whole life for this. Has it happened? Have I finally created something of significance?

This was her first piece of work to be exhibited. The *Loving Captive* sculpture had already been reviewed in three major newspapers and on its second day in the Daemonic Gallery, the crowds amassed again.

Inspiration for the piece had come quickly, exploding in her mind before racing through her long limbs until it tingled in every finger and toe, leaving the rest of her shaking. For days, she had worked like a madwoman, fasting and sleeping for only an hour or so until it was complete. Never had she worked so quickly or discovered so much of her darkest and most intimate self before exposing it in sculpture. The vision of a woman, contorted, bound, cuffed at the ankle and wrist, gagged, hooded, and left in an obscene position, had obsessed her. When it was complete, she knew part of her soul was inside it.

'You have touched something in all of them.' It was the cultured voice of a woman that crept up from behind. Poppy broke from her daze and turned her head to see a tall, thin woman smiling down at her. She had a noble face – almost gaunt but beautiful in a cold way – and her

5

discreetly shaded eyelids narrowed over bitter-blue eyes, possessing a scrutiny that made Poppy squirm. Instinctively, she lowered her face as if before a queen and the woman laughed, making a sound like ice chimes.

As she spoke, the slow movements of her lips and bright teeth seemed to mesmerise Poppy. 'See the shock and fear on all those faces when presented with a glimpse of the forbidden. But look a little closer, my dear, and you will see their desire too. They're hypnotised, every one of them. Each woman before the *Loving Captive* feels something tighten inside her. Each man experiences a moment of lust that frightens him. But they are all left baffled. Do you feel responsibility for creating so much longing in ordinary people?'

Poppy raised her eyebrow. 'What makes you think I'm the artist?'

The woman laughed again and, without invitation, sat close to her on the bench. A polar fire seemed to ignite and dance inside the woman's eyes, animating her whole face with excitement. And then the smile vanished, quickly, beneath the imperious forehead and fine bones of her face. 'News spreads quickly in this city when an original talent appears. The moment I arrived yesterday and saw the *Loving Captive*, I began to wonder who the artist was, and what she would look like. You see, I was sure it was not a man who created this masterpiece but a woman. A girl either experienced or deeply curious about the art of submission.' The woman paused and clenched her hands together. 'I had to know the identity of the artist, to congratulate her. So I decided to wait, like a relentless detective, expecting the criminal to return to the scene of her delicious crime. Today, intuition informed me the beautiful young woman, sitting alone, was the genius behind the creation. And here you are, my dear, unable to stay away from the epicentre of the shock waves you are already sending through the art world.'

Poppy stiffened and moved away from the woman.

The stranger smiled. 'Only someone who understands grace and sensuality could make torment look so enticing. Someone who loves the dark, dressed in black, who prefers

6

the moon to the sun. I sensed she would be beautiful, sensitive, maybe shy. A lone wolf. Privately suffering in some grim studio –'

It was as if the stranger were clairvoyant. 'You're just guessing. Those are all assumptions,' Poppy said.

She wanted to stay anonymous. Just as her new direction began, a glare of attention and notoriety would spoil the privacy she required to imagine and create greater extremes of passion. Instinct told her the *Loving Captive* sculpture was merely the first step towards an incredible and terrifying destiny. 'You are mistaken. I'm not even creative,' she said.

'Oh yes you are. Look at your clothes –' the woman stretched out a hand, gloved in soft leather, and stroked Poppy's coat '– furs, pearls, hat and veil, patent leather boots. Perhaps if you wished to stay anonymous, it would have been better to wear something more discreet.'

Poppy felt her face flush hot. She stayed quiet and turned away from the woman.

'Forgive me. I have been overzealous,' the stranger said, softening her tone. 'It was not my wish to make you feel uncomfortable, but to applaud you. I adore your work. Please don't turn away. Listen to me. I understand the mind of the artist. I have been a patron of unique and sometimes obscure talents for years. And it's a delight to see one so young with such honesty in her work. It takes courage. Nothing is jeopardised by my speaking to you. I also value discretion.'

The woman reached for Poppy's hand and squeezed her pale fingers, firing a little charge of electricity up her arm. She moved closer and crossed her slender legs, pointing the toes of her high-heeled shoes towards Poppy's feet.

Discreetly, Poppy eyed the woman's long skirt. It was black and hugged her legs to mid-calf. Two shapely ankles, hugged by sheer black nylon, were cradled by dagger-heeled shoes.

Perhaps she would understand.

'I only wished to inquire about the inspiration, nothing more,' the stranger whispered.

'It's a secret,' Poppy replied.

7

'A secret? I love secrets. And what a secret it must be. A young sculptor portrays the body of a woman mummified in black rubber, with her limbs manacled by the most elegant chains, and her behind raised in supplication to . . . Well, I suppose that is left to the imagination. Maybe, if I offered you the best of luncheons, you would entertain a little more of my curiosity.'

'Who are you?' Poppy asked.

'Baroness Nin,' the stranger replied.

'Have you eaten enough?' the baroness asked.

Poppy smiled at her host. 'Yes. Thank you.'

Reclining, with a crystal glass of claret in one hand, she allowed a vast red chair to engulf her body as she continued to survey Nin's opulent dining room. Like the rest of the apartment, in the exclusive southern end of Darkling Town, the room was furnished with an eccentric but expensive taste. There was a life-sized photograph of Betty Page being tied down by a blonde girl above the fireplace, and an Aubrey Beardsley print beside a marble sculpture of two blindfolded women making love.

'You like my home?' Nin asked.

'Very much,' Poppy replied, feeling sleepy and drugged, snug amongst thick crimson throw-rugs.

A few feet away, on the chaise longue, Baroness Nin rearranged her shiny legs, angled her head, and began moving a long fingernail up and down her shin. 'So tell me more about yourself, my dear. I believe we struck a bargain back at the gallery.'

'What do you want to know?'

'Have you been exhibited elsewhere?'

'No. I've been overlooked since art college. I was nearly homeless in London. Practically destitute, a failure, so I moved to Darkling Town this year to take a cheaper studio. It's a sad story with a Cinderella ending.'

'Oh, there is a Prince Charming?'

'Not exactly.'

The baroness leant forward on her seat, her eyes widening. 'Go on.'

'I received a gift that changed my luck by giving me a new direction. I still don't understand how.'

'A gift inspired you?'

'Yes. Even my dreams changed. They became sort of darker, and I began the *Loving Captive* piece, using a manikin I adapted with other materials. Now, I think my fortunes are about to change.'

Nin laughed and dug her nails into the antique couch, while her eyes flicked from Poppy's breasts to her legs. 'Evasive creature. The gift. What was it? From whom did it come? An admirer? I am sure you have many of those. A lover?'

'No. The gift came from an exclusive manufacturer, who wants me to test a product.'

Baroness Nin frowned. 'Really? I don't understand. What could you have received to inspire that masterpiece. A drug?'

Excited by the attention and feeling reckless after three glasses of wine, Poppy rose from her chair and stood before the baroness with her booted feet set apart. Bending over, she pinched the hem of her leather skirt. 'Do you really want to see my inspiration?'

Taken aback, the baroness said nothing but nodded her head once.

'And you promise to remain discreet?'

The baroness nodded again.

Maybe it was the rich food or wine, the eccentric company or decadent surroundings, perhaps a playful desire to flirt with this handsome madam, but Poppy never knew what prompted her to raise her skirt around her waist. She didn't think. Instead, she obeyed an urge – the same impetuous feeling that told her how to create the *Loving Captive*.

After a deft movement, Poppy's undergarments and legs were on display. From her feet to her knees, her long legs were bound by skin-tight leather boots. A pair of invisibly sheer stockings rose to the tops of her thighs, sparkling with a sheen and lustre in the dim afternoon light. Golden suspender clasps gripped her stocking tops, and through

9

the frontal slit in the transparent French knickers Poppy's blonde sex peeked out. Turning on her heels, she revealed her taut buttocks, enhanced by see-through gossamer. Another slit, above her concealed anus, exceeded the daring of its vaginal counterpart.

'These pretty things gave me the idea for the *Loving Captive*. Silly, isn't it?' she said, tipsy and giggling.

Silence filled the dining room.

Poppy began to lower her skirt.

'No!' Nin cried out. Poppy froze and the baroness softened her voice. 'Please, let me look for just a moment longer.'

Standing still with her skirt raised, Poppy heard the squeak of a spring. Turning her head, she watched the baroness move off the couch, approach, and then slip to her knees. While rocking back on her heels, close to Poppy's legs, the baroness muttered something to herself and her cool breath washed between Poppy's inner thighs. A look of ecstasy quivered on the older woman's face. When the baroness spoke, it was as if she were talking to someone else in the room. 'Beautiful. Made for a sinner with a mind destined for more than mediocrity. They make her feel more feminine than she could ever imagine. Maybe she wears them only to entice the fiercer passions of others.'

Poppy let her skirt fall and stepped away from the baroness, unsure of the dark waters she now waded through. But her reticence seemed only to increase the baroness's excitement. 'I'm afraid the informality of this luncheon must end, my dear. I have something valuable to add to this creative rebirth you seem to be enjoying. With luck, you'll see it as a gift.'

'What are you saying?' Poppy asked nervously, and took several steps away from her smiling hostess, who rose to her feet and strolled across to the dining-room doors. There was a heavy clunking sound and the doors were locked.

A cold but exhilarating fear grew through Poppy. Too shocked to react, she did nothing more than stand and watch the baroness pocket a heavy brass key.

'I'm sorry, Poppy,' she said. 'Sorry for the way I feel, but you're so precious. And I can help you. Make everything so much clearer for you. Believe me.'

Poppy stayed mute. Crushed ice seemed to be thickening inside every artery and vein. Something caught in her throat and she swallowed with difficulty.

'Poppy,' the baroness spoke as if she were talking to a child, approaching with her arms outstretched. 'There is no crime in being one of those rare and beautiful creatures who is excited by unusual cravings. As long as there is secrecy and guile what is wrong with satisfying your appetite? All you need is a suitable tutor. It can only help your art.'

Poppy glanced behind at the statue of the two female lovers, with their marble limbs entwined and long claws scratching. 'Please,' she said in a weak voice. 'I think you're mistaken. I wasn't thinking and should never have come here. It was not my intention to entice you.'

Breathing quickly, the baroness closed on Poppy, until she'd cornered her guest against a couch. Long fingers closed around Poppy's shoulders and held her trembling body still. The baroness narrowed the divide between their glossy lips. 'Poppy, I only want to aid you in exploring this new sensuality, your new beginning. Let art become life.'

Unable to think straight, Poppy felt a part of herself giving in to the fingernails trailing across her throat and jaw. As the handsome woman pressed forward, her hard nipples brushed against Poppy's tender breasts and her moist lips kissed Poppy's small ears and blew tendrils of blonde hair off her cheeks. 'There is no one here to see or hear us, Poppy, so relax. Are you not curious about your sculpture and the life you gave it?'

Looking towards the locked door, Poppy tried to pull away but was held fast by the baroness's hands.

'Did you not imagine yourself as a loving captive when you shaped it with your hands?'

'Maybe,' Poppy whispered.

'Did you not think of strange and assertive hands in the night? Of the danger and pleasure they may bring?'

Poppy was unable to speak. Her skin shivered and her strength seemed to be passing out from her body and through her lingerie. Feeling powerless, she closed her eyes and felt a part of herself slipping towards an abyss. With this odd but beautiful woman's body pressed against her, it was as if something were opening inside her – a vast virginal cavity waiting to be filled with a special kind of experience.

'Did you not imagine every second of your sculpture's bondage and pain and delight?' The woman's voice was inside her head now, dissolving her fear and caution. The fingers tightened around her shoulders and an expensive scent filled her sinuses. In the dark, she felt a small tongue taste her lips.

'I – I think so,' Poppy whispered, and opened her eyes.

A smile of satisfaction spread across the baroness's beautiful face. 'I saw you looking at my clothes in the gallery. You were curious about me, willing to play with a more experienced woman's affection. You enjoyed flirting with me. Am I right?'

Poppy blushed and whispered, 'I don't know.'

Suddenly, the baroness whipped her hand backward and let it descend to strike Poppy's hot face. A thousand refreshing starbursts of shock and pain obliterated her vision and she was pushed down to her knees.

Gasping and overcome with shock, as if plunged into icy water, Poppy shook her head. When her vision cleared, she watched the baroness step out of her hobble-skirt.

With her legs set wide apart, and her cruel nails digging into her own thighs, the baroness stood victoriously above Poppy, who could do nothing more than gape and hold her stinging cheek.

The woman's skin was brilliantly white around her black leather corset, and her toned legs, misted by dark nylons, drew Poppy's eyes to the hard triangle of the satin panties, submerged between eight suspender straps – four to each thigh.

Smiling, the baroness released her raven hair from a bun on the back of her head and let it sway across her cheekbones. 'Every artist with a vocation must fall before discovering their true genius. Poets compose from experience and so must you. Sweet Poppy, taste the bottom of your new world.'

Poppy tried to rise to her feet but was caught off-balance and pushed on to her back by the baroness's heel. Above her, the shining stiletto was removed and a slippery foot was placed over her face.

Writhing on the floor, Poppy snatched breaths through an exotic perfume of leather, nail polish and nylon, while her hands automatically shot up to grip the Baroness's calf muscle.

The baroness smiled. 'Lick the foot of your first mistress. There will be others, so accustom yourself to the ritual.'

Beneath her creased clothes, Poppy's underwear suddenly felt as if it were shrinking to bind her and her boots seemed unreasonably heavy. When something slithered forward in her mind to moan for humiliation, her tongue probed forward, tentatively, and began to glide across the heel and instep smothering her face.

A hand reached down and cold fingers entwined in the roots of her hair. Tears streamed from her eyes as she was hauled to her feet and dragged to the mistress's couch. From behind, quick hands shed her skirt and turned her sweater inside out over her head. Breathing hard, Poppy began to rotate her hips and buttocks, delighted by the sensation of this sudden vulnerability.

'A pretty slut,' the baroness said through gritted teeth. 'I know what you are. Did you think you could tempt the world with your icon of submission, while all the time you desired something hard against your young flesh? I'll teach you to flash your body in a stranger's lingerie.'

By twisting her head and peering through the loose strands of hair over her eyes, Poppy saw a white blur cut through the air above her buttocks. With a slap that echoed off the walls of the dining room, the baroness's hand met her silky backside. Pain and tingling pin-pricks of delight coursed through her. Another swish and smack followed. And then another and another.

Writing over the couch, Poppy stamped her heels and tried to raise her body with weakening arms. Light and fire spread under her punished skin and she could feel moisture gathering between her legs, at the top of her thighs.

The spanking paused when the baroness stepped away to retrieve something long and thin from a cupboard. Behind her, Poppy heard it slice the air and thought of running, but something kept her still with her buttocks raised in expectation. An exhilaration similar to the first lashing at school, and the hot flush of alarm after a pinch on the bottom by a mysterious hand in a nightclub, flowed from her memory and electrified every nerve ending on her back.

Grinding her teeth, Poppy pushed her backside towards her punisher.

The flogging was merciless.

Delivered in a flurry of strokes, the whipping razored her flesh from tailbone to golden stocking top. Fiery lashes fell evenly and rhythmically, making a wet sound she thought musical. Every inch of skin on her buttocks was consumed first by a sharp pain, which subsided to a smarting, and then became a warmth, until she felt as if her entire rear was glowing. And still the dampness of arousal seeped and spread between her thighs.

When the onslaught stopped abruptly, Poppy squinted through her briny tears and looked back at the dishevelled punisher. The woman was breathing heavily and tottering, drunkenly, on her high heels. Her hair was tousled and the pallor of her face had been invigorated by a rush of blood. One hand trailed beside her gartered thighs and gripped a bamboo cane.

Cool air buzzed around Poppy's striped cheeks. Although unable to see the damage, she knew her sheer knickers had been shredded above the swollen skin beneath.

'You have intoxicated me, girl,' the baroness whimpered. 'Forgive me. I have been a brute. I couldn't help myself.'

Poppy smiled and moistened her lips. She wanted something else to join the surface pain. The scalding

14

emotions inside her, responsible for creating the *Loving Captive*, had been set free. These feelings needed something deeper and crueller, forsaking every inhibition. Her mouth seemed to move of its own accord. A new spirit in possession of her young body began to speak. It said, 'Take me.'

'What?'

'Take me, please.'

The baroness exhaled loudly and closed her eyes. 'I . . . I have flogged her raw and yet she still submits.' Unsteady on her feet, the baroness walked to the bureau beside a large window overlooking the grey street outside. A drawer was opened and little chains and buckles clinked together as something was removed. There was a whisper of leather encircling leather and the sound of her heels returned to the couch where Poppy lay.

Unable to turn and look at the baroness's new prop, Poppy kept her eyes closed and braced herself for something she guessed would be both ruthless and thorough.

The baroness kissed at Poppy's buttocks, her tongue easing the edge off the pain. 'You beautiful mad girl,' she whispered. 'Has anyone ever stung your little, puckered rose?'

'No,' Poppy said with a sigh.

Long hands grasped her buttocks, and sharp nails found a purchase beneath her suspender belt.

'Forgive me,' Baroness Nin whispered and plunged something hard and inflexible into Poppy's tight, unbroken anus.

Three

Like the first package of lingerie, the second was delivered
by a courier, who waited outside Poppy's front door for
her signature before disappearing down five flights of stairs
to the rain-soaked world outside. This box was larger than
the first and secured by tape and twine.

Wondering what was inside and if it held the same magic
as the first sample, Poppy placed the parcel in the centre
of her one-room flat, which also served as a studio, and
positioned herself on her haunches with a bowl of sweet,
black coffee.

Radiators began to gurgle and all three bars of the
electric fire glowed hot. With the prospect of earning more
money than she had ever dreamt of, arising from the
bidding war her first sculpture had started, Poppy had put
the heating on full. The days of cold and hunger were over.

She let her dressing gown slide off her pale shoulders and
crumple on the wooden floorboards. Naked in the warm
air, above stormy Darkling Town, she felt her anticipation
mount.

Another message droned from the answering machine
behind her. It was the director of the Daemonic Gallery
informing her the papers were offering a generous sum of
money to interview the creator of the *Loving Captive*.
Everybody wanted to know if it was part of a collection,
and a new party had made an offer exceeding the first
generous bids.

With her scalpel, Poppy cut through the binding and
opened the box. While burrowing through layers of pink

16

tissue wrapping, she found five crimson-coloured parcels of different sizes which she laid on her brass-framed bed. While moving the mirror from a corner of her studio to the base of the bed, her stomach flopped over with excitement. She knew the contents of the packages would demand a dressing ritual and, if she were lucky, the garments might provide a fresh and frightening inspiration.

Inside the smallest box was a card and more tissue paper, this time red. There was a script on the card, and she recognised the words '*Enfer*' and '*Bonnetier*'. These words had been on the first pair of boxed stockings: the hose now running with ladders and clouded with stains after the baroness's onslaught the day before. Smiling to herself, Poppy remembered the luxury of the fine nylons and how they had recrafted her long legs. After peeling the tissue paper back, she rescued one of three pairs of flat stockings from the box. They were black and seamed. Holding them up to the window, she let the dim wintry light pass through the minute knit of the nylon before laying them on her duvet and opening the next box.

There was a glimpse of something shiny and black beneath the tissue paper. Poppy clasped it and pulled the strange garment free. It was an unusual garter belt with a thick waistband, designed to cover the area from sex to navel with a piece of the softest leather she'd ever touched, while the suspender clasps were heavy and crafted from silver. A pattern began to form in her mind – these black shapes were manufactured to cut and contour white skin.

Next, she unpacked the brassiere and saw that it too had been crafted from the most supple and shiny hide. In the centre of each breast-cup a hole had been made to entice a nipple through. Immediately, a little feeling of delight tightened inside her, eager to form and flow into the cold shiver of an idea for a sculpture. Would it need special nourishment?

Wasting no time, Poppy ripped into the last two packages.

The boots glistened like wet onyx as they uncurled across her hands and possessed a gloss that immediately

17

caught the eye. The first pair of knee-high boots had had zips on the sides, but these were to be laced up the front and would stretch to her stocking tops and the peaks of her legs. The heels were cruel stilettos and would push the wearer on to their toes, restricting movement and making their steps unsteady.

Inside the last parcel was an ankle-length dress that felt heavy and made a rattling sound as she pulled it from the tissue wrapping. Holding her breath, Poppy stood back and stared at a ring-mail gown.

Each hollow silver ring was no bigger than a tiny button and had been interlinked masterfully to create the cut of a stylish evening gown, offering glimpses of the wearer's body and underwear beneath.

Dare I wear it?

Carefully, she laid the dress on the bed beside the lingerie and began to feel dizzy with nerves.

Before her paint-spattered sink, Poppy prepared herself, widening the feline emerald of her eyes and enhancing the sensual cushion of her lips with cosmetics. She tied her blonde hair up, allowing two wisps to fall and tickle her throat and shoulders. After adding a pair of long crystal earrings, she felt ready for the new garments.

Kneeling on the bed before the mirror, Poppy put the brassiere on, immediately enjoying the fit that cupped and restrained her athletic breasts and made her nipples erect the moment they were encircled by leather.

Next, she slipped the garter belt around her flat belly and the suspender straps tickled her thighs as if anxious for sheer hose. Lying on her back and sinking into the mattress, Poppy rolled the black nylons down her legs from her painted toenails to her thighs, where she attached the stocking tops to the silver suspender clasps. Pointing her feet at the ceiling, she admired her own legs, on which the stockings looked like dark smoke curling around marble.

As she laced her legs inside each boot, the leather formed a clinging extra skin over her slippery calves and thighs. When she stood up to put on the dress, the inflexible grasp of the boots numbed her feet and she struggled to bend her knees, nearly losing her balance as the boot heels pushed her forward and on to her toes as if to dangle her over an edge.

Shivering, she squeezed into the metal dress and smoothed it across her hips only to feel mummified from toe to neck.

Standing before the mirror, she looked at the transformation. Only a month before, at the point of despair, she had trudged around her studio in grubby dungarees and workman's boots. Now she was a goddess, a queen, and a harlot, with a sculpture that rocked Darkling Town to its black foundations.

And her work would carry on. She felt the *Loving Captive* was merely the start of something grander. But would she need more experience, like the baroness suggested, to create something extraordinary with her second piece?

What the woman had done to Poppy had been thrilling, but how far dared she go to breathe more life into her work? It was almost as if the gifts had a price, she thought, and twirled around to admire her astonishing reflection.

Carefully, with her hands making little circles in the air for balance, she made her way to the phone and made two calls. One to the gallery to accept the highest bid for her first sculpture, and one to an art supplier for new materials. The blow torch and jeweller's tools were already in place on her workbench and only the ingredients were missing. Now, she could afford exactly what she wished and there would be no more hunting around junk shops, scrapyards and markets.

When the supplier answered her call, she reeled off a long list of her requirements, starting with stainless steel and latex.

In her mind, nightmarish ideas of the most extreme bondage began forming. With a sketch pad and stick of charcoal in hand, she took a seat on her bed. Squinting and breathing deeply in concentration, Poppy drew the silhouette of a tall woman wrapped in a latex skin. She detailed a series of chains, criss-crossing the compact breasts and shiny buttocks, before the chains led off to tugging hands that enforced her immaculate posture.

Maybe, when a certain chain is tugged the wrists can be pulled down to the ankles and her pretty head will be forced back. Perhaps she will be hung in a suspension harness, unable to resist whatever her master inflicts upon her. Yes, she thought, I'd like her to be set up high, above people's heads. As she sat and enjoyed the squeeze of her new lingerie beneath the mesh of the gown, the possibilities for going further than the *Loving Captive* seemed infinite.

When she had completed several preliminary drawings, Poppy attached them to a wall and then fell back on her bed and closed her eyes. Slowly, like a rare snake shedding its exotic skin, she slipped the gown up her body until it gathered around her waist. Knickerless, with her thighs parted, she slipped the fingers of one hand down to the furrowed lips of her sex and began administering a gentle pressure against her clit.

Squashing the tender and striped cheeks of her behind into the bed, she began to think of the smacks resounding off her body the day before. With a moan, she rolled on to her side and trapped her hand between her thighs. She closed her eyes and whipped her index finger around her pleasure bud.

With a deep groan, she imagined more forceful torments and tighter bonds on her body. And how it would feel with a man, whose body was brawny and firm, pounding in and out of her sex and anus after she'd enticed his most assertive passions forth with her sinful garments.

In her mind, she saw herself prepared exquisitely and perfumed, with only her red lips, vagina and anus exposed to whoever wished to take her, as savagely as they desired. There could be one lover, two lovers, maybe more. She could be led on a leash through the dark to something brutal. Anything was possible.

To be vulnerable, and reduced to an object of pleasure, made powerless and strangely powerful – who had explored this in sculpture? What would cuffs really feel like? How would a gag taste?

Tears filled Poppy's eyes and she made a final, throaty moan before a climax relaxed her body and left her lying on her side, sucking at her own fingers.

What's happening to me? she thought. Why do I feel so restless? Her appetite and curiosity had grown beyond anything she'd ever experienced. And caressing herself was insufficient. Denial was useless. Lunch with the baroness had opened her eyes to other possibilities.

Before her materials arrived from the art supplier, she would go out in her new finery and see what Darkling Town thought of her.

Hungry eyes followed Poppy to her table.

In the restaurant, her scent haunted the far recesses of the booths and kitchens, seeking a special kind of predator. Wafted outward by the ceiling fans, her perfume captured the attentions of many male diners, but only one of them interested her – a man with a broad and scarred face.

From where she was sitting she made sure the slit in her ring-mail gown allowed him a generous view of a booted and stocking-sheathed leg. Her smooth white neck, circled by a diamanté choker and tickled by loose strands of hair, held her face aloof as if it were indifferent to the many admiring glances, and her eyes seemed distant and unimpressed by the plush surroundings and excellent food. Sitting alone, and careful not to engage a single stare, Poppy sipped her claret and cleaned her red lips with a careful tongue.

What is he thinking? The man whose eyes have eaten me since my arrival. Is he wondering if someone is missing from my evening? Why is a young woman, in full evening dress, eating alone in Darkling Town's most exclusive restaurant? Would it be a relief to see a male partner arrive late to greet me with flowers and a kiss? Maybe that would end his misery of longing and indecision. But is he right for me?

By stealing glances at his image, reflected in a gilt-framed mirror opposite his table, she admired his shoulders and arms. They were powerful and moved slowly beneath a loose-fitting shirt, while his slicked-back hair and earrings suggested the eccentric. But it was his face that inspired her the most. It was square, tanned, and flecked with tiny scars on the cheeks. An uncompromising face. But is he capable of extremes, of going beyond the pale of normal liaisons?

Poppy hoped so, because she was hungry.

Raising her glass, she peered over the crystal rim at the diner and held his stare with her heavy-lidded eyes. Without a blush, he returned Poppy's gaze with honesty while his hands tightened around a white napkin. Unconsciously, he appeared to be pulling it taut, then knotting the cloth. The action of his brown hands on the napkin appealed to her. Is he a severe man after all? she finally asked herself, and her instincts answered yes.

There was only one way to test the depths of this situation. Poppy wrote a note and beckoned for a waiter to come to her. Smiling, the slender waiter took her message to the diner's table, where it was collected and read several times. The diner smiled, folded the note away, and looked up to the ceiling as if to thank some obscene god. Then, he raised his glass to her.

As she returned his toast, she smiled and thought of the daring of her discreet note:

If my instincts are to be trusted then you are a man with assertive tastes. I am not insensitive to such passions and would consider entertaining the consequences, if discretion and anonymity are observed. If you are curious about me, pay our bills and meet me outside. I'll be waiting in a cab.

The Woman in Black.

When he climbed into the rear of the taxi, purring outside the restaurant's canopied reception, he began to introduce himself, but Poppy held a finger to her lips and silenced him. As the taxi pulled away from the kerb, he shuffled along the seat to be closer to her, but she looked straight ahead and continued to smoke her cigarette, as if oblivious to his presence.

Amongst the stops and starts in central Darkling Town traffic, his rough-palmed hand found her thigh. Looking down to her lap, she watched the arrogant passage of his hand inside her dress. Occasional bursts of pink light, from the flashing neon outside, illumined the gradual brush and sweep of his fingers along the smooth contours of her thigh-booted legs. When the hand tickled her inner thighs and toyed with a suspender clasp, she uncrossed her legs and parted them.

Hard fingertips found her sex to be knickerless and immediately probed through her blonde floss. A cool cologne from his nicked cheeks seeped up her nose and his warm breath played with her ear. She did not react, however, until his teeth found her throat.

When she whimpered, the cigarette dropped from her lips and created an explosion of tiny orange sparks on the cab's dusty floor. Via the rear-view mirror, the driver's eyes flicked sideways and focused on the darkened back seat.

The diner's tongue lapped at the subsiding pain on her neck and three of his fingers slipped over the damp lips of her sex to force a stabbing entry inside. They slithered up to tickle the furthest reaches of her vagina and forced a sigh from her. As more of his rough hand entered her delicate passage, his free hand clutched the hair at the back of her head. His grip dislodged several hairpins and he forced her to face the cab ceiling. Again, his hot mouth engulfed her throat and the rear-view mirror reflected the cab driver's eyes – this time wide with shock.

A quickly rising fire of arousal spread through her body with every stubborn pump from his hand, sending the fingers deeper inside. Poppy stretched her feet across the cab's floor and thought he might split her, but still found the pain to be exquisite. His mouth moved from her throat to her lips – biting, sucking, kissing, sometimes tearing, but always adding to her pleasure.

Despite teetering on the edge of orgasm, she wanted more – something harder and more desperate, exceeding the pumping hand and merciless mouth. When the cab stopped outside her apartment, she guessed further delights would not be far away.

While she rummaged for the front-door keys, he paid the pale-faced driver. Taking the steps two at a time, Poppy fled upward to her front door with the metal dress hiked around her slick thighs, listening to the soles of her lover's boots pounding the wooden stairs behind.

Inside, Poppy had cleared some space on the floor earlier in case an illicit eventuality resulted from her dinner. Around the bed, she'd arranged four red, cherry-scented candles and mounted them on silver stands. Hurriedly, she lit the candles and glanced over her shoulder to watch her guest unbuttoning his shirt as he admired the sketches she'd pinned to one wall.

Poppy walked across to where he was standing, put her hands together and lowered her head to emulate the posture of submission in her sketch. Smiling, the stranger moved away to her workbench and selected his materials. Carefully, he unhooked several thin steel chains from her equipment and found, to his delight, a pair of cuffs.

Poppy moved to the foot of her bed, where she unhooked her dress and let it fall in a silvery ripple to the floorboards. There was a sharp intake of breath from her guest and she shut her eyes on his approach. Standing tall in thigh-high boots, seamed stockings, leather garters, and a black peep-hole bra, she waited, wanted, and expected something brutal.

Like a leopard before a succulent goat, he circled her, making the wood creak beneath her spike-heeled feet. Unable to bear the darkness any longer, she opened her eyes and saw him standing beside the bed, stripped naked. The broad and hairless chest was scarred with small flowers of pink tissue, suggesting the non-fatal passage of bullets. She trembled, knowing her mysterious guest understood pain in both receipt and delivery. A dark shadow seemed to pass under her pale skin and she guessed her love would reach a new peak.

Thin silver chains fell like water over the hard rocks of his knuckles, and his blue eyes, ringed with gold, burned with something that terrified her. Cuffs were snapped over her wrists and chains were wrapped around the small of her back and across her front, trapping her arms to her belly. The pinch and embrace of cold steel caused a little moan to issue from between her lips, but he just tugged her around to inspect and finger the traces of Baroness Nin's cane on her buttocks.

By mapping the scars from the baroness's lashes a vicious passion ignited inside the diner and he pulled Poppy back against his hard chest and thick penis, which passed between the tops of her legs where her stockings peeked above her boots. Slowly, he pumped his veiny shaft through her thighs, gripping her leather-gartered hips with his hands.

The shaft was withdrawn; Poppy was twisted about to face him, and his eyes set on her nipples – exposed and succulent in black leather. Bending down, he licked, sucked and bit her little pink gems. Crying out, she watched his shoulders and biceps tensing, while his mouth moved from her nipples to feed in her cleavage with a savage appetite.

Falling to his knees, his mouth slid from her breasts and found her exposed sex. He gripped the silver chains around her waist and pulled her on to his mouth. Unable to throw out her arms for balance, Poppy fell forward, but was kept on her feet by his hands, which held her steady, reinforcing her awareness that she was in his power and at his mercy.

She began to moan as his mouth tongued, lapped, and chewed at her clitoral bud and the velveteen skin of her sex. With his thumbs, he pulled her lips apart and smeared his bristly chin and hard teeth with her honey, before inserting a long red tongue inside her dewy canal.

Poppy came with a whimper, and her lover's sticky face, still nestling between her open thighs, broke into a smile. Before her dizzy mind could guess his next move, her long body was hoisted from the floor and dropped face down on the bed. Like a rag doll, she was tossed on to her back and he straddled her face. The weight of his body, pressed through his knees, indented the mattress on either side of her head and a thick and fully erect penis was slipped between her open lips. Her mouth was filled immediately but the shaft was still pushed on to the rear of her welcoming throat.

After raising his groin off her face, he clasped the brass railings of the bed frame to support his lunges inside her head. Lying still and breathing through her nose, Poppy lapped at the hard muscle that rutted her mouth and was delighted by the taste of it.

A vein pulsed on his forehead, and sweat broke across his tanned and battered body as he moaned and grimaced down at the pretty, painted face and the smudged mouth that suckled him expertly. When he withdrew to prepare for the next thrust, her tongue would rush out to meet the sensitised tip of his phallus, before her soft cheeks closed to hug the plunging rigidity packing her mouth.

Grunting, he strained to hold his cream back with no success; her mouth was too skilled in extracting his strength. When the muscles on his stomach tightened and his pumping increased in speed and vigour, she braced herself for the jerks and pulses that would fill her mouth with a briny milk. Thick, heavy dollops of hot cream splashed on to her tongue, gums and teeth, and Poppy gulped the luxurious food down.

With a sigh, he collapsed beside her and began to kiss her cheeks and damp forehead in thanks.

Lying still and soundless, Poppy pondered on what he would do next to her carefully prepared body. Her curiosity was soon satisfied. When his cock had retained an ample solidity, she was turned about and pulled to her knees. Without her arms to sustain her torso, her body was angled down so her face sank into the pillows.

A glorious pain electrified her buttocks when his open palm met her backside with a loud smack. The force of his blow pushed her up the bed and collapsed her bent knees. His rough fingers tugged her back into position and the beating continued. Soon, the scarred diner was slapping her buttocks with all his might. Overcome by the hot explosions on her cheeks, Poppy began to sob.

It was as if he was punishing her for being desirable and yet unobtainable through her absolute compliance. She could not be tamed, or made his own, and dreams of her beauty and pain would haunt his sleep for the rest of his life. This self-imposed vulnerability at the hands of a stranger seemed tantamount to insanity, but the pain and humiliation did nothing but thrill her. With each successive blow she was giving everything to the barbaric – living for a moment of primal hunger. From this, her next piece of art would come.

After a flood of tears had cleansed her face of make-up and her backside had become numb, the spanking ceased and his hands reached over her back to seize her shoulders. Anticipating a more ferocious pleasure, Poppy bit down hard on the goose-feather pillow and braced herself.

His thick cock forced itself into her tight anus. No lubrication was used. He had no patience. The sight of her thigh-booted legs and wanton face made him insensitive to such preliminaries and her backside was taken with a doglike technique that stretched and rifled her deeply. Her vision slipped into a swirl of crimson lights and her body began to shake from a climax. Sensing her response, the man pumped harder and more savagely while snarling through his clenched teeth.

Bucking like a wild horse, the bed frame shrieked and lurched across the floorboards, ridden hard by two sweat-slicked riders – one spitting, the other croaking. There was no opportunity to marvel at his stamina and power because Poppy was lost to the delight of being tightly chained, held down, and rutted by the animal inside this man. At the point when she knew her bruised rectum could take no more, but her mind still demanded further punishment, she felt him come. Finally, inside her rear passage, alight with so many sparks of hot pain, she enjoyed the pulse and throb of a penis unloading its gratitude.

When he fell across her back, sweating and gasping for breath, he whispered one word into her ear: 'Beautiful.'

Poppy wept.

The diner unlatched her chains and cuffs and let them drop to the floor beside the bed. He lay against her and kissed her shoulders, before turning her warm body round to cradle it against his hard chest. After kissing her forehead, he rediscovered her compliant mouth and sucked her little tongue, perhaps tasting his own fury.

They rested and kissed for a while until he'd regained his strength, still saying nothing to each other. Then, he unlaced the boots from her hot legs, and kissed her nylons from toe to thigh, before easing himself between her parted thighs to enter her sex. This time, his loving was gentle. The passage of his cock inside her was both smooth and slow, encouraging her to hug his waist with her slippery legs so her stockings creased and pulled at her garter fastenings.

They rolled, moaned and perspired on the wide bed for what seemed like hours. He led and she accommodated every angle and position he selected. With his hands he would press her shoulders down, raise his body and slowly pump her from the front. When his arms ached he'd twist Poppy on her side, hold one of her legs high and tease the entrance of her sex with the head of his cock. When she grew impatient for his length, he placed her ankles on his shoulders, pushed her knees down to her breasts and filled her with a deep lunge.

Only at the end did he utilise his power and size to make her entire body shake from the force of his onslaught. To hold her body steady on the bed, so her sex could take the full impact of his cock and pelvis, she stretched her arms up above her head and pressed her palms into the wall. Immediately, the outside of her sex was bruised, but she wanted more and began to whisper obscenities at him to taunt him and make him explode.

He gripped her waist, clawed her skin, and yanked her on and off his shaft, until her cries rose to a crescendo and drowned out the thump of their slamming flesh.

The moment his final plunge settled at the neck of her womb and the hot splashes of this stranger's seed landed inside her, Poppy groaned through another orgasm.

Exhausted, she clutched his body close and rested against his chest. While he stroked her tousled hair and kissed the top of her head, she drifted off to sleep. With the produce of their passion drying in every entrance to her young body, she dreamt about this new world of strange beds and lovers. It was as if she had discovered a new island in a distant ocean and wanted to drown in its deepest lagoon.

In her dreams, tight fastenings held her still and assertive desires were endured and adored. She saw herself willing and eager, manipulating her life into weird situations where the only result could be a delicious pain and the deep pleasure beyond the first sting. But she was unable to see her own screaming or panting face. It was always concealed behind a veil or mask, as if this was a private identity – a separate character living purely for experience.

When the cold woke her, early the next morning, the diner had gone.

Sometime in the night, when she was lost to her dreams, he'd stolen away. There had been no word of introduction between them, no names or preliminary chitchat, only the satisfaction of a deep and mutual hunger. This was how it must be, and he must have realised the futility of attempting to make it any other way. To him, she wanted to be nothing more than a night-time phantom, once seen but never forgotten.

Poppy lit a black Russian cigarette and removed her bra, garters and stockings. She dropped them inside the plastic bag that came with the garments from Sheen Couture and strode naked to her kitchen area, where she made strong coffee with lots of sugar. While smoking, she glanced over the sketches of the next project. In three dimensions, she hoped to twist the sculpture's posture to make every onlooker feel uncomfortable but unable to look away.

She had a new relationship with her art. The baroness was right: she should live through her inspiration before giving it immortality. She'd only been able to guess at the state of mind with the *Loving Captive* piece, but, from now on, she vowed to experience the dangerous and the compromising, the spontaneous and the unpredictable, before re-creating it with her hands.

29

Four

'You were told not to interfere!' The man's voice cracked through the freezing air, followed by the clatter of high heels as the baroness retreated across the tiled floor of the chamber. The room had a vaulted ceiling and steel mirrors had been fixed into every wall. Unshaded bulbs threw a pale yellow light to the four corners of the vast area and illuminated what looked like an old-fashioned washroom in an asylum.

'Everything could have been jeopardised. She was to be left alone, to go her own way, but you couldn't wait. The whole project is at risk, you stupid, greedy woman.'

'It's all right. She suspects nothing. I promise you,' Baroness Nin answered, her voice undermined by emotion.

A tall and distinguished figure stepped through the clouds of ice vapour towards her. In either hand he held a Doberman at bay. 'How can you be so sure? Could you not, even for me, control your appetite?'

The baroness bowed her head.

'This isn't the first time you've let me down. You're becoming a liability, my dear.'

The two dogs strained on their chains and tugged the man's arms towards the baroness. She pulled the collars of her fur coat around her pale throat and took another faltering step backward. In response, the hounds tensed and bared white canines before pulling forward to sniff at her long stocking-clad shins.

'Sir, show a little compassion. Please understand, I just had to see the sculpture. Our sculpture. You see, it's all

30

working, and the samples have done more than just alter her habits. The transformation is incredible. And she is so pretty, so graceful, everything and more you desired. I will never meddle again. I can promise you.'

The man stayed silent and studied her face for a short time. Finally, he smiled. 'You're right on one account. After today, I'm certain you'll never upset me again.'

When his smile vanished, he approached her.

To escape the dogs she scuttled to the rear wall of the chamber, where her thin, black silhouette became highlighted against the dripping steel tiles.

In the past she'd enjoyed many observational or active roles in her master's secret world, but today she was no longer sure of her status in a place that drew pleasure from pain.

The master relaxed his arms and the dogs leapt forward. With a whimper, she slid to her knees and hid her face behind her gloved hands. Reaching the end of their short chains, the dogs were suspended airborne for a moment before recoiling to their owner's feet. Tensing his muscular arms, he held the excited brutes still.

The baroness peeped between her fingers and exhaled a plume of condensation that clouded around her face.

'Henry!' the master yelled over his shoulder. 'Henry! The boys are hungry!'

Another man entered the chamber, wrapped from collar to ankle in a black woollen overcoat. After approaching his master, he clicked his shiny boots together, military style, and took the dog's leashes. His handsome face betrayed no emotion and seemed indifferent to the baroness's quaking presence.

The master turned his face to Henry. 'Take the boys out and give them something red and wet.'

Henry nodded and led the Dobermans from the chamber.

Smiling, the master turned to the baroness, who remained in a crouch. 'My dear baroness, you did not think ... surely not, that I would let the boys have their way with your long bones?' He laughed and she joined in with a giggle. 'What a beastly idea,' he cried. 'You're far too well dressed for such a fate.'

'Thank you, sir,' she answered, and a little colour returned to her cheeks. Slowly, she rose to her feet and smoothed out her furs. 'You were so angry with me. I had no idea what you had in mind for a bad girl.'

'One must, however, set a precedent in these matters.'

The baroness stiffened.

'Strip down to your silkies,' he said pleasantly.

As if stupefied by the request, she mouthed the word 'no', tried to smile and then shook her head gently.

'Go on. Do as I say.'

Although standing perfectly still for several seconds, she saw something in his eyes that urged her to begin undressing. After removing her gloves, she unbuttoned her furs and black suit jacket. She held her breath for a moment and then gasped when the air rushed in to embrace and goose her pale flesh. When stripped to her black silk bra and short skirt, she paused to throw a begging glance in the direction of her master.

His long face refused to move.

Raising her chin with the last of her pride, she unzipped her skirt quickly and let it drop to collect in a dark pool around her ankles.

Eyeing her legs with interest, he said, 'Leave your heels and stockings on. Nothing else.'

When he turned and left the chamber, the baroness remained behind with the ignominy of removing her bra and French knickers at a temperature of two degrees Celsius. By the time he returned, carrying a small silver attaché case, the baroness was rubbing the outside of her arms and stepping from one foot to the other.

'We must be quick before the cold gets to you,' he said. 'We do not want the temperature to dull your senses. Do we, dear?' Kneeling down, he unlatched the case and opened the lightweight alloy lid. His favoured implements shone in the yellow light. From the velvet lining, he withdrew a leather collar and laid it like a priceless treasure on the tiles. Two short chains dangled from the collar. At the end of each chain there was a sharp-toothed nipple clamp, with jaws shut tight. A long steel chain with wrist circlets at both ends followed the collar from the metal case.

Inhaling sharply and closing her eyes, the baroness was unable to even look at the black riding crop and beaded whip.

'Turn and face the wall,' the master ordered while rolling the sleeves of his linen shirt up to his elbows. Next, he removed the chunky Rolex from his wrist and a ring from a finger before tucking them inside a trouser pocket.

Baroness Nin complied with his first command. She looked upward and trembled at the sight of the wall hook, which was poking through the steel mirrors four feet above her head. Her captor threw the chain up and looped it over the hook with an expert's ease. After collecting the two swinging steel circlets in his hands, he nodded to the baroness, who raised her hands above her head. Standing on his tiptoes, he snapped the cuffs around her wrists.

'There must be some other way I can atone for my error,' she muttered. 'This is not necessary, sir. After all, I am one of the select –'

Before her words reached a desperate conclusion, a rubber ball-gag filled her mouth. Kneeling down, he stroked her legs, tickled her inner thighs and kissed the rear of her seamed knees. Her body relaxed and something like a moan slipped from her stuffed mouth. Smiling, he slipped his hands down the outside of her shiny legs until they reached her ankles. After grasping the slender joints and squeezing until his knuckles whitened, he yanked her legs wide apart.

With the collar in hand, he slipped between the baroness and the mirrored wall and chuckled at the sight of the silent scream in her eyes. He slid the collar around her sinewy throat and buckled it fast at the nape of her neck. When the hard jaws of the clamps oozed on to her erect nipples, her eyes rolled back inside her skull.

Slipping a hand between her thighs, he stroked the lips of her sex, teasing the clitoral bud with the rough pad of

33

his thumb. 'Oh sweetness,' he cooed. 'You're all dewy down there. Do you mind if I take a sip?' She tried to move her body away, but when his cold lips found the outer drapes of her sex she slipped both legs over his shoulders and swung free in her chains. In tune with the skilful dance of his tongue, she threw her head back and began a rhythmic moaning.

Removing his face, he licked his lips and swung around behind the baroness, freeing himself from her raking heels. He placed his clean-shaven jaw on her naked shoulder and kissed her right ear. 'Remember, my dear, this is a punishment. I'll stop if you start enjoying it.' He laughed at her muffled cries before concentrating on dispensing his justice.

Starting with the whip, he targeted the lower portion of the baroness's buttocks. In no time at all, he was delivering full lashes. The wet slap of nine beaded strips on the baroness's wriggling backside was nothing short of a symphony to his ears. For a while, he lost himself in a frenzy, staring through a red haze at the long stocking-clad legs kicking and buckling beneath his assault. When her eyes were wild with hate and desire, he changed the whip for the crop.

Henry entered the chamber and walked solemnly through the fog to where his master laboured. In time with every loud crack produced by wood connecting with flesh, Henry blinked, but nothing else moved on his face. The master paused to smile at his silent valet. 'Henry, your arrival is most opportune. In my experience, a mature woman is only at her peak when sired by a young buck.'

Overhearing the comment, the baroness turned her head and looked over her shoulder. Mascara ran from her eyes to her chin and, around the ball-gag, her lips moved.

'Henry, will you do her the honour?'

'Yes, sir,' the young man said, approaching the striped rear of the baroness while unzipping his dark trousers. Although Henry seemed unmoved at the prospect of taking the handsome and thoroughly lashed baroness, the rigidity of his thick penis betrayed his inner glee.

34

'Take her deeply, my boy,' the master whispered. 'Front and rear.'

After seizing the baroness by her slender hips, Henry effortlessly eased her, with one hand, on to her toes and his groin. With his free hand, he then inserted his erection in her tight vagina and both participants groaned.

From his position behind Henry, the master could tell, by his servant's long and even strokes, that he was pulling his manhood out to the tip before plunging it back to the hilt in the squirming baroness. All she was able to do was press her hands into the mirrored walls to steady herself against the vigorous thrusts.

'Been some time since you had it against a wall, my sweet,' the master said. 'See this as a little appetiser before that trainer returns for the summer.'

The baroness seemed to flinch at this remark.

'Oh yes, darling Nin, I know all about the young lad. Did you think you could keep such exquisite depravity from me? But I wonder if your young trainer takes you properly like young Henry is about to.'

Smiling, the master folded his arms and savoured the taste of a captive's enforced submission on his lips. Before him, Henry withdrew his glistening penis from the baroness's sex, only to slip it between the red cheeks of her buttocks. The baroness's whimper, which immediately followed the presence of Henry's large erection by her anus, brought a laugh to the master's blue-tinged lips.

With a groan, Henry slipped his groin forward and buried himself inside her back passage. The baroness threw her head back but the rest of her body stiffened. Releasing her buttocks, he smoothed his hands up her ribs and slipped them around her torso to seize her breasts. Slowly, he began to pull her on and off his shaft, using her chest as a handhold. Over the gag, her mouth unleashed a deep groan every time his penis sank into her.

Developing his rhythm, Henry began to pump her harder and more quickly, and she began to kick her legs backward until one of her high heels dropped off a foot. He bit her back and began to yank her body against him, to double the power of his thrusts. The chains supporting her weight slipped about on the hook and her cuffed hands fisted. Despite the restraint in her mouth, she began to utter a muffled 'yes' during every thrust.

Grinning, the master rubbed his hands, thrilled the baroness had begun to betray her delight at being punished, despite the humiliation of anal interference from a mere servant. 'The others need not know of this, darling Nin,' he said. 'But one more mistake and I'll invite every member of our clan to partake in, shall I say, your court martial.'

For a second, her face turned and in her streaming eyes the master detected a look of alarm that encouraged him to clap his hands and laugh out loud.

After Henry's hips began working like pistons and the baroness stretched her legs backwards to loop them around his knees, the master turned on his heel and left the chamber.

Outside in the hallway, when he heard Henry's final groan and a soprano shriek from the baroness, the master smiled and made his way to his favourite room.

Eliot Rilke, a man accustomed to the titles of 'sir' and 'master' from the select few who had met him, retired to the cavernous living room in his penthouse apartment and poured a drink. After the incident with the baroness, his long and stiff body needed the revitalisation of vodka and tonic in a tall glass, complemented by frosted ice cubes and a slice of lime. As he sipped the drink, he checked one of the ten thermometers in the room: the temperature was exactly two degrees Celsius.

Smiling, he made his way to the package Henry had collected from the post office box on the western side of Darkling Town – where the freaks, misfits, and Poppy the sculptress lived. The large padded envelope lay on the vast oaken table in the centre of the room. Before he opened the parcel, Rilke leant back in his red leather chair and surveyed the walls of his favoured haunt with satisfaction. This was his empire: undisturbed by the outside world, and the private house of one of the world's most eclectic collections.

His eyes roamed over leather-bound books, a bank of security monitors, and neatly arranged black and white photographs before finding the place where his antiques were arranged. Marlene Dietrich's transparent black gown was the first artefact he had acquired. Ten years before, he had set it high on the wall, shielded behind glass, to begin his collection. Beside Marlene's gown, Lana Turner's basque was on display, shaped around a white marble torso. Further on, his eyes stopped to survey one of his enduring favourites: a pair of pewter-grey nylons worn by Marilyn Monroe, delicately held by a thin wire frame and kept pristine in an airless glass case. Betty Page's five-inch Cuban heels, worn once in a photo shoot and then stolen by a fetishist, stood tall between Monroe's exhibit and Janet Leigh's brassiere. The collection stretched on, from wall mountings to marble pedestals, around the living room and out into the hall and bedrooms.

'So many riches, but none, I wager, to rival her delights,' Rilke whispered, and rapped his fingers on the table top. It was as if he could not bring himself to even touch the package from Poppy. He just stared, sipped his drink, muttered to himself, and threw glances across to his archive, fondly remembering the adventures of his agents when acquiring the precious merchandise.

Outside, in the marbled corridor that passed the open doors to his living room, he heard two sets of footsteps before Henry walked stiffly into view, escorting the baroness. Hastily gathered clothing hung off her body while hair dropped in strands across a drained face. There was, however, still a certain grace in her carriage, and Rilke was pleased to observe this.

'Take her home, Henry,' he called out from his chair. 'She is forbidden to leave her residence until I say otherwise. And she is to have no guests. Now get her out of my sight.'

'Yes, sir.'

Both figures disappeared from view and Rilke heard

Henry twisting the handle of the main air-tight portal. Outside in the main reception, the reinforced and sound-proofed double-doors swung shut with a clunk and hydraulic wheeze.

Rilke smiled and turned his attention back to the parcel on the table. Slowly, he withdrew the polythene interior from the padded envelope and switched a desk lamp on to illuminate his booty.

Poppy had followed the instruction explicitly. After wearing the first set of garments, she had sealed the soiled cast-offs in the reinforced polythene bag, slipped the bag into the protective padded envelope, and posted them to the dummy company's post office box.

He swallowed hard and stared at her fragrant treasures, flat and folded, inside clear plastic. The temptation to remove them and inspect the scars inflicted by the baroness was overwhelming, but he did nothing more than stroke the plastic. Self-discipline was vital. It was too early to indulge himself. But his darkest and most creative scheme to date would reach its conclusion soon enough. And then he would be lost to the greatest of pleasures, for ever. And so would she.

Five

Around the base of an onyx step pyramid, a row of steel chairs was angled upward to seat an audience below the figure of a woman. Sealed within a skin-tight suit, made from red rubber, her erect posture had been enforced by the bonds attached to her body. Her ankles were locked together by a hobble-bar; her wrists were cuffed and, from a tiny ring in each nipple, silver threads as thin as fishing twine ran in taut lines to brass fastenings on the bottom step of the pyramid. Between her legs a section of latex had been cut away from her suit to reveal the slit of a shaven vagina, which glittered with the tiny silver hoops that pierced the labia. Her creamy buttocks had also been exposed through cuts in the suit, and a chain, attached to the figurine's collar, ran from her neck to a bolt on the gallery floor.

As if in response to the torments inflicted upon her body, her head was thrust back to face a large circular mirror, suspended from the ceiling. A piercing set of green eyes and a mouth frozen in a gasp were captured in the reflection. At the base of the mounting a white perspex square offered the title of the piece: *Please*.

At six o'clock, Poppy heard a voice buzz through the gallery intercom system to announce closing time. The crowd began to thin around her, taking a host of blushes and giggles with it. When she stood alone on the central court of the floor for 'Modern Art', she whispered a goodbye to her second sculpture. There had been many difficulties with the piece. Trying to manipulate the limbs of the manikin into perfect lines and angles had brought her close to despair.

For over a month she had bent, moulded, stitched and machined her new creation into life, seeking to capture the moment when bondage passed from discomfort to freedom – an escape from everything save the immersion in the pleasures of another's will. Something she now craved.

She had taken no lover since the diner, but the clothes from Sheen Couture continued to fill her drawers, line her wardrobe, and whisper to her as they embraced her skin. Certain items had been worn while she worked: transparent brassieres, high heels, French knickers, and panties made from the finest black silk – all feeding her creativity through the long hours she worked alone.

Now, with the second piece complete and another seed planted for a collection destined to blossom beyond the expectations of a jaded art world, she felt ready to venture back into Darkling Town and seek fresh inspiration. Like an animal in the wild, she experienced a need to mate. Beneath her long coat, she wore a fresh set of secrets. As she'd dressed for the unveiling of her second piece, she'd wondered if a stranger would enjoy them with her. Dressing that afternoon in a directoire corset, seamed nylons, and a flimsy black slip-dress, she'd felt the heat ignite inside her, only temporarily appeased by the pressure of her own fingers between her legs.

Through the flimsy treasures from Sheen Couture, it was as if she'd been granted an opportunity to become another woman. For the first time in her life the desire to seduce and be seduced commanded her will. But what had created this change inside her? Success? Freedom from poverty? An end to denial? The town, with its spires, spidery bridges and black towers? The clothes? Was it possible, she'd begun to think, for a garment to change a person's character? Could a pair of seamed stockings make her more vulnerable to illicit and previously buried cravings? Or could a pair of sheer panties, cupping her buttocks and drifting across her sex, make her desire penetration? It seemed preposterous. But, as the fine fabrics from Sheen

Couture continued to envelop her young flesh, it was as if the rooms of her mind had darkened and become insufferably hot. Now, her new direction seemed at risk of becoming an addiction. In quieter moments she worried how far it would lead her, and to whom.

She drifted out of the gallery to the main boulevard, where a light snow fell through a windless night to powder the city. It always snowed in February and she hadn't dressed for the weather. The silk dress beneath her coat and the new pair of stiletto sandals on her feet offered no resistance to the freezing temperature at street level. Shivering, she closed the fur-lined collar of her overcoat under her chin and made her way to the nearest underground station.

Amongst the rush of commuters and beggars, she hurried down to her platform in time to catch the next shuttle leaving for the western side of Darkling Town. After boarding the metro, she wandered down the length of the train, glad to be back where it was warm, while secretly loving the whispers between her thighs and the grip of the corset on her breasts. As she moved amongst the commuters these sensations created by her underwear seemed to increase her inner heat. No one knew what she wore beneath her overcoat and she fought a smile by tightening her lips. Twice, though, she found it necessary to stop walking in order to catch her breath and to allow a flush to subside. Never had silk or nylon felt so similar to a lover's dry tongue tickling her flesh.

Looking about, as she wandered through the cramped carriages seeking space, Poppy noticed several men leering at her. There was nothing in their eyes, however, beyond a tepid carnal fancy, and she ignored their attentions. When she entered the third carriage, though, something caught her eye. Through the jostling passengers at the far end of her compartment, she could see a muscular arm and broad hand, holding a book. This was no ordinary arm. Every square inch of skin, from shoulder to elbow, had been tattooed with intricate designs in bright inks.

Curious, Poppy made her way between damp office

workers towards the arm. Soon she was able to see more of the owner – a young man with a shaven head, pierced nose, and dark eyes that were engrossed in a book titled *Crime and Punishment*.

Poppy approached the solitary figure and stood beside him. Eyeing his body, she presumed he was one of the many freaks peopling her side of town. Through his leather trousers and white vest, she could see the outlines of what looked like an acrobat's body, and the man's face had an intensity she found intriguing. Perhaps he too was an artist. There were flecks of paint around the hem of his vest, and the edges of his hands were nicked with little scalpel cuts.

Oblivious to her presence on the train, which seemed to draw nothing but envy or admiration from the other passengers, the man continued to read, allowing her a closer scrutiny of his tattoos.

Immediately, something tightened inside Poppy and her secret heat spread further through her body. Stretching around his left bicep was a depiction of a busty woman trapped between thorned vines. Tiny splashes of red ink flecked the design where her blood had been let by the barbed restraints. On her legs she wore polished knee-length boots with the pointed toes disappearing into his elbow.

No sooner had she begun to squint at the finer details of the tattoo, when another batch of commuters pressed themselves into the carriage and pushed her within an inch of the man's body. Immediately, her sense of smell sharpened and she found his scent to be raw but well tempered by a strange cologne. Turning a page, the man sighed, and continued to read.

As the train raced around a bend in the tunnel system, Poppy lost her balance on her extreme heels, slipped, and grasped for a ceiling strap, only to end up hanging from the leather support. As she righted herself, she heard the tattooed man say, 'You wear beautiful shoes.' He had a rough though cultured voice. She tried to offer her admirer a smile but, when she looked at him, his eyes, once again, were occupied with the book.

Poppy felt her stomach rumble. 'And you read books, which is also beautiful. You never see it these days.'

'Long live the book,' he murmured. 'And hail the spiked heel.'

She looked down at the shoes he'd been able to admire without a turn of his head. Raising her leg, she straightened the seam running down the back of her calf. Out of the corner of her eye, she saw him fidget.

'Those are also rare,' he said. 'Are they authentic?'

'I think so, they're French.'

There was another stop and soon the carriage was loaded to maximum capacity, creating a wave of human bodies that squashed her against the tattooed passenger. While moving her body back away from him, she turned and grazed the front of his leather trousers with her backside. There was a quick inhalation of breath from the stranger.

Acting impulsively, she leant forward and allowed more of her weight to hang from the ceiling strap. Then, she pulled her ankles closer together and assumed a pose of submission that emphasised the parallel seams on the rear of her legs.

When his cool breath brushed the nape of her neck, Poppy closed her eyes and felt his erection settle against her buttocks. Slowly, as her body began to sway back and forth with the rhythm of the train, the pronounced clips of her suspenders and the bottom edge of her corset rubbed his crotch.

'Have you any idea what you do to a man?' he whispered.

She smiled but said nothing.

'You should be careful with whom you flirt, madam. Some men have strange ideas about beautiful, well-dressed women who parade themselves on trains. Women who offer the signs of submission.'

'I'll take my chances,' she said over her shoulder, and noticed the woman beside her leaning towards their whispered conversation.

'So you know what it means to give yourself to another, completely?' he asked.

Turning around, she let her beautiful face drift close to

the man's mouth. She raised an eyebrow and stared into his eyes. 'Yes, I know something of submission.'

'And do you have a master? Maybe someone sent you out to find a special kind of passion.'

'No. I'm free.'

'Free?'

'Yes.'

'Sure you're not a cop?'

She laughed. 'I'm on a special journey, that's all.'

He gave her a quizzical look.

'A journey where I can see and feel different things, before I put them in a special place.'

This seemed to please him. 'Some kind of artist?'

'It's possible.'

'I see. And do I inspire you?'

'I'm curious about anyone who'd endure pain to decorate their body.'

The man smiled. 'So what kind of experience is a pretty artist like you looking for?'

'Something unforgettable.'

He held her stare for a second before dipping his head to kiss her hand. The man introduced himself as Hector, the skin artist.

'Tattoos?' she queried.

'Skin illustrations. And no two of my designs have ever been the same.'

'I'm intrigued.'

'So am I. And flattered that such an elegant young lady would speak with me about her – special journey.'

A wry smile creased her mouth. 'My journey has brought good fortune. Perhaps I should have an illustration to commemorate my success.'

'Then follow me. This is my stop and my business is always open for special guests.'

People began leaving the carriage but Poppy hesitated.

'Frightened?' he asked.

She said nothing and searched his face for more clues.

'Understandable,' he added. 'But if you don't accompany me, your journey may miss an interesting detour.'

She looked at the man's musculature – at the tensile power in his sinewy arms, the length of his legs, and the solid pipe hidden beneath the heavy-duty zip of his leather trousers. She swallowed and deep inside her sex something stirred. At first it tingled, but the tingle grew to a contraction. There was a rush of blood to her head and she felt dizzy. She needed cool, fresh air. Anything to relieve the unbearable heat under her skin. But it wasn't like feeling ill, or feverish. It felt good. It was the desire to be taken firmly and to be loved hard.

Banishing her caution by refusing to think of the consequences, she looked into Hector's eyes and said, 'After you.'

He took her arm, led her off the train and out of the station to his neighbourhood.

Before they ventured more than a few feet across the snow-covered pavement, Poppy felt one of her heels slip forward. She gasped and prepared to perform the splits. Acting quickly and instinctively, Hector caught her around the waist and helped her stand up. 'You're far too pretty to lie in the street,' he said, and smiled to ease her embarrassment.

'Thanks. These shoes are not very practical,' she muttered, and put her hand on her chest to calm her heart.

Holding her steady with his large but gentle hands, he looked down to admire her heels under the illumination of a street light. 'Have you been somewhere special?' he asked after a long silence.

'The Daemonic Gallery to see the new exhibit.'

'I see. I caught it this morning; it's wonderful. Do you like it?'

Poppy didn't answer, looking away to hide her knowing smile from his eager face.

'But you dressed for the occasion?'

She nodded and then moved to disentangle herself from his hands, but he held her fast. 'Tell me, Poppy,' he said softly. 'What interested you in the sculpture?'

She raised her chin. 'I wanted to think about the girl.'

'Who?'

'The girl all wrapped up, and stared at by the people sitting in those metal chairs.'

Hector tucked a strand of hair behind her ear. 'What do you think she feels?'

'Anticipation.'

He moved his face closer. 'What do you feel now?'

She kept her face straight but her heart skipped a beat. 'Something similar,' she whispered.

Hector squeezed her hips and began to kiss her neck. She didn't resist, just closed her eyes and felt the stranger's lips move to her ears, cheek and then mouth. Can he feel my heat? she thought, convinced the skin on her face was burning up.

When his groin pressed forward, she felt the length of his penis press against her stomach. Impulsively, she rubbed her tummy against the lump. In response, he licked her jaw before telling her she tasted wonderful.

Poppy opened her eyes. 'Before we go any further, can I ask you a question?'

'Of course.'

'If the girl in the sculpture was at your disposal, what would you do with her?'

Something changed in the man's expression. 'That's something I can only show you,' he replied, and seized her hands.

As her heart began to beat faster and her pulse thundered against her temples, she felt herself being marched down the main street until the mouth of a darkened alley presented itself between a Mexican restaurant and a massage parlour. This is it, she thought, and then laughed. I'm about to give myself to another stranger. I've gone mad. Is this really happening?

But although she'd taken a moment to question her sanity, she'd become light-headed with excitement. Like the diner, Hector was rough looking but handsome. Battered but virile. And the very thought of his hard, labourer's body smashing itself against her softness started a fire in her womb.

By the alley, Hector stopped walking. 'Find me,' he said, and disappeared into the gloom.

46

Poppy hesitated and looked about at her surroundings. This was a dangerous part of town and the street was deserted. Beneath her coat her skin began to shiver, but not from the cold. Before her reason could interfere with her desire, she walked after him.

In the dark, a shape darted before her and a pair of rough hands slipped inside her coat to seize her breasts. Her gasp was silenced when his teeth smashed into her mouth, bruising her lips. He sucked at her tongue, lapped at the crimson paint on her mouth, and shoved her further down the litter-strewn alley before pushing her against a wall.

Despite being crushed beneath him, Poppy responded to his aggression and dropped her hands to waist height seeking the long bump of his penis. For a moment she struggled to yank his zipper down, before the clasp was pulled from her fingertips as the man dropped to a squat.

When he found her vagina to be both pantyless and freshly shaven, his ferocity increased.

Clutching the back of his smooth head, Poppy gasped and pushed herself further on to his tongue, adoring the combination of its insistent probing and the bristly chin nuzzling against her inner thighs.

After seizing her buttocks, he raised her up the wall, straining every muscle in his shoulders and biceps to hold her aloft while his mouth nibbled and bit at her silk-covered breasts.

'Now,' she said, losing control. 'Give it to me.'

Hector released her arms and she fell to her knees and freed his cock. A large strawberry-tipped phallus appeared between his legs. Poppy dragged his jeans and pants down to his ankles and slipped her lips over his glans. Purring through her nose, she swilled her tongue around the swollen head and pumped her hand up and down the solid base of the shaft.

'Face the wall,' he gasped. 'I can't wait.'

She swivelled about on her heels, dropped her coat and spread herself against the bricks, moving her backside in readiness.

'Perfect,' he muttered.

'Always wanted to do this,' she whispered. 'To know what it feels like.'

His hands mauled her buttocks and then slid down the outside of her legs, pulling a stocking top free of two suspender clasps.

'If I stand on tiptoe, you'll get it in,' she said, feeling exhilarated, but also frightened by what she seemed capable of.

With a push, he sank his penis inside her in one quick motion. At first there was pain, and then, once the seal had been torn, his length glided between her slippery vaginal walls, forcing a gasp of relief through her teeth. With several deep thrusts, controlled by his hips, he drove his thickness right up her until she became aware of his pubes tickling her backside.

'Your cock is beautiful,' she whispered, and Hector increased his pace. Harder lunges pushed her flat against the wall and she became unable to stifle her whimpers and squeals of delight. The noise of his groin slapping against her buttocks was music, and the bestial and desperate nature of the situation felt so glorious. Losing control, she began to thrust her hips backward to increase the force and friction of their impromptu coupling.

'That's it,' she murmured, feeling the first tremor of orgasm.

His thrusts became more aggressive, even savage.

'Harder,' she demanded. 'Just shove it in me.'

'Did you wake up today and need this?' he said with difficulty.

'Yes. Sometimes a girl needs to be a whore – Oh yes! Really bang it into me. Like that. Oh that's so good – to get dressed up and high on her own –'

Poppy never finished. She'd touched a nerve. Quickly, her body was snapped double and she felt his hard body squash against her back. Hands reached around her torso, squeezed her breasts and she was forced down to all fours. On the ground, he pumped at her with such vigour she was unable to prevent herself from crying out. But she didn't

48

care. Without any thought of who might hear or be watching, Poppy shrieked into the dark, thrusting herself backward to take in more of him.

She could hear his grunting mouth close to her left ear and was shocked to feel her entire body, inside and out, judder from the force of his thrusts. Clenching her eyes shut, she felt herself soar towards climax. Together – they would come together, in a furious and spitting consummation. That is what she wanted. An end to sophistication and rules. To be so free. To feel like a devil. Almost there, she thought, before her thoughts disintegrated.

Overwhelmed by the delights of his savagery and eager to feel him strain and then empty himself inside her, she whispered several obscene prompts back to the stranger. When he embedded himself inside her with what she sensed was the final stroke, her legs gave way.

On the garbage-strewn floor of a darkened alley, they came together. He thrust his head back, swore, and emptied himself inside her. Racked from head to toe with a series of tremors, Poppy was capable of little else beside whimpering through her climax.

For a while they crouched in the dark, panting and squashed against each other, before Poppy eased herself from under her lover, on shaking legs, to make reparations to her attire. 'Not again,' she whispered, staring at the tears in her stockings.

'You'll get cold out here,' he said, gulping at the foggy air to regain his breath. 'We better move. My place isn't far.'

'There's more?' she said, smiling.

Hector grabbed her, pulled her against his chest, and answered her question with a vicious kiss.

Because the extremity of her heels forbade too much footwork, Poppy hailed a cab from the main street and they took a short ride to his studio and flat combination, which was situated in the backwater of a suburb modelled on Prague.

'It used to be a funeral parlour,' Hector said, unlocking

the studio's rattling door. 'But the cheaper municipal disposals put them out of business. Around here, no one can afford wooden caskets.'

The interior walls were covered with runes, swirling Celtic emblems, and shapely silhouettes grasped by cuffs and chains. Between the designs she could see patches of velvet wallpaper, from the days of the funeral directors. By way of furnishings, there were only two sofas, an orderly workbench, a stainless-steel sink and a large adjustable dentist's chair upholstered in padded leather.

Poppy's heels dragged across the linoleum tiles as she gazed at the walls. 'You're accustomed to unusual requests?'

He laughed. 'Yes, but rarely on a train. I'm lucky: my work is also my passion.'

'Inflicting pain?'

His broad grin revealed two gold teeth at the back of his mouth. 'A necessary by-product of the craft.'

Behind a wall there was the sound of heels descending a staircase and then, at the far corner of the studio, a thick crimson curtain was thrust to one side, making Poppy jump. A tall, busty girl, sporting a spiky haircut, entered the parlour. She wore knee-length boots, a leather miniskirt and a biker jacket. The resemblance was obvious: this was the girl tattooed on Hector's arm.

He appeared at Poppy's side and offered a tumbler of bourbon. 'This is Chloë. A little surprise for you. She's my partner.'

'In business and pleasure,' the girl said, her face not moving while she gave Poppy a dismissive once-over with her pale blue eyes.

'I'm Poppy,' she said, and fumbled for a cigarette she could hide behind. Although about the same age as Poppy, the girl was taller and her punky make-up added something sinister to an already formidable face.

'She's here for something unforgettable,' Hector said, smiling, and with his eyes he seemed to be conducting a secret communication with Chloë.

As Chloë took her coat, Poppy felt the girl's fingers run

50

down the back of her dress. 'Nice threads,' the girl whispered.

Despite her embarrassment, Poppy managed a smile and returned a compliment about the girl's outfit. Chloë acknowledged this with a nod and then brazenly stared at Poppy's breasts. 'Are you wearing foundation garments?' she asked.

Poppy nodded.

Chloë removed her jacket. 'A girl after my own taste.' Between the underwired panels in her black corset, a transparent gauze revealed her magnificent breasts above a pierced tummy button. Each of her shoulders had been tattooed with tiny purple bubbles, framed inside delicate circles. 'He's very good,' Chloë said, angling her head towards Hector, who busied himself by the workbench.

'I know,' Poppy muttered, and offered the girl an apologetic smile.

For a moment, Chloë's body seemed to stiffen. She turned on her heel and flopped down on a couch, staring hard at the back of Hector's head. Draining her glass, and a refill for courage, Poppy sat on the sofa beside the girl.

'Are you afraid of needles, Poppy?' Hector asked from the other side of his studio.

'No,' she answered, and smiled at Chloë in an attempt to diffuse the atmosphere.

'Just here for a tattoo?' she asked Poppy, sulkily.

'Thinking about it. Look, I'm sorry, he never mentioned a girlfriend. I feel so –'

The girl smirked. 'I'm not his bird. We go beyond that. He might have fucked you, but he'll always be my master.'

'Master?' Poppy muttered.

'That's right.'

'Perhaps I should go.'

Although Chloë's face didn't crack, she seemed relieved by Poppy's readiness to desert her territory. Without invitation, and perhaps worried that her frosty attitude would incur her master's wrath, she placed an exploratory hand on Poppy's knee and ran one painted nail down her shin. 'Love your shoes, girl. You've got nice things. Are you loaded?'

Poppy ignored the question but asked her if she'd like to try them on.

'Can I?'

Poppy unbuckled the tiny straps while Chloë slipped off the couch to sit by her ankles, drawing the shoes off Poppy's feet before rubbing some warmth into her cold toes. Hector appeared behind the sofa. 'If one of my needles was to pierce your skin, Poppy, where would it prick you?'

'Above the V of my groin.'

'Good choice.'

'I think so.'

'And would you like to sit in my chair?'

Poppy nodded, and Chloë, having buckled herself into the shoes, began to trace her fingertips up and down Poppy's legs, fascinated by the seams on the rear of her calves.

'You have a nice touch,' Poppy said.

The girl's sulk seemed to be wearing off and she smoothed her hands across the tops of Poppy's thighs.

'It's not often we meet someone like you, Poppy, outside of an organised gathering,' Hector whispered from behind the couch. 'Perhaps we three can become friends.'

'You two had a good start,' Chloë said in an emotionless voice while caressing Poppy's ankles.

Poppy smiled at Chloë and said, 'I'm just a guest,' before glaring at Hector. 'And I wish your master had told me he had such a beautiful lover.'

The girl looked away, but Poppy detected a blush on her cheeks.

'Darling,' Hector said, frowning, 'don't I always share?'

This made Chloë pout, but Hector ignored her. 'Poppy, I think I have the perfect illustration for you,' he added, his face beaming with sadistic delight. 'Something personal.'

'Good,' she said. 'Let me see it.'

Hector showed her a circular design on a piece of linen paper. It reminded her of a Viking rune.

'What is it?'

'The circle of freedom. Awarded to a slave by the ancient Celts. Slaves who had earned their freedom with an act of significance.'

'Love it,' she murmured. 'So pagan, but so pretty. Does it really signify freedom?'

'Oh yes.'

'I want it. Perhaps it's the design I would have chosen anyway.'

'Part of my gift, knowing which illustration suits an individual. And feel free to leave whenever you wish,' Hector assured Poppy, brushing a hand over her hair. 'But until you say "no more", you are ours. You see, there is a small ritualistic aspect to my work.'

Poppy reclined further into the couch, enjoying the movements of Chloë's fingers on her legs. 'I understand. When you mark me, though, make it perfect.'

'Naturally,' he replied, with a nod of his smooth head. 'I'll let Chloë prepare you, our way.'

Chloë leapt to her feet, as if on command. She placed her hands on her hips and cocked her head at a challenging angle. 'Undress,' she ordered.

Unabashed and determined to impress the sulky punk, Poppy removed the slip-dress and revealed her dark corset. Silk panels formed the bodice beneath two half-cups, which served to push out her breasts. Attached to the waist were six suspender straps framing a freshly shaven, coral-pink sex.

'You like?' she asked the girl, who had become unable to remove her eyes from Poppy's breasts.

For a moment, the girl looked into her eyes with a combination of longing and something more aggressive, before falling to her knees and dipping her face between the legs of her guest.

Poppy found the sudden and uninvited presence of Chloë's lips so near her sex to be irresistible. She'd only aimed to tease the girl out of her mood but the prospect of making love to another woman, so soon after the baroness, was beginning to make this the sexiest night of her life. Reclining back on the sofa, she raised her legs and draped them over Chloë's back before shuffling further forward to press her sex against the girl's mouth.

The rough surface of Chloë's tongue lapped at her tender outer lips before burrowing and parting them to discover her tiny fleshy jewel of delight. Humming through her nose, Chloë began rubbing her two front teeth, gently, across Poppy's clit to make her squirm on the couch.

The thought of returning Chloë's passion and having a woman's sex on her mouth made Poppy shiver. It would be new. Something she'd been curious about but never brave enough to instigate. This was her chance – buried in the wrong side of town with two deviants who wanted to exhaust themselves on her compliant body. 'I want yours,' Poppy whispered, and Chloë immediately clambered upon the sofa, forcing Poppy horizontal so they topped and tailed each other among the cushions.

Despite one tipsy fumble with a girlfriend at school, it was the first vagina Poppy had seen so close and she marvelled at the size and texture of Chloë's sex. But no sooner had she begun to stare in fascination at the girl's wet treasure, so near her lips, when Chloë wiggled her backside and prompted her to begin the feast. Tentatively, she stretched her tongue forward and touched the salty lips of the girl's damp flesh, before whipping her tongue back as if she'd been electrocuted. When Chloë moaned with annoyance, Poppy slipped her tongue forward again and let it glide and flick through the girl's furrowed intimacy.

'I like to be sucked hard,' Chloë gasped, her body shivering from the first touches of Poppy's tongue. With her eyes closed, Poppy opened her mouth and sank her face into her lover's soft fruit, making the girl moan and press her hips down for more.

Breathing gently through her nose, she sucked and nibbled at Chloë's fragrant petals, gradually increasing the speed of her tongue's craft. It was good to taste a woman, to feel the weight of a body on her face, and to have the sharp scent of arousal in her nostrils. It was so easy and seemed so natural. She'd do this again. Yes, she'd even seek it out. Go to bars where aggressive and experienced panthers prowled the shadows looking for younger, more feminine women. Delighted by her daring and the strange visions that filled her head, Poppy slipped joyously towards climax.

Chloë responded to her freshness, no matter how clumsy Poppy's mouth became at times. Using her fingers, she opened Poppy wide and suckled her with a hasty though deft affection. Soon, they clasped each other's buttocks, moaned through mouths that were full, and rocked from side to side, eating until their jaws began to ache.

Poppy came first, but, despite her desire to pull her face away and bite a cushion, she continued to service Chloë until the punky beauty began to writhe and then stiffen above her. Gyrating her hips, Chloë whimpered to announce the arrival of her own peak and Poppy trapped her lover's face between her legs to prevent the slippery mouth from escaping. Entwined, they fell sideways and Poppy thrust an arm out to prevent them from tumbling to the floor. Despite the lack of grace, they still managed to lap each other through a mutual, sighing completion.

When Chloë was finished with Poppy's sex, she slipped up the couch so they could lie together, flushed and smiling, and clean each other's lips with the tips of their tongues. As they snuggled side by side, Poppy began to massage Chloë's sizeable breasts through the slippery gauze of her corset. The beautiful punk whispered in her ear, 'I wanted to hate you for screwing Hector, but I can't. He usually lets me have a say in who he fucks, but I understand how he felt about you. I'd have done the same.'

Poppy squeezed Chloë's nipples and then rubbed the nylon covering her breasts with the palms of her hands until it hissed. Chloë closed her eyes and said, 'How do you feel about rough trade? Umm? Something harder?'

Poppy poked her tongue out and licked the girl's hot cheek. Chloë gritted her teeth. 'I warn you, I like to slap pretty girls.'

Carried away by the increasingly harder ministrations of Chloë's hands now busy on her breasts, Poppy said, 'I like to tease tough bitches until they lose control.'

With a groan, Chloë rolled Poppy on to her tummy and

dug ten red fingernails into her backside. 'I could show you something, girl,' she said under her breath.

Poppy smiled at her, wrinkled her nose and raised one elegant leg off the sofa, moving her foot in circles. Kneeling beside the couch, Chloë began moving her hand, palm down, over the area of soft backside she intended to punish. Poppy rotated her buttocks to speed the process up. Chloë, however, seemed determined to tease her, promising a slap but not delivering until Poppy said, 'What does your master's hand feel like?'

Not even Baroness Nin wielded the same power and precision as Chloë's hand. This girl was younger, stronger, more agile, and capable of making Poppy pass close to a faint from the sudden explosion of pain created by an open-palmed delivery on her backside.

'Ouch! That's so hard,' she cried out.

'You slut,' Chloë hissed.

With a leather cushion stuffed into her mouth, Poppy was unable to reply. Tears blurred her vision and her nose began to run. She tried to squirm free but Chloë forced her down with an elbow while her other arm rose and fell, repeatedly, until she hurt her hand. 'Don't take liberties with me, OK?' Chloë said, with her face pressed against Poppy's wet cheek. 'I love the taste of your posh pussy, but if I cop any attitude off you, girl, you won't sit down for days.'

With that, she kissed Poppy on the cheek and walked across to Hector, who greeted his slave with open arms. Smiling, he whispered into his partner's ear before pressing something into her hands. When Chloë turned around, a broad grin had set on her mouth.

She walked back to Poppy, concealing something behind her back. 'Time to build your tolerance for the tattoo. Close your eyes, pretty.'

Poppy swallowed but kept her eyes open.

'Close your fucking eyes,' Chloë demanded.

Wary of the girl's temper, Poppy complied and a blindfold was wrapped round her head. Lying still, she allowed the girl to position her on the couch. Both her legs were gripped at the ankle, raised in the air, and then parted. Instinctively, she moved her hands to cover her damp vagina, but Chloë slapped them away and, without ceremony, plunged something inside her sex.

Stretched to an almost unbearable degree, Poppy swore and then moaned, but Chloë forced the appendage further inside her, until her entire sex seemed to have been filled with a frightening length and girth. Above her in the dark, she heard Chloë gasp and then speak: 'Don't worry, girl. My half is just as thick. Move with me, slowly.'

There was a rustle and squeak of leather and Chloë's high-heeled feet were planted on either side of her head. Poppy moaned and knew Chloë had leant back on the sofa to press their impaled vaginas together. Keeping with the rhythm Chloë set, Poppy pushed and rotated her hips, grinding the lips of her sex against her lover's. Reaching down and finding Poppy's clit with her fingers, Chloë began rubbing them in circles to increase her partner's pleasure. Groping through the dark, Poppy stretched her own hand forward and found Chloë's dewy bud to return the favour.

'It's so big,' Poppy whimpered, as Chloë began banging her crotch against her, forcing the toy even deeper inside them both. Unable to resist, Poppy swiped the blindfold off her eyes and looked down her body to see Chloë writhing and banging on the truncheon-sized shaft that joined them together. Turning her face to the side, she uttered a heartfelt moan of delight and chewed at Chloë's ankle, rooted into the leather cushion beside her head. 'Go on, Chloë. Harder. Just take me.'

Immediately, Chloë began a rhythmic gasping and slapped her hands about on the sofa. Kicking out with her legs, Poppy slipped towards a climax, joining her lover in grinding hip-surges until their bodies finally relaxed.

From the side, seated on a stool, Hector applauded and then zipped his erection away. 'Chloë darling, must you always exhaust our fairer guests?' he said, and walked across to the couch to collect Poppy from between his slave's thighs. With his strong arms, he effortlessly lifted

Poppy from the couch and carried her to the dentist's chair, where he positioned her sitting upright and unlaced her corset, giving her breasts the freedom they'd screamed for all evening. As Poppy examined the marks her corset left under her breasts, he unclasped her ruined stockings and rolled them down to her ankles. 'Cold?' he asked. Poppy shook her head and allowed him to arrange her backside more snugly upon his macabre throne.

Angling his head like a bird of prey, he surveyed her naked body and began caressing her limbs as if stroking delicate porcelain. 'Chloë gets a little jealous,' he whispered. 'But don't worry: she likes you. She likes you a great deal.'

Poppy smiled. 'You're a lucky man. I don't know why she feels threatened. It's you who should worry.'

Hector raised an eyebrow and turned a lever at the side of the chair to tilt it in the middle, raising her upper body as if to invite observation of something below. 'Don't forget who's holding the needle-gun,' he said, and Poppy felt the smile die on her face.

From a satchel on his work surface, he withdrew a cluster of scarlet ribbons. 'Open your legs so your feet reach the sides of the chair.'

Poppy hesitated and Hector glared at her until, slowly, she moved her legs into place.

'Now put your arms along the rests.' Poppy obeyed. 'Good,' he said, and smiled.

Hector peeled off his vest and revealed a well-muscled torso completely inked to the waistline. Each illustration featured an act of extreme love and Poppy's eyes were immediately drawn to the image of a blonde woman hanging inside a gibbet while a horned creature impaled her from behind. As he moved across her body to check the fastenings, the second illustration that caught her eye revealed the head of a woman, concealed by a rubber mask save for her bright-red lips that were poised as if ready to accept something of size. In Poppy's stomach, an exquisite sensation of both dread and excitement began to grow.

'See something you like?' he asked, smiling at her

fascination. 'They are all taken from experience. Perhaps you too will find a place on my body.'

'I think we'll both help each other's art.'

He lowered his face and gorged himself on her breasts. Electrified by the teeth on her hard nipples, Poppy arched her back off the table and began to moan. With her nipples trapped between his incisors, he stretched them from her breasts before bathing the sting with a gentle tongue. There was the sound of a descending zipper and his erection was free. 'I want your mouth again,' he said. 'I remember my desire to fuck you in the alley interrupted some expert fellatio.'

Poppy smiled.

Using his foot on the lever, he lowered the chair almost to the floor, stood on his tiptoes, and fed his swollen glans between her lips. Her jaws were stretched to their furthest extreme, but she still managed to flick her tongue around the head of his cock. Hector rose to his toes and began to pump his manhood through her lips. Instinctively, she attempted to move her arms, forgetting about the ribbons which only pulled tighter, anchoring her beneath his hard body.

As the speed of his lunges quickened inside her mouth, it was as if he'd impaled her entire head and throat with his penis. The scent of his arousal crept through her sinuses and the feeling of utter helplessness, before a stronger body, thrilled her. Gradually, she relaxed beneath his pumping ferocity and Hector began to work his hand along the base of his cock until he could hold back no longer. After he released a long groan, she felt the cock spasm inside her mouth, repeatedly, and a tasty cream was spilt across her tongue.

With his fury spent, a glaze passed over his eyes. Smiling, Poppy swallowed his seed, knowing she'd pleasured him well. She experienced a curious satisfaction too, at the conquest of another assertive lover.

'Lie back and relax,' he whispered, and motioned for Chloë to approach.

The girl appeared, raised the chair back to waist height

and wiped a trail of semen off Poppy's chin. 'You're such a slut,' she whispered, but Poppy was pleased to see the excitement in the girl's eyes. 'A posh slut who'll do anything. And they're always the best.'

'Hood,' Hector said, standing by his workbench.

Frowning, Poppy whipped her head to the side, to see what Chloë had produced from beneath the chair and was currently stretching open. She only had time to mouth the word 'No' when the lights went out.

Inside the hood, which had a scent of stale perspiration, she could only hear her heart and the clatter of Chloë's heels on the floor. Before she had time to think, fingers busied themselves between her legs and something was inserted in her vagina. Poppy gasped, but soon enjoyed the length of the unexpected probe, which, unlike the last toy, was ribbed. Another hand slipped under her back and raised her buttocks a few inches off the chair. A new object, which felt cold, probed around the rim of her anus, searching for an entrance. The rushing of blood through her ears became a roar and Poppy whimpered, fondly remembering the dimensions of the baroness's tool. Her body contracted and then stiffened as a solidity, harder than aroused flesh, forced an entry into her back passage. It pushed on, as if determined to spear her heart, and she choked through an ecstasy of complete violation. Only when the device in her rectum could go no further did the hands disappear from beneath her.

Taking shallow breaths, and determined to endure his ritual, Poppy eased her body flat against the couch and waited.

'Keep still,' Hector whispered in her right ear.

The next thing she heard sounded like an insect. A small creature buzzing with annoyance and determined to sting. Outside of her hood, it drew closer, insistent, angry, and attracted to her pale skin. A hand caressed Poppy's head through the hood and someone's lips kissed her nipples. 'Relax,' she heard Chloë whisper, before the needle sank into her belly.

Speared in the anus and vagina and pricked by the

insect, Poppy began to feel faint. She could cry 'No, stop' and run from this underworld of freaks, but something kept her still and quiet. It was the same urge for self-sacrifice that prevented her from escaping the baroness, and the same desire to be a plaything that incited her to seduce the diner. These emotions frightened her, but were too exhilarating to deny.

On her belly, it felt as if the needle had disappeared beneath the top layer of her skin so the glinting shaft could touch her soul. Again and again it dipped and stung, illustrating patterns on her divine complexion.

Inside her sex, Chloë's toy was pulled and pushed, slowly, to take the edge off the sting and lead her towards a climax. The blend of stimuli, inside and outside her body, disorientated her. This was a continuous stream of pleasure and pain, coursing through her. Every nerve ending on her skin seemed to add itself to a symphony of sensation until she could think of nothing but the sting on her tummy and the glorious pressure on her womb.

In time, the pain numbed and then disappeared, superseded by the delight of Chloë's skilled attentions between her legs. Poppy moaned and tried to raise her hips as an orgasm crashed through her, but strong hands held her still, bottling a storm of ecstasy inside her until she thought her mind would shatter.

As she whimpered and peaked through her climax, the buzzing stopped and the needle was removed. Before she regained her breath, cotton wool was dabbed on her stomach and her wrists and ankles were untied. When the hood was pulled off, all was revealed.

Within a tender patch of skin, no bigger than a large coin, the series of interwoven circles had been carefully etched upon her groin. On either side of her shoulders, Chloë and Hector smiled down at her. Poppy pushed her head forward and examined it more closely.

'What do you think?' Hector asked.

'It's beautiful,' she whispered.

'The skin has been traumatised, but only temporarily. I'll give you a gauze to protect the ink.'

Still dazed, she reached between her buttocks and felt the end of a small steel plug. Chloë smiled and eased Poppy on to her side to remove the tool from her weary rectum. Poppy glanced at Chloë's hand and saw a tiny butt plug, shaped like a little mushroom, between the girl's fingers.

As if reading Poppy's thoughts, Chloë said, 'In the dark everything is amplified.' She kissed the tip of Poppy's nose, making her whimper as the other thick toy was extracted from her sex.

'Nearly finished,' Hector said. 'Let me clean you up and then I'd like to extend an invitation. An offer, if you like, for something very special.'

Poppy smiled. 'You're spoiling me.'

'Tonight was a mere kiss compared to this.'

'What is it?'

'There is a date on the rear of this card. On that night, there will be a gathering in a place designed for people who live for their passion – be it servitude or power. But think carefully before you accept. This place is tough, real hardcore. That's why it's accessible by invitation only.'

While Chloë dabbed a numbing antiseptic on the tattoo to remove all traces of pain, Hector produced a small card from his wallet. 'Not even the authorities know of it. That is, those who aren't members.'

On the card, a black script read:

Seasons in the Abyss. Members Only.

On the back of the card there was a date plus an address in the docklands sector of town.

'Is it a club?' Poppy asked.

Hector nodded. 'Where extraordinary and sometimes important people lose themselves, in private. I think you should pay a visit.'

'Are you sure?' Chloë asked her master.

'After the delights I brought home for you tonight, Chloë, how can you doubt her suitability? I think Poppy's perfect.'

Poppy looked up at her hosts. 'Thank you, but can you tell me anything else?'

Hector and Chloë gave each other a look. 'No,' they said in unison.

'Just be aware, though,' Hector added, with an air of finality, 'it will either give you nightmares for the rest of your life or you may never want to leave.'

Six

And the next blow was delivered at frightening speed. Like the prelude to the previous ten strokes, the baroness took a deep breath as she raised her arm to deliver the corrective measure. Then a whooshing sound followed as the heavy leather strap swooped through the air to slap on her valet's buttocks.

'The cold-hearted bastard punished me,' she said, panting. 'He actually disciplined me. After all I've done' – the pitch of her voice rose and the young man flinched in anticipation of another lash – 'it was me, he said, who'd taken a liberty. Me!'

Fisting his hands on a cushion, Thomas readied himself. As expected, the blow came sharp. Even the sound of the slap ricocheted off the crystal and glass in the dining room. Lightning streaks spread from the numb centre of his cheeks to the top of his thighs. It felt as if his backside had been covered with brandy and then set alight.

This was too much of a good thing. Tempted as he was to remain on all fours and receive her bullying for another month, the flesh of his buttocks would soon harden and be insensitive to even a bed of nails.

After the dishevelled and shell-shocked figure of his mistress and keeper had staggered back to the apartment, following a meeting with Eliot Rilke a month earlier, she had vented an incessant rage on him. When she awoke, so did he. When she spoke, he flinched. There were calls on the intercom every ten minutes, demanding food, drink, relaxants, hot baths, massages, readings from her favourite books, company, a sympathetic ear. End to end, she'd worn Thomas out.

'I believe in loyalty, Thomas. And in fairness. Paying in kind, if you like. An old-fashioned girl, that's me. We have a good working relationship, do we not?'

Thomas thought of the last four years of his life: of how many times he had painted her toenails, polished her boots, laundered her clothes, been humiliated on shopping expeditions, cuffed, whipped, trodden on, and kicked. Yes, he thought with a smile, it's been heaven.

'Yes, ma'am,' he whispered. 'I'm very fortunate.'

'You are. And you have the intelligence to realise it. You went to the best university in the country and I'm glad to say your time was not wasted. You know something about the nature of partnerships. You understand the hard work and the sacrifice I have endured for that man, and yet our benevolent leader sees fit to humiliate me over a girl. The girl I saw first, whom I nurtured, and am forbidden to see! A second sculpture has been unveiled while I'm a prisoner in my own home. Where is the justice, Thomas?'

A twelfth lash licked across the back of his thighs and brought a fresh welling of tears to his eyes.

Typically, she suddenly lost interest in the flogging and dropped the belt to walk across to the bay window. Another random thought or whim had entered her head and distracted her. Thomas turned and watched his mistress parade through the room. For the third day running she had neglected to dress fully. Chic dresses and Italian suits had been left untouched in her expansive wardrobe. Instead, she remained stripped for the kind of action that left Thomas constantly nursing an erection and unable to sit down. Black nylons, sling-back heels, and a waist-pinching corset – she'd not made it any further in the customary dressing ritual that usually consumed two hours of their mornings together.

He'd never seen the baroness in such a state. What did this sculptress have? To defy Eliot Rilke and interfere with the girl was tantamount to insanity. A person could disappear for less. Why had his mistress risked everything for one luncheon with that girl? Thomas had served Poppy lunch and had to admit she was young and beautiful, but the baroness had entertained a seemingly endless supply of pretty girls and youths over the last four years. Why was this one so captivating? It was a mystery to him, even though he knew his mistress better than anyone.

Currently, she was bored and that spelt trouble. His mistress lived in a continual cycle of fresh stimulation. Parties, dinners, clubs, appraisals of new initiates – her social engagements were her life. Take that away and she would crack. After her confinement at home, he doubted whether his stamina, let alone his inflamed buttocks, could withstand another day of her captivity.

Not even Rilke seemed fully aware of his actions. According to Henry, the man had spent a small fortune on Poppy's first sculpture and intended to buy every one of her creations. Plans were already being drawn up by Rilke's lawyers for the sale of several valuable assets in order for him to purchase her future work.

Following Eliot's own brand of justice, his mistress was still too embarrassed to confide fully in Thomas and confess the true nature of her punishment. During one of their walks together, however, in the Francis Bacon Memorial Park, Henry had related the full details of the incident to Thomas and he'd immediately needed to sit down to digest the news. Not only had she been flogged, but also taken forcefully by Henry, a mere manservant. The very idea was heretical to the cult she and Rilke had developed together. One of the select had been forced to submit; it had never happened before and both valets dreaded the aftermath.

'Here,' the baroness demanded, and pointed to a spot on the floor before her heels. 'You haven't listened to a word I've said. You're not interested in how I feel.'

'Ma'am, that's not true, I –'

'Don't interrupt. Do you disrespect me too? Happy with your pots and pans, and little errands I am good enough to provide? Selfish. Everyone is so selfish. For once, boy, consider me.'

'Ma'am, you know, my first thought is always for you.'

'I know nothing of the kind.'

With his head bowed, Thomas walked to where she stood.

'Look at me,' she said, quietly.

He obeyed and saw her face soften. The rage had passed, momentarily, and now she would indulge in self-pity.

'Take me for a ride, boy.'

'But the restraining order –'

'Not in the car, fool. On your back. Remember the game we had, when you were a student and you tended my garden. It helps me relax.'

Delighted, Thomas dropped to all fours and braced himself for her weight. Her naked behind settled in the small of his back and she slid her legs over his shoulders so that her high heels rubbed against his cheekbones. Slowly, Thomas began to crawl around the dining room rugs and, while the baroness jabbered away, he closed his eyes and lapped at her spiked heels.

'Has Poppy given me a second thought?' she asked.

'Sure she has, ma'am.'

'Why are you sure?'

'Because of your taste and beauty. Any girl in her position would be glad of such an eminent mentor.'

'There is wisdom in your words, but why hasn't she come back to me?'

'Been working on her sculptures, ma'am.'

'Yes,' she said softly. 'And I deserve her, Thomas. I could make her happy.'

While she distracted herself with thoughts of the girl pining for her, Thomas began to push his back upward, gently, so he could feel the soft flesh of her sex on his spine. As he turned to crawl back across the dining room, he allowed his lips and nose to swiftly pass across the top of her slippery foot – his favourite delicacy. In response, the head of his cock moistened.

'Well, would she?' the baroness asked.

Too frightened to admit to missing the first part of her question, because he'd been preoccupied with her slender foot, Thomas said, 'Of course.'

67

Suddenly the baroness clapped her hands and leapt off his back, taking her foot away. 'Darling,' she shrieked. 'For a member of the serving masses, you surprise me with your rare bouts of genius.'

'I do?' he said, frowning.

'Of course, why ever did I not think of this before?'

'Of what?' he dared to ask, but the baroness was too excited to hear.

With her arms spread wide, she walked around the room. 'Everything she needs is right here! Privacy, comfort, good wine and food, my tutelage, staff to attend to her needs. Poppy will be delighted with the idea. And that frozen bastard need never know.'

Thomas stiffened. What was she considering? What had he inadvertently encouraged her to think?

'But ma'am –'

'But nothing! My mind is made up. Prepare yourself for a treat, my little man. And after that you will prepare her room, and I want it to be splendid.'

Despite his anxiety, the sight of his mistress slipping off her shoes made his blood rise. He swallowed hard and rolled on to his back to accept her feet on his face. With her heels in his eye-sockets and her toes on his chin, she stood tall and balanced her entire weight on his face.

'Do you have to play with yourself when I do this? It's beastly,' she said, and must have been eyeing the movements of his hands along his erect penis.

She stepped off his face. 'Shan't let it go to waste. On the couch, boy.'

Mesmerised by the sway of her pale buttocks and the length of her legs, Thomas hurried after her to the chaise longue. Reclining on a throw rug, with her thighs parted, she reached behind her head and slipped a riding crop from a Grecian vase.

Thomas nearly came at the thought of what he was about to receive, but clenched the muscles at the base of his penis, determined to make the rarest of pleasures last. She hadn't asked him to service her in this manner for over six months.

Gently, he slipped between her legs. She closed her eyes and he mouthed the words 'Bitch. Beautiful bitch' at her, delighted she couldn't see. The head of his cock nuzzled at the mouth of her vagina and she clasped his waist with her legs to draw him in. Moaning and shivering, Thomas sank his length inside his employer. The baroness's eyelids fluttered and she exhaled a plume of fragrant breath over his face.

Leaning forward, Thomas lowered himself so their nipples touched and his face hovered no more than an inch from hers. Kissing was forbidden. In four years he'd never kissed anything above her waist, but he mouthed the words 'I love you, beautiful bitch', which pleasured him more than any kiss he could remember. Slowly, he penetrated her to the hilt, slipped back out and repeated the stroke. Tingling with excitement at the thought of what was coming, he increased the vigour of his thrusts.

'Faster,' she muttered.

He obeyed and gritted his teeth.

'Faster, you bastard!'

Gripping the armrest behind her head, he raised his body off her softness and rammed his shaft home.

'Yes!' she shrieked, and raised the hand holding the crop.

With all his might, he thrust inside his mistress so the couch squeaked and rocked on the wooden tiles she'd imported from Bucharest.

'Ride boy. Ride hard!' she said, gasping.

Thomas thrust down and ground his pelvis against her clit. With a deft flick of her wrist she caned his backside, and shouted, 'Harder.'

Unleashing a long, pent-up moan, Thomas moved the lower half of his body like a machine, spearing his erection down evenly and quickly inside the now kicking baroness. Hours of ironing, carrying shopping bags, mowing lawns, and cleaning the indoor pool had developed his strength for this task.

After each of his strokes had rested inside her for a split-second, she'd strike down on his body with the riding crop. The faster he thrust, the harder she raked his back, buttocks and thighs with lines of fire, until the weapon flew from her fingers and bounced off a marble statue. Without the crop she used the flat of her hand, and to the fast rhythm of her slaps Thomas thumped his groin against her until her breasts shook and her face contorted.

'Fuck me,' she began to say between her throaty gasps, and Thomas knew he'd soon pass the point of no return.

'Fuck me!' she screamed, and he used the last of his resources to ream her so hard they tumbled from the couch and rolled across the floor, still attached at the hip.

'Mouth,' she whispered, her voice barely audible. Thomas wrenched his shaft free of her sex and, as he'd been taught, milked every drop of semen between her lips.

Capturing his essence, or so she called it. It was an honour to feed her in this manner. For years, as he stood by or drove her car, he'd often been forced to watch her swallow the essence of other young men. And when he lay alone in his quarters, stroking an erection, those images of her excesses would haunt him.

Her throat made squelching noises as she gulped his cream down, and Thomas felt his elbows weaken. For a moment after he came, there was a rare display of affection from his mistress and she clasped him against her chest to hug him. After seeing him smile, however, she bit his mouth and pushed him away.

Curled up on a rug, Thomas mouthed the words 'I love you, beautiful bitch'. And he did, knowing full well he'd carry her suitcases and hat boxes to the frozen wastes of hell just for one caress from her foot or hand.

Looking at the ceiling, with a dreamy expression on her face, the baroness was lost again to her scheme. 'Her room will be marvellous. Full of the finest things. She'll eat breakfast in bed – Thomas's special omelettes – and then she'll swim in the pool before working on her sculptures. In the evenings she and I will retire together and learn so much of each other.'

But what if she won't come? Thomas thought. Or what if she does and the master finds out? What will become of us then?

'Thomas darling, I want to offer you an incentive. When you have made the necessary preparations and her room is fit for a princess, there will be spike-heeled boots for your back and Italian sandals for your stomach. If I see fresh flowers in vases and chocolates in crystal bowls then I might flush you.'

Crossing Eliot Rilke was insane – an assured method of self-destruction – but the thought of an enema delivered by his mistress would inspire him to prepare the most beautiful guest room of his career.

'Now,' she continued. 'Prepare my lunch. I have an important phone call to make.'

'Why hasn't she answered my messages? Do you think she's been out all evening?'

Thomas sighed as the baroness continued her slow passage up his back with patent-leather boots on her feet. As he enjoyed the prods over his kidneys from a pair of six-inch heels, her obsession with the sculptress was the last thing he wanted to consider.

'Ow!' he shrieked when she pressed her right heel under his shoulder.

'You're not listening to me, boy.'

'I am. Really, ma'am, I was just considering the possibilities.'

'She has a lover?'

'Not so.'

The heel depressed further into his shoulder. 'How can you be sure?'

'Ahh . . . She works and is impatient with distractions. Consider the artistic temperament.'

'Maybe you're right,' she replied tersely, and stepped off his back. 'But I don't like to wait. No one keeps me waiting. Was I too rough with her? Am I too rough, Thomas?'

'Oh no, ma'am.'

'It's this infernal waiting and imprisonment. I need to redirect this energy.'

Thomas pushed the pair of high-heeled shoes towards her.

71

'I'm tired,' she said, and flopped into an armchair to finish a glass of wine.

'But you said, if I fixed her room –'

'All right! Will you stop whining?'

Smiling, Thomas unzipped the boots from her legs, and kissed her hot feet. Taking his time, he slipped the spaghetti-thin straps of the sandals around her ankles. Gazing at the ceiling, she raised a foot and Thomas suckled the heel while stroking his erect penis in the palm of his hand.

'Front or back?' she muttered, and began examining her nails.

'Front, please.'

'Very well,' she said with a sigh, and rose from the chair.

Thomas closed his eyes and waited for her feet. The leather soles came first as she eased herself on to his tensed stomach. Seven-inch heels, with a gold sheen, touched home next and Thomas groaned. He opened his eyes and looked up at the baroness, still resplendent in her corset and black stockings. When her careful steps reached his chest, he gazed at her sex and a sudden urge to taste her gripped him.

Bending her knees, she crouched down. As if sensing his desire, she said, 'I have another task for you. I want you to watch her very carefully. If she fails to make contact tonight, go and follow her tomorrow and every other day after until an opportunity presents itself.'

'An opportunity?' he muttered.

'Umm, to approach her.'

'Is that wise?'

'Do you want to taste me or question everything I suggest?'

Thomas stayed silent but continued to eye the lips of her vagina, squashed between her hips.

'Well?' she said, with one eyebrow raised.

'Taste,' he whimpered.

She smiled and placed her ankles on either side of his face. Right away he could smell her, all musky and aroused, with a hint of his seed in her odour. Thomas moistened his lips.

Darkness and warmth engulfed his face and he stretched out his tongue to flick across her dewy labia.

'That's good,' she whispered.

He lapped between her outer lips and the tip of his tongue slithered across to the pink tenderness, probing forward when it passed across the tight entrance to her vagina.

'You'd have been out on the street, boy, if your mouth didn't make me shiver so.'

Thomas moaned and began circling her clit with his tongue. After a gasp, the baroness pressed her wet sex down to cover his lips and chin.

'Can't get her out of my mind,' she whispered in a confessional tone. 'Am I a fool, boy?'

'There's no crime in a little foolishness, ma'am,' he said, in a muffled voice.

She laughed and began to rub herself on his teeth. 'Am I wet?'

'Ummm.'

'Would you like to fuck me, with my toes in your mouth?'

Unable to contain himself, Thomas grasped her shins and began stroking them aggressively.

'Steady, boy. Don't get me riled.'

He pursed his lips and began sucking her noisily, making her wince and moan.

'Now,' she gasped. 'I want it now.'

Gently, he lowered her to the rug, removed her shoes and stockings and then slipped her toes into his mouth. He massaged his cock inside her sex and gripped her thighs, making sure he was still able to see her face between her knees. The baroness had rolled her eyes back and begun to twist and pull at her own nipples.

Thrusting forward, he added a tremor to her moans, while lapping at the underside of the toes he manicured weekly.

'Oh yes. That's good,' she cried, pinching her nipples.

Why am I not enough for you? he thought, and began swishing his tongue on the ruffled underside of her feet. Do you know how you torture me with your lovers? he wanted to ask, but pumped her harder instead. I hear you punishing young men at night, and slapping that pretty schoolteacher who calls you Aunty. Do you know what you put me through, you beautiful, depraved bitch?

'Faster, boy. Get it in deeper, or I'll find someone who can!'

Thomas pressed her thighs down to her breasts to assist his efforts at deep penetration, and began banging his groin against the base of her buttocks. Her red claws gripped the rug and tore bits of white fur free. She tried to speak but only groaned, and he kept on thrusting into her, daring himself to whisper, 'I love you, my beautiful bitch.'

'Coming,' she gasped.

Thomas felt a boiling sensation at the base of his cock. 'Please say it, ma'am,' he whimpered, feeling his thoughts disperse like a gas at the point of ejaculation.

'Make me yours,' she whispered through her grunts. 'All yours.'

Thomas came. Hot dollops of cream pulsed from his phallus and splashed at the back of her sex. It worked every time. She was fifteen years his senior but when she uttered those words he climaxed, instantly. For a short while he could pretend he'd tamed an aggressive and insatiable feline who would look no further – a moment when a slave suddenly became all his mistress could ever want. He'd feel ashamed afterwards, and the baroness would tease him.

Sighing with his eyes clenched, Thomas emptied himself inside her, shaking his buttocks to free every last drop from the end of his penis. Perversely, he had the master to thank. While the baroness was in exile, he was her only available means of satisfaction.

'Good, Thomas,' she whispered. 'Oh you good boy. I'd forgotten how eager you can be. That was the best orgasm I've had, darling, since that barbarian, Henry, ravaged me.' An evil smile flicked across her mouth and through half-closed eyes she watched his sudden discomfort.

'There are ways,' she said, 'for an old fool to keep a young man hard.'

'Yes, ma'am,' he muttered and blushed.

'And, tomorrow, we track the beauty.'

He nodded and bit his bottom lip.

'Won't be so bad, Thomas,' she cooed at him.

'No, ma'am.'

'And perhaps a quick flush will assure your vigilance on the morrow.'

His eyes lit up. 'Shall I fetch the apparatus, ma'am?'

'Yes. And be quick in case I change my mind. You've been spoilt today.'

Thomas sped to the box where the hoses and pump were kept, while his mistress reclined behind him and dreamt of someone else.

Seven

'Why have I been brought here? If you're thinking of kidnap, forget it, my husband's broke.'

Eliot remained silent and continued to smile at Molly – the pretty young wife of one of his prominent clients, and debtors. Behind her, Henry stood with his arms folded and the usual blank expression on his face.

'Why is it so cold in here? It's freezing,' she added, chattering to allay her fear. 'What is this place?'

'My home,' Eliot said, finally breaking his silence after taking the time to enjoy the sight of Molly's exquisite figure, and the scent of fear surrounding it. Dressed in a pinstriped suit, a black fur coat and high heels, she had been removed from a shopping excursion in central Darkling Town by Henry and two cycle cops on Rilke's payroll.

'Look, I've had enough of this,' she said through gritted teeth. 'Who are you?'

Eliot said nothing.

'It is because of my husband then, isn't it? He owes you money.'

'Smart girl,' Eliot whispered.

'But he owes everybody money.'

'Maybe, but I collect.'

'But he doesn't give a damn about me. You should have abducted his golf clubs.'

'He will give a damn.'

Molly swallowed. 'I have some jewellery – I can get it from a safety deposit box –'

76

'Please,' Eliot interrupted. 'Don't be vulgar. You're embarrassing me. The only collateral that interests me is you.'

'Me. What can I do?'

'We'll know soon enough.'

Fidgeting in her narrow-heeled shoes, Molly seemed to be catching on.

'Molly darling, I want your soul,' Eliot said with a smile, spreading his hands across the surface of his desk. 'But don't worry, I'll give it back once I've had a look inside.'

'This is illegal. They give you the therapy for kidnap.'

Wafting his hand, as if to knock an annoying insect away, Eliot said, 'The law? What power has the law between consenting adults?'

'But I don't consent. I demand you –' she turned to glare at Henry '– set me free, right now.'

'You will consent, my dear. On that issue I am never wrong.'

'Are you fucking insane?' she said, frowning in disbelief.

A wide smile broadened across Eliot's mouth and he began to chuckle. 'Henry, introduce Molly to our guests. You know how keen they are to make her acquaintance. In fact, my dear, we've all had our eyes on the pretty executive's wife for some time. So many of my special friends have recently asked, "When is Molly coming to the party?"'

'You are crazy,' she whispered. 'You are completely out of your mind.'

'Not yet, darling, but soon you will be. And then you can start working off your husband's debt.'

Gripping her elbow, Henry attempted to lead Molly towards the door of Eliot Rilke's office. With anger now exceeding her bewilderment, she snapped her arm from Henry's hand and took several steps towards Eliot. With a quick nod, he gave Henry the next command and Molly was seized around the waist, hoisted into the air and dropped over the valet's shoulder as if her weight was of no consequence. Despite the blows she drummed on Henry's back with clenched fists, his stride out of the office remained unbroken.

'And what a career I have in mind for you, Molly,' Rilke said, following the pair. 'Never thought you'd end up a high-class call girl, I bet.'

She stopped fighting and twisting on Henry's shoulder and raised a red face to stare in mute horror at Rilke. 'That's right,' he continued. 'You'll perform the most beastly deeds on command. With all that style and spark, my customers will adore you. Smart and sexy, my dear, that's what the market demands and that's just what it shall get. And don't look so outraged: you've been enjoying the favours of a young hotel porter for months. Episode two in the elevator is one of my enduring favourites. The days of paying a working man to cane you are over.'

From the office, Henry carried the now silent Molly through the penthouse to the correction chamber – where everybody was waiting, impatiently. At the sight of Molly, a wave of sighs and whispers immediately rose from the assembled elite, who stood close to the walls, half-obscured by clouds of vapour.

'Master, you have even exceeded your existing standards with this pretty little thing,' a tall woman said as she stepped forward to the edge of a wide rubber mat that created a black pool in the centre of the mirrored room. As if poured like a coat of glossy paint across her slender contours, the woman's dress moved with every sinew and muscle on her body. Fine leather gloves squeezed her pale arms to her elbows and the seamed stockings that shone on her legs were exposed between patent ankle boots and the short hem of the dress. But it was her head that made Molly gasp. Latex as thin as skin formed the hood concealing her features and hair. Only her glossy lips, bright teeth, and eyes shielded by opaque contact lenses were visible. Around her neck, the hood descended into a choker, made from a thicker rubber than the mask, to hold her chin upright in a permanent display of arrogance. After Henry lowered Molly to the padded mat and moved away from her, the tall woman began tapping the ground around Molly's heels with a tipped cane.

'Stay away from me,' Molly said through clenched teeth, trying to rekindle her fight while proving herself incapable of looking at the cane with anything but excitement.

Smiling, the rubber-skinned mistress raised her cane and prodded one of Molly's breasts. Before Molly had time to retaliate, there was the sound of a second pair of high heels behind her. After turning quickly to face the new threat, Molly gasped and began walking backward until the tip of the cane, placed in the small of her back, held her still. Like a hellish parody of a widow in mourning, the second figure was bound rather than dressed in a floor-length gown made from black hide, which parted down the front and allowed a glimpse of her legs, mummified in thigh-high boots. Inside the borders of her magnificent and multilayered head-dress, a mask, fashioned on the image of a young Elizabeth Taylor, offered an unchanging smile.

In a symphony of squeaks and rasps, other women materialised through the fog to gather around the now breathless girl, whose small nipples had risen to spikes beneath her blouse. Turning on the spot, Molly watched the bizarre creatures form a shiny corral around her. There was a sinister-looking bride clad in a black lace gown and veil, two women wearing gasmasks to complement patent-rubber body suits, and a statuesque, shaven-headed woman wearing nothing besides severe heels, a china mask and a belly chain. Every face in the group was shielded to reveal nothing but the odd nose, or mouth, or eyes. Each woman reeked of expensive perfume. Where visible, their nails were red and cruel. Heels and boots were spiked, and every hushed voice was clipped by its owner's breeding.

Standing back from the shiny squad of his followers, Rilke anticipated the submission of Molly with a grin of delight on his face.

There was a shriek as she was seized and brought down to her knees by the woman with the cane, assisted by the shaven-headed giantess. A sudden stampede of tipped heels and boot soles then signalled a free-for-all, as every coven member jostled and shoved to get at the girl. Sounds of tearing cloth were heard above both her cries and the excited yelps of her tormentors. From afar, it seemed Molly was being ripped apart by the mob, but when it parted she appeared again, stripped down to her black underwear, her skin scratched in places and her limbs securely tied. Bent double, with her head gripped between her own knees, upon which her weight was supported, her wrists had been lashed to her ankles, leaving her unable to move freely besides a gentle rocking motion from one kneecap to the other.

Every masked face turned towards Eliot and awaited his signal. He nodded, and a tall, busty woman stepped through the crowd to stand above Molly. From the rear of her hood, long hair – dark though streaked with silver – fell in a ponytail to her waist. Tight riding breeches with the crotch neatly removed covered her hips and legs to her knees, before a pair of boots with spurs gripped her calves and long feet. Despite the cold, her torso had been left naked to display a large bosom and the silver rings that pierced each nipple.

Without a word, she sat in the small of Molly's back, gripped her garter belt like a horse's reins and began to thrash her backside with a short leather strap. Muffled moans of satisfaction could be heard through the leather bit in Molly's mouth, and no quarter was shown as the executive's wife began to reveal more of her unusual tastes. The severe belabouring continued, making a crisp slapping sound that left a ringing in the ears, until Molly's cries were finally silenced. More than a score of blows had registered on her ruddy backside during the flogging, and the cheeks of her face were now wet with tears. As if pleased with her initial response to the treatment, the two girls in gasmasks removed the ropes from her wrists. This time, beside a brief struggle after the bonds were gone, Molly's resistance had lessened.

Another four of Rilke's followers approached and held her down while the girls in gasmasks retied her wrists to her ankles. In the new position, her legs were stretched apart and she was placed on her shoulders so that her high heels spiked into the air. The gag was left in place and

Molly's large green eyes were frantic with excitement. They flicked left and right as several shadowy figures circled her on all fours, whispering obscenities as they drew near. It was not long before they pounced. When both of her large nipples were completely encircled by rubber-fringed mouths, and loving caresses stroked along her muscular legs and the tenderness of her belly, it seemed her eyes were becoming heavy with sleep.

'Now she is ours,' Rilke whispered to Henry, the moment the change passed over Molly's face. 'Even if we were to let her run free right now, her sleep would be haunted by this moment for ever. It would be a nightmare from which she would wake screaming, only to find her fingers damp and clasped between her thighs.'

Only the widow had remained standing until this moment, and soon it became apparent she was merely biding her time. When she finally moved towards the captive, she opened her long cloak and raised her apron to reveal a rigid appendage, suspended between her thighs. Suddenly catching sight of it above her exposed buttocks and sex, Molly squirmed in anticipation and several pairs of gloved hands righted her and then pressed her into the mat. The masked widow dipped her crotch and allowed the tip of her false penis to tickle the outer drapes of Molly's sex. After jerking her body forward, Molly then relaxed and succumbed to the thickness that began to pass through her, one inch at a time.

Eliot approached Molly, whose pale body now shook and bounced as the mighty baton seemed to almost raise her from the mat before thrusting her down. He was afforded a view between her gartered buttocks of her pink sex stretched to its widest extreme by the black pole that oozed so deeply inside her he almost expected to see the phallic head emerge inside her mouth to fill out her cheeks. Every muscle tensed beneath her pale skin and each one of her fingers stretched out from her hands until her knuckles whitened. On her face, only the eyes stood out amongst the pretty features suddenly engorged with a flush of humiliation and uncontainable arousal.

Increasing the rhythm of her thrusts, the widow began plumbing the very extremities of Molly's sex, making her groan and cease tugging against her bonds. Instead, her body seemed to soften and, by bending her knees, she placed her ankles on the widow's hips. When she closed her eyes and her hands became fists, Eliot said, 'Remove the gag.'

The woman with the cane crept forward, removed the leather bit from Molly's mouth and tenderly kissed the girl's damp forehead.

'Now,' Eliot whispered, 'let us hear her shame.'

'Is it good?' the widow cooed at Molly, and pressed the shaft inside the girl until even the hilt had been swallowed by her soft insides. Molly stayed silent, so the widow began to slowly withdraw the glistening pillar from her sex. When only the thick head was left inside, Molly whimpered, 'No.'

Around the couple on the mat, a sighing chorus of approval sounded and Eliot's grin broadened.

'Louder,' the widow coaxed.

'No. Don't take it away,' Molly whispered.

'You want me to fuck you some more?' the widow said, breathless with excitement.

Molly mumbled something that no pair of straining ears caught.

'Speak up!' the widow demanded.

Molly winced, her lips parted, before a groan slipped out and she said, 'Fuck me.'

'What?'

'I want you to fuck me.'

'Like this?'

Molly shrieked with delight at the force of the thrust.

'Or like this?' Seizing Molly's ankles, the widow began a series of quicker but shallower plunges in and out of her sex.

Groaning and biting her bottom lip, Molly threw her head back and began to croak in time with every stroke inside her. To the surprise and delight of everyone present, she then turned her head and gasped, 'Harder, you bitch.'

Closing his eyes, Eliot savoured the sound of Molly's

music. Beneath him, the rest of the coven applauded before creeping forward in unison to feast on the girl's body.

'Hood her,' Eliot commanded the seething mass of shiny latex and clawing nail, before turning to Henry and saying, 'It is time.'

With a nod, Henry left the correction chamber and Eliot turned back to the massacre on the mat. Molly's writhing shape was now almost entirely concealed by the swarm of glistening sadists. The shaven-headed girl wearing the crotchless riding breeches had straddled Molly's face and ground her shaven sex on the captive's chewing teeth. Both of Molly's nipples had been clamped and the fleshy expanse of her bosom was indented with the bruises left by prodding fingertips. Between her thighs, where her expensive stockings now ran with ladders, the woman with the cane lapped around her clit. Inside the eyeholes in the cane wielder's mask, heavily painted eyelids had closed over the opaque lenses as she concentrated on bringing the executive's wife to another climax.

At the far end of the chamber a beam of light fell through the main doors and a group of men entered. Eliot walked across to greet the individuals, who were all dressed in dinner suits and overcoats. In their midst, a red-faced man, reeking of alcohol, laughed loudly. Supported by two smiling men at either elbow, he was led forward to stand before Eliot. A look of panic suddenly appeared on his face and he stopped laughing. 'Mr Rilke, I had no idea this was your home. The boys should have told me.'

Smiling, Eliot said, 'It's all right, Frank. There's no need to apologise. Relax, you're a guest here.'

'About the money,' the man stammered. 'I can explain. My new secretary is hopeless. I only received notification of your messages today. That's why your calls weren't returned –'

'Please, Frank,' Eliot said, placing a hand on the man's shoulder. 'There will be plenty of time to talk about business. In fact, I have resolved the small matter of your credit problem.'

'You have?'

'Yes, so let's not hear another word about it. This evening is a time of celebration in my home. An unusual affair, you'll soon see, but treat it as an opportunity to unwind. I trust the boys have warmed you up, because tonight's entertainment is very special indeed.'

'Yes, we've had a great time,' he said quickly, his words carrying the relief of a condemned man offered a reprieve at the moment of execution. 'And thank you, Mr Rilke, for this hospitality. I'm just overwhelmed by all this –' He paused and looked over Eliot's shoulder. 'What's going on over there?'

'Come and take a look, but keep your voice down: the girls are really enjoying themselves and we don't want to distract them. Let's get a little closer.'

'Good God,' Frank muttered, his eyes widening. 'Who are these women? What on earth are they wearing? That girl's in a wedding dress. Gasmasks? I've never seen anything –'

'Oh, we have these little get-togethers all the time, but only my special friends are allowed to attend.'

'There's a girl in the middle.' Frank's eyes shone and he rubbed at the stubble on his chin. 'That is definitely a girl.'

'Absolutely,' Eliot said. 'A pretty creature who came to me of her own accord, some time ago, and requested an invite to one of my little gatherings. She has a problem with her emotions. Adores sex, this one. Married too.'

'Never.'

'Yes, she is, but never stays faithful. The things this girl has done.'

'Is she nuts?'

'No, she's as sane as you and I, but she likes to let off steam at the weekend. She came to me and said, "Mr Rilke, give me something to occupy my time. I'm sick of shopping and coffee mornings. I want to really use my freedom when my husband's at work."'

'Naughty girl,' Frank muttered through a smile, and began breathing more quickly.

'I know it's only your first time here, Frank, but would you like to love her? She'll never know it's you, because she likes to wear a hood. It's the anonymity she craves. You know, the feeling of strange men and women inside her.'

'I – I don't know whether I could. I mean, with all the boys watching.'

'Go on, Frank,' someone muttered.

'You'll love it,' another piped up from the back.

'Watch this,' a third said, and moved towards the orgy, unbuckling his trousers.

'You old dog, Ted,' Frank cried out as the man eased the widow from between Molly's thighs to create his own access. After Molly placed her high-heeled feet on his shoulders, the man sank his length inside her and began thumping his crotch against her pelvis. Delighted by the sensation of a real organ inside her, while a dozen hands attended to every other part of her body, Molly began to issue a series of loud moans through the hood. Shuffling her buttocks up the mat, she moved closer to her new lover to swallow more of his manhood.

'Look at that, Frank,' Eliot said to the open-mouthed man beside him. 'Have you ever seen a girl with such an appetite?'

'No, I haven't. Sure she's not a professional?'

'That's the beauty of my relationship with her. You see, she's going to become a professional and work for my escort service, unsalaried. No fee, nothing. She'll work solely for the sheer joy of these encounters with strange men.'

'I want her,' Frank muttered.

'Then take her.'

'I don't deserve this, Mr Rilke. Really I don't,' Frank said, and moved towards the hooded girl, upon whom her most recent lover had just ejaculated.

Eliot smiled. 'Oh yes you do, Frank.'

In his haste to enter the salacious creature writhing before him on the mat, Frank tugged his zipper down and unleashed a stubby penis. Beneath him, two of the leather-clad girls enjoyed Molly's breasts and navel, so most of her body was still concealed from his eyes. But this only served to increase his excitement. His hands shook as he clumsily fed his cock inside the girl's sex. With a groan, he began a quick prodding and his face became waxy and beaded with sweat. Breathing heavily, he began ramming himself inside the hooded beauty, who responded by kicking her shapely legs into the air. He lost control at the sight of her rapture and seized her ankles to tear through her stockings and bite her ankles.

From the side, Eliot nodded to Henry.

Henry approached Molly and pinched the top of her hood between the finger and thumb of his right hand. In one quick motion, he whipped the garment off her head and the two women who devoured Molly's breasts suddenly sprang away, leaving her and Frank, still joined at the hip, in the centre of the mat. And after five years of marriage, they needed little introduction.

Relaxed in his chair and shielded within his study – a private sanctum and the very heart of his arctic retreat – Eliot inspected the latest batch from Poppy. By moving the polythene wrapper this way and that under his desk lamp, he could see a pair of tangled stockings. They were stained, and at least one seemed to have been ripped, but the fine knit still shone like the skin of eels under the surface of shallow water. Several pairs of the daintiest panties ever manufactured for a woman's loins could also be detected inside the sealed package, screwed up and spotted by milky droplets. Creased panty-girdles slipped about beneath the plastic also, as did brassieres of the finest gossamer – now frayed by misuse and torn by impatient teeth.

What had she found, out there in Darkling Town's alleyways and gutters? By which hands had her scantily clad body been twisted and caressed? The answers were inside the package. Every stain and tear, odour and crease had a whisper sealed inside it. A depraved secret for him to interpret at the appointed time. But for now he must wait and exercise the discipline and patience that had served him well throughout a life made unusual by an incurable taint in his blood.

Staying away from Poppy, however, was proving harder

than Eliot had originally thought. Schemes hatched daily in his mind: plans to have her photographed with company; to have strange masculine faces married to the cruel rends in her finery. Should he have her followed? What if she were to desert Darkling Town? Or find a permanent lover?

No, stalking her would destroy the mystique of the venture. As much as he ached to know everything, to watch her writhe and hear her cries, Eliot needed to maintain distance. It was all part of the plan; the ingenious formula to create the greatest act of voyeurism in history.

Like an addict, however, discovering a new and intoxicating supply of stimulation, Eliot realised he had become haunted by Poppy. For the three hours he managed to sleep each night, he saw her perfect face, increasingly contorted by pleasure as her innocence mingled with the sadism in their corrupt town.

He would look at the original passport photo, included with her application to Sheen Couture, now enlarged to cover the entire wall opposite his desk, and imagine how her features must change in the intense period between the choosing and discarding of her lovers. If only he could see the rest of her: the long and graceful limbs, and the skin as pale as cream. And the very thought of her wearing his garments could suffocate him with desire at any given moment. His appetite would flee, his stomach churn, his head spin, and his heart beat until it was fit to burst. He had become bewitched and enchanted by her, as she had become enslaved by the magic in her attire. That was the curse of the garments and he had been warned by the tailor.

Photographs of her new work, which he intended to buy at great expense, were littered across his desk. After the successful acquisition of the *Loving Captive*, which would be delivered to his apartment after the collection was complete, her agent was asking a king's ransom for the second piece and the bids were still flooding in. But he would have them; the sculptures were already his in spirit. It was he that had enchanted her by placing a second skin over her life to induce her inspiration and the actions it fed. He would acquire the entire collection upon completion, by whatever means necessary.

But what of her? What was to become of the beauty when her journey was finished and immortalised in sculpture? Of one thing he was sure: no one else would ever own her. She was a strange and precious treasure, re-created by him and him alone. It was only right, therefore, that he should keep her once the sculptures were complete.

'The guests are changing,' Henry said from the doorway, breaking into Eliot's thoughts.

'Pour me a drink, Henry.'

'Yes, sir.'

While Henry busied himself with Polish vodka and ice cubes, Eliot relaxed deeper into his chair. 'I think tonight was a success, Henry. The coven seemed delighted with my latest offering, and I can only hope their patronage will equal their enthusiasm for young Molly. Tomorrow you will make my bid for *Please* and send the Japanese buyer the photographs of his wife with our German agent. I don't like competition, Henry. It's unhealthy for a monopoly.'

'Yes, sir. What about the bid for the *Please* piece.'

'Increase it by twenty per cent, and if the Colombian is seen in the Daemonic Gallery again, fanning his fat face with a cheque book, I'll have to think of something to cool his ardour for Poppy's work.'

'He's dangerous, sir.'

'And so am I,' Eliot said, sharply. 'I've liquidated too many assets to come this far. I will have the sculptures.' Breathing out, Eliot touched his brow with trembling fingers, suddenly afraid of finding the signs of a raised temperature. Henry brought the drink over and looked at his employer with concerned eyes.

'Don't give me that look, Henry. I'll be all right, but get my apparatus ready all the same. I told you to stop looking at me like that!'

Henry lowered his eyes and Eliot saw him swallow.

Shaking his head, Eliot said, 'I'm sorry, but stop fretting. Everything's under control. I'm just a little tense, and will be until the sculptures are in my hands. And then Poppy can follow –' Eliot stopped speaking, and saw Henry's shoulders and face stiffen. This was further than he had ventured in sharing the final part of his plan with anyone.

'Does it surprise you, Henry?' he said in a softer voice, as if appealing for sympathy.

Henry said nothing.

'You know how I feel about that girl. I had no way of knowing that my relationship with Poppy would become so fruitful. Don't disapprove, Henry. You have no right. Think of what I've endured in this prison, and for how long. Am I not also entitled to feel what a healthy man does?'

'I – I am afraid for you, sir,' Henry said in a low voice.

'You think I'm a fool for risking everything? Why can't we go on like always? Is that what you're thinking? Understand, Henry, that my needs have changed. The ghosts displayed on these walls have taken the edge off my suffering, but they are not the same ...' Eliot's voice trailed off and he looked down at the blue skin on his hands. 'They are not the same as a living woman who thinks, feels and loves as I do. On this earth, I believe she is the only woman capable of being my lover and companion.'

A knock sounded against Eliot's study door.

Eliot cleared his throat, took a breath and nodded. Henry walked across the study and opened the door. In single file, a group of well-dressed men and women entered the study. Each face was flushed and smiling, and most of the crowd sported a champagne flute. Most of the women wore chic dresses or tailored suits beneath their furs, and the men remained in their overcoats.

'I hope it's been a pleasant evening,' Eliot said, smiling again.

Everyone bowed and muttered their thanks.

'In the absence of the baroness, Molly will go home with

89

the widow for tutoring. I want her working in a fortnight. As for Frank, throw that piece of garbage in the snow. He can have his wife back when the debt is cleared. Which brings me to my next request, a matter of overheads.'

There was a perceptible shuffling amongst the coven as Eliot's instructions moved to the question of money. 'As you are all aware, my new project requires a high level of maintenance, but you've all been to the Daemonic Gallery and are aware of the astounding results produced so far. No one will disagree this project deserves investment.'

The tall woman, who had masqueraded with the cane and latex mask in the correction chamber, looked towards the enormous photograph of Poppy's face on the wall and raised an eyebrow. 'Will you share?' she asked, and amongst her neighbours a ripple of fear spread.

Eliot smiled. 'Imogen, your appetite is exceeded only by your forthright manner, and I thank you for it. You've never been afraid to speak your mind in any situation, and you deserve – all of you – an explanation.'

Imogen nodded and blushed.

'All of you are aware of my collection. In fact many of you have supported it for years and aided its development to the present state of magnificence. In fact, the widow's gift of a president's wife's slip, stolen by a White House domestic over fifty years ago, made the best Christmas present I've received since childhood –' Eliot paused. 'Yes, I was young once.'

Everyone laughed and the beautiful redhead known as the widow performed a small curtsey.

'My personal resources, however, need support, and I know I can count on each of you to support this remarkable and unique opportunity. The Sheen Couture charade has directly influenced the work of an artist. Poppy has captured our creed. She has our vision and has unwittingly unveiled our philosophy to the world. Although we remain a secret, we now have a powerful voice. Her work must continue, and once the public has been offered a brief glimpse it will be displayed solely for our enjoyment in this gallery. Where it belongs.'

The coven remained silent until the widow, moved by

her leader's rhetoric, said, 'Sir, I pledge my support, as always.'

Eliot smiled and bowed his head.

'I was merely inquiring about a shareholder's return,' Imogen added. 'You know you can always count on me, sir.'

Other votes of confidence followed.

'My friends, the debt will be repaid twofold,' Eliot said, desperately wanting to add, 'Follow me and I will give you a queen like no other.' But instead he only said, 'Now, I'm tired and I must bid you all good night until the next summoning.'

Henry ushered the chattering coven out of the study.

When alone, Eliot shuffled from his chair and checked the thermometers on account of the slight discomfort he usually felt as summer approached. With everything in order, he moved through the central corridor towards his bedchamber. Although his body was exhausted, his mind still sped through every plan and scheme involving Poppy. Sleep would come slowly again, and be interrupted until dawn. To draw comfort and find his usual inner resilience, Eliot began to touch the glass surrounding several of his finest exhibits. If I can secure a corset worn by Frances Farmer in 1942, authenticated as hers at the height of her Paramount career, he thought, then I can have my princess. Beside the slip, a bottle of Lauren Bacall's pink nail polish, imprisoned within a tiny cube, brought a smile to his lean face, and the sight of Lupe Velez's French knickers – a gift to her from Weissmuller no less – never failed to fire a shiver of frost along his stomach lining. Before the iron doors to the master bedroom, Eliot paused and placed both his hands, palm outward, against the glass protecting a black negligée owned by Greta Garbo. Softly, he said, 'Poppy,' and then entered his room.

Beside the gigantic bed – draped in dark curtains – Eliot raised the lid of a vast alloy chest and dropped Poppy's soiled undergarments into the padded interior. He said her name once more and undressed for bed.

Eight

Surgery was complete. Wearing nothing but sheer white stockings provided by Sheen Couture and an old pair of biker boots, Poppy crept around her third sculpture and admired it. It had been set on a huge platform, the size of a wrestling ring, which in turn had been covered with artificial black bear fur.

As she crouched in the shadows of her most elaborate creation to date, she began to think of it as a strange altar offering sacrifice to an even stranger god. From where in the dark recesses of her mind had it come?

At waist height to an onlooker, a wall of surgical trolleys had been fixed in a perfect square around a vast operating table. Affixed to the top of each trolley, a range of instruments had been placed on red baize to encourage the audience to walk around the outside of the entire piece, in order to see every artefact on display.

Resembling exhibits in a perverse museum, the accessories had been purchased from an exclusive craftsman whom Hector, the skin artist, had recommended. Silver bars, studs, chains, and rings for body piercing occupied one trolley. Another housed a collection of artificial female limbs, to be attached by the black harnesses that trickled off them. Legs already sealed inside spike-heeled boots and arms coated by black latex lay amongst artificial breasts of a lifelike quality. Surgical twine and darning needles lay beside the grotesque but alluring limbs. Other trolleys were covered in a bizarre assortment of cuffs, body harnesses, hoods, gags, straightjackets and china masks. At the rear of the piece, the last wall of trolleys contained a variety of steel implements designed for purposes that even puzzled Poppy. They were the tools of madmen, she decided, but despite the cruel hooks and strange braces they were not without beauty.

A vast operating table, covered in black satin and set in the middle of the instruments, formed the centrepiece. The height of the platform had been arranged so the edges of the table would be higher than the average eye level. The design made it impossible for anyone, besides those with the benefit of a ladder or stilts, to see the entire contents of the table.

Above the centrepiece, a chandelier made from black iron hung on a chain as if to illuminate the aftermath of an operation. But the haze of red light that fell from the tallow candles in the chandelier offered nothing more than a suggestion of the table's contents. The centre of the table was deliberately dipped and only the patient's ankles, hands and hair could be seen.

These glimpses, however, told their own story.

Beautiful locks of ice-blonde hair fell in a torrent over the back of the table to gather on the fur below. From one angle, a tall man might argue the forehead and eyes of a pretty girl were visible. But while denied access to the actual set no one would ever be sure. Draped over either side of the rectangular table were the elegant hands of a woman, whose nails were lacquered with a rich crimson varnish. There was something peaceful about the pose the hands assumed, and between two fingers on the right hand was a cigarétte holder, tipped with a black panatella. An empty champagne glass, its rim stained by bright lips, was cradled in the other hand. Upon the end of the table bed the patient had arranged her feet with one heel poised upon the toes of the foot beneath. She wore high-heeled sandals, with straps as thin as electrical wire hugging the marble-white feet inside. Her toenails, also, were coloured a bright red.

There was nothing to suggest entrapment or unease in

93

what appeared to be the figure's elegant lounging upon the table, but on a stool beside her lay a pile of discarded clothes. Men's clothes. There were polished wing-tipped shoes, a pinstriped suit, cufflinks, striped braces and driving gloves. All discarded as if recently removed from a body.

With a long sigh of satisfaction, Poppy climbed her stepladder, leant over the table and placed a trilby hat on the body's midriff before declaring the work officially finished.

Four security guards had been posted, one at each corner of the exhibit's perimeter, to protect *Surgery* on the day of its unveiling. A thin chain had not been sufficient to deter the squash of people eager to see Poppy's new sculpture, and two men had already been caught attempting to steal accessories. Additional plain-clothes security staff confiscated cameras wherever flash bulbs exploded, and prevented the moralists from defacing *Surgery*. Two zealots had been caught smuggling cans of white paint inside the gallery and a daily vigil of sign-wielding fanatics had camped outside the building, protesting against what they called 'Devil Puppets'.

Poppy had gone beyond even the dreams of her past life. Darkling Town was a strange garden in which the rarest species of plant could grow. Amidst the daily routine of shootings, robberies, kidnappings and terror, she was the only artist exploring the sensual freedom in the city, and some people found it hard to accept.

Surgery had been assembled inside the Daemonic Gallery behind closed doors. It had taken more than two months to finish and only from above could the full scenario be observed in detail. She had thought about erecting a mirror above the black operating table, but decided it was best the viewer's imagination solve the puzzle.

Several hours after the unveiling, Poppy took a seat in the security control room of the gallery. Surveillance cameras fitted in the ceiling of the studio, dedicated solely to her piece, relayed the black and white faces of the crowd back to her as they stared at what she had created. After the usual routine of sleepless nights and skipped meals endured while working on a sculpture, she had intended to relax in the booth and watch her public. But no sooner had she made herself comfortable, stretching her legs out and lighting a cigarette, than she caught sight of an unusual woman on the monitor.

Clad from head to toe in a black yashmak, with only her hands and eyes visible, the curious figure was standing as close to the sculpture as she was able. Using the manual zoom on the control board, Poppy focused the camera on the woman's face and, even in two-tone, found the large eyes intriguing. They were full of excitement and something else: passion, or possibly hunger. It was the woman's hands, however, that enticed Poppy out of the booth. Although dressed in a restrictive Eastern garb, the woman's nails were long and lacquered.

Puzzled, Poppy walked downstairs and mingled with the throng, making sure her thin cape covered her dress. Made from a glossy rubber, as thin and light as nylon with lycra, the dress had been fashioned in a back-laced vest cut and would quickly make her the centre of attention if not covered. It tapered her bottom into a compact heart shape and displayed the creaminess of her back between thin criss-crossing laces. The neckline plunged all the way down to her navel, where it framed her skin illustration. On her feet she had chosen patent Cuban heels from Sheen Couture's latest delivery, and enhanced her legs with vintage nylons. And it was no more than a whim that had enticed her into a salon to have her hair fashioned after Lana Turner from a photograph taken in the fifties. Or was it? Ever since she had been a girl, she'd worn her hair long and free, besides the odd occasion when she tied it up for something special. But for the duration of her work on *Surgery*, Poppy had craved a genuine fifties look with Marilyn beauty spot, cherry lips, long lashes and dark eyeliner. Until the unveiling of the sculpture, her face and hair had been maintained by the best salon in Darkling

Town. This desire for change puzzled her, but when she had thought about the recent series of bizarre twists in her life she shrugged the query away.

Once on the main floor of the gallery, Poppy could see the cowled woman easing her way through the crowd in order to view the entire display. She occasionally rose on to her toes to peer at the artefacts arranged on one of the surgical trolleys. Hugging the wall, Poppy teetered around the outside of the crowd and peered above everyone's head to keep the Persian cowl in sight. She hadn't thought of anything to say, or even decided if she would speak to the girl, but was determined to take a closer look at her beautiful eyes and hands – to wonder what the shaded eyes had seen and what the elegant hands had touched.

While attempting to close on the girl, a sudden rush of German tourists eagerly pursuing their guide passed before Poppy. When the obstruction cleared, she had lost sight of her quarry. Disappointed, Poppy made her way to the chain surrounding *Surgery*, where she had last seen the woman, but she was no longer there.

Turning on her heel to escape the jostle and heat, Poppy caught her breath. She had stumbled into the petite Arab girl. The hooded figure with her flashing Egyptian eyes moved backward. Somehow, it seemed, Poppy had passed her in the crowd. But how? Lost for words, she smiled at the girl, who immediately lowered her eyes. In a heartbeat, the girl then twisted and ducked away through the crowd.

'Wait. Sorry . . .' Poppy called out, but it was too late: the girl had vanished.

Feeling a little foolish, Poppy realised she had probably frightened her and with reluctance decided to give up the chase. Baffled, she gave in to her pangs of hunger and moved towards the stairs leading to the gallery offices on the third floor, to order lunch. The gallery restaurant would be too crowded and, as usual, she would order from Little Russia.

'There has been another bid,' someone whispered in her ear.

Poppy jumped and then turned to face the gallery

manager, who fidgeted beside her with eyes inflamed by excitement. 'That's three this morning, and this one's huge,' he added, his plump face glistening with sweat.

'Who?' Poppy asked.

'Anonymous bidder. It came through an intermediary who arrived in a limo.'

'Great,' she said, distractedly.

'My phone's going,' he said, scrabbling for his mobile. 'I think it's the fashion magazine. Look Poppy, I'll speak to you later; I need to take this call.'

'Sure,' she murmured, and left him with his phone pressed against his ear. Climbing the stairs to the manager's office, Poppy found herself unable to shake the image of the cowled woman from her mind and still felt deflated at the reticence of the girl to acknowledge her smile.

At the summit of the stairs, however, her heart skipped a beat. The dark-robed woman reappeared, seemingly from nowhere, at the end of the corridor on the administrative floor. Only the young woman's eyes and sharp fingers were visible. Her dark robes blended into the black decor of the surrounding walls.

'Sorry,' Poppy said. 'You gave me a fright.'

The woman said nothing and continued to stare at her. Feeling giddy with excitement at the possibility of being pursued, Poppy approached the door to the manager's office. As she put her key into the lock she glanced at her pretty admirer and saw that the girl's bright eyes were transfixed by her legs. The scrutiny, she intuited, was a combination of innocent wonder and that of a trader excitedly inspecting an interesting bargain.

Inside the office, Poppy made her way to a phone to dial for food she no longer had an appetite for. The woman followed and stood beside her. This time her eyes were engrossed with Poppy's chest – tightly packaged inside the rubber cups of her dress and appearing as appetising bumps beneath her cape.

'Can I help you?' she asked the pretty-eyed shadow.

Remaining silent, the girl continued to stare at Poppy's breasts.

'I said, can I help you?' she repeated.

'*Non*,' the woman said, before speaking in broken French.

'Oh, you don't speak English. Let me order my lunch and I'll find a curator who can translate for you.' Before Poppy finished dialling the number, she felt the girl's fingers touch the back of her head, just above the nape of her neck. In her mind, she pictured red nails gliding through pale hair and shivered.

'Blondee,' the girl murmured, and by the expression in her eyes Poppy could tell she was smiling beneath her mask.

'Yes, I'm a blondie,' Poppy said softly, and returned to the phone. Discreetly she indented the STOP button to kill the call but still made the pretence of a conversation with the restaurant owner. As she chatted, Poppy felt the girl's fingernails explore her cheeks, ears and throat. In the grip of a thrilling apprehension, Poppy said 'goodbye' to the dialling tone and replaced the receiver. As she turned to face the girl, eye to eye, Poppy's cape fell from her shoulders to the floor. While her back was turned, the girl had craftily unclasped the gold brooch by her collarbone.

'Oi,' Poppy said, frowning at the big-eyed creature. But the girl's reaction to her apparel stalled her reprimand. Having taken a step backward, the Arab girl stood and stared at Poppy as if she were a miracle. She raised one hand and pointed at Poppy's dress.

'Blondie pretty?' Poppy said, narrowing her eyes. 'You like blondie?'

'*Oui*,' the girl said, understanding the gist of the question, and she reached for Poppy's hand.

'What?' Poppy asked, trying not to laugh. 'You want me to go somewhere with you? Stop pulling me. Don't be silly.' The tugging increased and, laughing, she was led from the manager's office to the stairwell, where the girl pointed at her veil and smacked her hidden lips.

'Dinner? You want me to have dinner with you? Or take you shopping so you can buy a dress like this for the sheikh?'

'*Oui*,' the girl said, before jabbering first in broken French and then in what sounded like Arabic.

'*Non*,' Poppy said. 'I can't just go.'

A look of puzzlement appeared in the beautiful veiled eyes and the girl dipped her hand inside her gown. When it emerged, a roll of bank notes lay in the palm of her hand.

Poppy laughed. 'So you think I can be bought because of my clothes, is that it?'

Giggling, the Persian beauty began tugging at Poppy's hand again and motioning towards the stairs.

'OK, we'll have lunch in the restaurant and I'll try and find out who you are.'

Before they had descended the first flight, a man came pounding up the stairs towards them. There was a look of panic on his face and from one ear a thin white wire trickled from a tiny ear-piece to disappear inside his black suit. Relief flooded his face the moment he saw the girl. He immediately bowed to her and then spoke quickly in Arabic. She responded quickly and sharply, wafting one of her beautiful hands before his face, which made him flinch.

Looking at Poppy with beseeching eyes, he said, 'Mademoiselle, forgive me, but I must return my ward to her hotel before it gets dark.'

'Of course,' Poppy said, feeling bewildered as the girl continued to pull at her hand.

Words were exchanged between the pair, with the girl's voice rising above the man's to drown out his appeal. Reluctantly, he then turned his face to Poppy and said, 'My ward wishes to know if you would dine with her.'

'What's her name?'

'That is not possible for me to say,' he replied, while his eyes seemed to be begging Poppy to refuse the invitation.

'Well, who is she?'

Clearly uncomfortable with the question, he dipped his head.

'I see,' Poppy said. 'Someone quite important who's a real handful to look after.'

He nodded, and his black eyes pleaded with Poppy again.

Reluctantly, she decided it would be best to obey the bodyguard, but when she took a final peek into the girl's eyes she saw something that immediately filled her with sympathy. It was the look of the lonely she had seen in her own face, staring back from a mirror after the move to Darkling Town. 'You can trust me,' she said to the bodyguard. 'I don't want her money. Let us just have lunch together.'

The man began to rub his mouth while the girl not only glared at him but issued a string of whispered curses through her veil.

With terror in his eyes, the bodyguard looked at Poppy and said, 'Please follow.'

It was the first limousine Poppy had ever been inside. Where it was heading, she had no idea, but after the exhausting months' work on *Surgery*, she realised how much she missed company – even if she was unable to speak with the Arab girl whose big eyes continued to stalk her in the wide rear of the limousine. Not for a moment did her adoring gaze leave Poppy's lips, breasts, or legs. And in order to maintain the flattering attention, Poppy removed her cape inside the car and made sure her dress rode up her thighs.

Why the young woman was in Darkling Town, if she was married, or whether her intentions were innocent or not, was still a mystery. When the limousine pulled into the preferred guests' car lot at the Fritz Willis Hotel, however, Poppy's suspicions that the girl was not just wealthy but probably worth a fortune were confirmed. Only the millionaire club could afford a room at the Willis, and once installed few ventured beyond the palatial walls. There was a constant threat of kidnap in the city and even the hotel porters were armed with pistols.

Following the girl, who made a swishing sound as she sped across the marble reception to the elevators, Poppy gazed about the ground floor, astounded by the hotel's opulence. It had been designed like a New York hotel from the forties and gave one the impression of walking across a film set.

When the elevator reached the highest floor of the building, housing the penthouse suites, Poppy's excitement gave way to anxiety. Those who could afford these apartments could afford anything, including legal immunity. Displeasing the cowled minx, for all she knew, could lead to an unfortunate eventuality.

Inside the girl's apartment, another black-suited bodyguard took Poppy's cape without making eye contact. Remaining silent, he did nothing more than bow to the ladies before making himself scarce, with Poppy's cape neatly folded over the crook of his arm. The girl motioned for Poppy to sit upon a white leather couch in the living room, which afforded a spectacular view of Darkling Town's spires and domes. No more, however, was seen of the bodyguards, and Poppy began to feel more at ease. The guards had secreted themselves away, she supposed, hoping the ordeal of the strange female guest would soon be over.

On the low-level coffee table before them, the girl placed a basket of fruit, a large box of chocolates and a magnificent cake stand populated by vividly coloured sweetmeats. Helping herself, Poppy scooped up a cinnamon croissant and a baked apple tart, while the Arab girl knelt at her feet pouring a thick, strong-smelling coffee into two thimble-sized cups.

Sipping the bitter-tasting liquid and devouring the pastries, Poppy reclined on the soft couch and let her host remove her shoes. Gently, the girl smoothed her hands over Poppy's feet and played with the chain around her left ankle.

'Blondee,' she whispered, and slipped her fingernails up the rear of Poppy's legs.

Feeling her face flush, Poppy looked into her host's eyes and said, 'Blondie nice to touch.'

By angling her head, the girl tried to take a peek between Poppy's knees. 'Bad girl,' Poppy whispered, but was unable to resist inching her thighs apart. Instantly, the girl became mesmerised by the shadowy cleft at the peak of Poppy's thighs. Moving her bottom off the couch, Poppy slid the hem of her dress to her stocking tops and stretched her legs out until her feet rested in the girl's hands. Fascinated by the length and presentation of her guest's legs, the girl's quick breaths began to stir the silken veil on her mouth. Slowly, her hands began to caress Poppy's shiny legs from her ankles to the rear of her knees.

'Careful,' Poppy whispered. 'I know you like to look at pretty things and touch them, but you probably don't know what your fingers are doing to me.'

Raising her hands, the girl began pushing upward at the air, indicating that she wanted to see more of what was concealed beneath Poppy's dress. Tiny hairs on the back of Poppy's neck prickled. She stood up and pointed at the laces on the rear of her dress. With determined fingers, the girl began unthreading Poppy from her rubber attire. When the tight bodice slackened around Poppy's breasts and it was loose enough for easy removal, she turned to face the girl and hesitated long enough to ask herself whether undressing before a strange Arab girl in Darkling Town's most expensive hotel was an adventure or an end.

The kneeling girl made the decision. She reached out and tugged Poppy's dress down to her ankles. Suddenly naked from the waist up, Poppy covered her nipples with her hands. Rocking from side to side on her shins, the masked girl devoured every inch of Poppy's fresh skin with her wide Cleopatra eyes. After more than a minute of enduring her scrutiny, Poppy watched the girl reach out to begin fingering the transparent panties she wore over her garter belt. Pinching the ivory-coloured fabric between her finger and thumb, the girl rubbed the expensive gossamer and nodded her head in approval.

'Blondee,' the girl whispered again and batted her luxurious eyelashes, continuing her inspection of Poppy by tweaking her suspender clips and pushing at the welt of her stocking tops.

Blushing, Poppy squeezed her thighs together, aware of a subtle moistening on the petals of her sex. She thought it best to fight the urge, but it had been so long since her night with Hector and Chloë.

'Maybe this is far enough,' Poppy whispered, suddenly remembering the two bodyguards, but the Arab girl was insistent on exploring her guest. Kneeling before her, the girl slipped her hands around to the rear of Poppy's thighs and stroked her nylons, as if entranced by the texture of the thin fabric on shaven skin. 'Really,' Poppy said, stepping away. 'You've had your fun. If your guardian comes in . . .'

Cursing herself for being led into what could be the most dangerous situation she'd encountered so far, Poppy made a move to put her dress back on. Seeing it as a game of cat and mouse, the girl giggled and whipped the dress from her fingers.

Soon, Poppy's smile had changed to a frown and she found herself chasing the girl around the apartment. After several unsuccessful attempts to retrieve the dress, because her heels restricted her mobility, Poppy was forced to watch the girl take a good lead and then skip through a wide arch to leave the lounge. Feeling increasingly vulnerable, and remembering her cape had been spirited away to a cloakroom, she had no choice but to follow the mischievous creature through the archway.

Anger began to mingle with her excitement as Poppy walked into a spectacular bedroom, equipped with a large bubbling pool and a row of fitted wardrobes large enough to house livestock.

From the far corner of the bedroom, there was a sound of a lock being unbolted. When the door opened, the girl stepped out of what must have been a bathroom. She was naked except for her veil and held Poppy's dress out in front of her.

Despite her annoyance, the sight of the slender, coffee-coloured body fired a pleasant shudder through Poppy. Around her veil, the girl's dark hair had been cut into a chic bob that shone beneath the bedroom lights. As she turned about before the mirror, Poppy caught sight of her small dark nipples and shapely bottom. Her little feet were well manicured too, and her toenails were coloured in the same rich shade as her fingers.

Poppy was taller and broader than the girl so the dress wouldn't fit, but a sudden and reckless desire to see the Persian beauty scantily clad appealed to Poppy in a way that surprised her. What, she thought, had the encounter with the baroness and Chloë started?

Moving from her wardrobe to the imperial-sized bed, the girl began dropping parcels on to the satin sheets. She looked at Poppy and pointed at the packages, intimating she should help her dress. Tearing through the boxes, feeling the girl should be placated first before she made an escape, Poppy uncovered a startling array of deviant underwear. Although not as well crafted or designed as her samples from Sheen Couture, the garments had been purchased from designer boutiques and did possess the potential for turning the Arab girl into something extraordinary.

Sitting on the bed, the girl began tugging a pair of black stockings over her little feet, until Poppy knocked her hands away and sat beside her. Slowly, she showed the girl how to roll and smooth the sheer hosiery up her legs, avoiding the creases or twists capable of marring the desired effect.

When the slippery fabric had coated her legs, the girl's pretty mouth released a single, melodic sigh, and Poppy wasted no time in slipping a suspender belt around her narrow waist. With a transparent black negligée in place over the girl's small, tight breasts, Poppy was unable to resist stroking her open palms along her ribs. It was the first time she had touched the young woman, and possibly, she realised, the first time anyone had touched her in that way – slowly and sensually. Before her, the girl's eyes flashed wide and the veil moved upward with her cheekbones, signalling a smile.

To support herself while she slipped into a pair of stilettos, the girl placed her hands on Poppy's shoulders and giggled again. Elevated by six inches of patent heel, the girl's eyes drew level with hers, enabling Poppy to look into them more deeply.

Teetering about in her new shoes, the girl moved closer.

Poppy cupped the girl's elbows in the palms of her hands and leant forward to taste the fragrant breath that slipped through the veil. When there was nothing but a narrow space between their lips, the girl slipped her hands inside Poppy's arms and abruptly seized her breasts.

Taken by surprise, Poppy tried to step backward, but the girl continued to squeeze her breasts, painfully, to make her stand still. 'Ow!' Poppy shouted, but the girl just giggled, removing one hand from a breast to snatch at Poppy's gartered backside. Suddenly enraged, Poppy knocked the girl sideways so she fell down to the bed.

Looking shocked, the girl stared up at Poppy.

'Yes,' Poppy said. 'You weren't expecting that, but you don't grab. Blondie's not a toy. Unless she wants to be. You're too clumsy for rough stuff.'

Sensing her guest's refusal to obey, the girl ripped the veil off her face. Her succulent and heavily painted mouth pouted and then spat at Poppy.

'Little bitch,' Poppy said, and wiped the saliva off her cheek. Overcome with rage, she leapt upon the girl, seized her by the shoulders and twisted her over so she lay on her stomach. They wrestled for a few seconds, but Poppy soon had the girl's two thin wrists clutched behind her back. She freed one of her own hands from the grapple and raised it above the girl's thinly covered backside. Over a smooth shoulder, frightened and confused eyes peered up at her.

'*Non, non, non,*' the girl repeated, and Poppy looked down at a mirror image of her own fear after Nin lured her home to a special brand of luncheon.

Feeling empowered by anger, she felt compelled to slap the girl across her backside, to punish her for the spitting. She took a deep breath, focused her stare on the small bottom beneath her, and lashed her hand down to make contact.

There was a soft *whump* sound as her hand connected with the contours of the girl's buttocks, wrapped in dark silk.

For a moment, Poppy stared at her hand with shock. What had she just done? But before she had time to reflect on her violence, the captive spat again. Instinctively, Poppy responded by delivering a flurry of open-palmed blows to the captive's behind.

Wriggling free, the girl made a dash for freedom by scuttling up the bed. Poppy pursued. Blinkered by the adrenaline of chase and conquest, she repeatedly aimed slaps at the girl. The silken buttocks were missed but a noisy contact was made with the girl's upper thighs, just above her stocking tops. The spitting madam collapsed into a pile of soft pillows.

Suddenly remembering where she was, realising what she had done, and recalling she had not been this aggressive in a confrontation since school, Poppy stopped slapping. She was about to apologise and reach out for the girl in order to comfort her, but the minx rolled on to her back and smiled.

'Blondies,' Poppy whispered, feeling a sudden sense of relief. 'You like doing this with blondies. Is that why your shadow with the ear-piece was tearing his hair out?'

Writhing on the bed, the girl kicked her high heels off and slipped a foot between Poppy's thighs. Catching her breath, Poppy grabbed the girl's ankle to hold it fast. Slowly, with the girl's foot positioned at a certain angle, she began to slide her sex up and down on the hard bones behind the girl's toes.

'Good,' she whispered, and the girl giggled before stretching her other foot forward to play with Poppy's breasts. Gripping the ankle tighter, she began to rub her clit harder along the top of the slippery foot. She felt her eyelids growing heavier and her breathing quickened. Insistently, the girl's other foot pressed against Poppy's lips until her little toes squirmed inside her mouth. Sucking the toes hard and jerking her sex furiously on the girl's other foot, Poppy ascended to her peak.

Her lover laughed, coaxed her down on to the bed and began licking the dew of perspiration from the small of her back, where tiny downy hairs, the colour of gold, grew. Delighted by the way the girl's tiny hands explored her curves and warm hollows, Poppy relaxed into the soft mattress. The tongue tasting her skin was tickling and Poppy sighed when she felt it roam between the cheeks of her buttocks and down to the moist lips of her sex.

This was a new experience for her but pleasant – a broad soft bed, an attentive lover she had spanked into submission, and the sensation of rich food dissolving in her belly. She began to see the assertive passions of her old lovers with fresh eyes.

Rolling on to her back, Poppy opened her legs and let the small, dark shape nestle between her thighs. The tongue that found the pip of her clit must have travelled along similar paths before. As it licked and flitted around her intimacy, Poppy released herself into a deep and languid arousal. Here was experience – perhaps obtained in rolling deserts, or marble palaces, or with musky-smelling Bedouins who drew blood. There was the voice too, embellishing the actions of her eager mouth. Short sentences of French, hummed rather than spoken, vibrated between her warm thighs. Wrapping her legs round the girl's neck, she began to squash the little, burrowing face against her sex. The head clasped in place, she rubbed the sweet face hard against her lips, making sure the girl's teeth ground her clit against her pelvic bone.

'This is good, really good,' Poppy murmured, going dizzy as the pretty features of her lover's face, both hard and soft in turn, were forced to deliver satisfaction. Being strapped, restrained, and then fucked had given her pleasure beyond anything she had previously enjoyed in sex. She had been able to take anything. She had given herself willingly to strangers to be curiously freed by pain and humiliation. But what of the other side? Where one will overcame another will made weak by nature or choice.

Biting her fingers and pushing her legs down the bed until her heels caught on the satin bedspread, she moaned through her second climax and rejoiced at the discovery of what she could give.

After delivering a final, cleansing lick over the lips of her sex, the girl disentangled herself from between Poppy's splayed legs. She slipped up the bed, kissed Poppy's forehead and then nuzzled her face into the crook of Poppy's neck. Between the kisses she planted on Poppy's throat, the girl whispered long sentences in which the word 'Blondee' appeared frequently.

'See how good it can be when you're not such a spoilt bully,' Poppy whispered, stroking the girl's hair. When she raised the girl's chin and kissed her full lips, she tasted a sweetness, like caramel, in the princess's lipstick.

Murmuring in Arabic, the girl rolled off the bed and padded across to her wardrobe. After rummaging through a vanity case, she scuttled back to the bed clutching what appeared to be an ivory-coloured rod in both hands. Taking it from her, Poppy held it out before her eyes and admired it. It was a long and well-girthed replica of a penis. Fine carvings circled the base of the smooth shaft, depicting Jinn creatures and sloe-eyed women joined in sinful embraces.

As she studied the toy, the Arab girl climbed across Poppy and slipped her thick lips over the end of the penis to moisten the tip. Closing her eyes and humming through her nose, the girl withdrew her mouth slowly to leave smears of crimson on the pale shaft. Staring deeply into Poppy's eyes, she began poking the index finger of one hand through the small 'o' shape she made with the finger and thumb of her other hand.

'Time you were put out of your misery,' Poppy whispered. 'I've been greedy.'

The girl rolled off the bed and ran across the room, where she unashamedly arranged herself on all fours before a large dress mirror. While purring through her elegant nose, she began to move her backside in small circular motions.

Needing no further encouragement, Poppy joined her. Lying on her back, she slid between the girl's legs and poked her tongue out until it found salt. The fabric of the negligée that clung to the girl's sex was drenched with a strange spice. Poppy greedily suckled the girl's honey, sharp to the taste and opaque in appearance, and enjoyed the mild sensation of burning it produced at the rear of her throat. When the girl began to make gentle groaning sounds, Poppy slipped out from under her and promptly worked the shaft inside her lover.

'How's that, umm?' she whispered at the svelte shape who'd dipped her head between her shoulders and stretched one stocking-sheathed leg out to tense her toes. When she raised her face, the wide eyes looked drugged, lipstick trailed off her bottom lip and Poppy could just see the small breasts juddering from the quick thrusts her hand made between the girl's legs.

'Good,' Poppy murmured. 'Say good. Go on, say good. Good. Good. Good.'

'Gourd,' the girl said before biting her bottom lip. 'Gourd blondee, gourd.'

'You little slut,' she said, relishing her new role. 'It's good to be a slut. You can do what you like here and no one knows.' But no sooner had Poppy whispered this to the girl when, in the mirror, she saw two sweat-slicked faces peering into the bedroom from the lounge outside. It was the bodyguards with their eyes now closed while their hands moved in the pursuit of relief.

'Poor boys,' Poppy whispered, and began to push the baton deeper and more vigorously inside the girl.

'Teased all day by her highness,' Poppy whispered through gritted teeth. 'Who, no doubt, is foolish enough to let them wash her undies.'

In her mind she pictured the tortured faces of the girl's servants risking everything for one pair of skimpy panties carelessly discarded beside her bathtub.

Below her, the girl collapsed to her elbows and panted into the carpet. To finish her lover, Poppy whipped the ornate shaft in and out of the girl's stretched lips until her wrist ached. With a final gasp, the girl collapsed on to her stomach and began to mutter as she came.

Peeking at the mirror, Poppy saw that the appreciative and well-behaved audience had disappeared. But there was always the possibility, she thought with a smile, that the girl liked to be watched and deliberately left the door open.

'Let's take a bath in our skimpies,' Poppy ordered and

slapped the girl's backside to regain her attention. 'Come on,' she added, and squeezed the dozy creature's waist.

Holding hands, they walked across to the tub and slipped beneath the bubbling surface to feel their bodies suddenly clothed in hot, foamy water. 'Oh, this is good,' Poppy said, enjoying the sensation of lingerie clinging to skin. 'I'm not supposed to wash these,' she added, and raised one dripping leg from the water. 'They'll smell of bubble bath and all the stains will be gone. Won't matter just this once.'

Keeping only her head out of the water, so the rest of her body was nothing more than a black smudge beneath the bubbles, the girl curled around Poppy's knees. Leaning forward, Poppy raised her from beneath the water and tongued her chin and neck, making the girl squeal with delight.

Beneath the ripples and foam, Poppy and her lover's fingers were soon busy in an illicit kind of underwater irrigation. While two slender fingers explored her deep inside, Poppy rubbed her knuckles against the girl's sex. Hot breath clouded between their damp, sucking lips as they whispered salacious taunts to the other in words never to be understood.

With her legs climbing to wrap round Poppy's waist, the girl pulled Poppy off the tiered seat and into the centre of the pool. Jets of bubbles, fired from the floor of the wide tub, fizzed and tingled around her anus, adding to her arousal and making her claw the back of her lover's head. Standing up, the girl placed her hands on Poppy's shoulders and pushed her sopping sex on to her face. With her fingers, Poppy ripped the sheer gusset of the negligée apart and sank her mouth on the trimmed but dripping sex that had been offered to her. Catching the girl unawares, she slipped her little finger between the girl's buttocks and inserted it in her anus. Squealing, the girl tried to escape the finger, but Poppy seized her hips with her free hand and used the girl's body weight so that the eager probe was swallowed whole.

With the girl skewered on her finger, Poppy could feel

the tremors of delight coursing through her lover's body. At the same time, she serviced the girl's sex with her tongue. Moaning, the girl clawed Poppy's hair into disarray and stamped her little stocking-clad feet under the water.

'That's it, honey,' she whispered. 'Let go.'

Her lover obeyed and started to weep for joy as her body, gripped by climax, slumped against Poppy in the water.

Kissing the young woman, in the drowsy warmth of steam and post-coital fatigue, Poppy realised she felt different. Is this how a man feels after satisfying his wife? she wondered. Or how a master feels after fulfilling his servant's dark and secret need for punishment? She had been assertive and seduced the young woman in her arms, who could buy anything. With the 'Seasons in the Abyss' gathering only one day away, she began to wonder how she would behave. She had made her art from the art of submission, re-created passion from passion, but now her curiosity about power demanded succour.

Nine

Clack! Clack! Clack! The sound of her heels, full of purpose and confidence, filled the night, echoing off the red-brick walls of the factories and warehouses that stretched for miles around her. With her chin held high and her fists pressed deep into the pockets of her trench coat, she enjoyed the bite of cold wind on her face and the passage of its icy influence beneath her garments.

Poppy wasn't surprised the cab had sped off the moment she'd paid the driver, one block away from 'Seasons in the Abyss'. Even within the relative safety of a car, few ventured into the docklands area during daylight hours, let alone after dark. But she felt little anxiety in the most dangerous zone of Darkling Town. Instead, she obeyed the power inside her, the strength that pawed about, desperate to get out.

Despite the fatigue waiting in the wings of her overworked body and mind, that waited to claim her, Poppy's journey was altering. Something was at work in her imagination; something similar to the fury she'd seen in the faces of her lovers as they indulged their passions on her body. I'll sleep when I'm dead, she had decided earlier when applying her make-up. After her reduction to the role of a willing puppet, seeking taut strings in masterful hands, it was as if these strings were now being handed to her. What she had done to the Arab beauty the day before seemed to offer the first glimpse of this new attitude. And now, the desire to be impetuous, regardless of the result, was stronger than ever.

She could be anyone and do anything, but just as her instincts had made her yield to the desires of others, no matter how cruel, the restless spirit beneath her pale skin now wanted, if not demanded, to explore the other side of sensuality: power.

Sex as power, sex as a weapon, sex as the conqueror and sex as a dominant – she wanted to taste it. Taking lashes, having her limbs moulded like a manikin, and being restrained, had been unforgettable, but if her art was to evolve she needed to switch roles. In the same mode of rashness that had led her to the baroness's couch, Poppy decided to let her imagination and emotions lead her astray down in the 'Abyss'.

After turning the corner of Vargas Street and strutting along the wet tarmac to the address on Hector's invitation, her thoughts were broken into by the sound of a passing car. The vehicle slowed down to draw level with her and she saw that its windows were tinted. Sensing an intense scrutiny from behind the opaque glass of the driver's door, she stopped walking and glared at the sleek, rain-speckled car.

Almost immediately, the car accelerated away.

If she wasn't mistaken, the same vehicle, or one very similar, had often been parked near the Daemonic Gallery while she worked on *Surgery*. She had liked the look of the dark car with its old-fashioned features, like the chrome grille and pointed wings, and had assumed it belonged to an art dealer. But why was it here? Although anyone suspected of having money ran the risk of being kidnapped by an organised-crime outfit, it was unlikely she would be a target after remaining incognito. No one beside her agent, and the baroness she'd met only once, knew for certain she was the artist behind the bizarre sculptures.

For a moment, though, she wondered whether the once persistent baroness would stalk her. A few weeks before, the demanding woman had left messages, or rather instructions, at the gallery insisting she phone. There was something about the baroness that made her uneasy. And there was little she hated more than those who were preoccupied with ownership. As a result, she had decided to ignore the woman.

It was possible the car contained nothing beside a leering businessman on his way home, or a curious pimp, as hookers were a popular feature in this part of town. She continued walking towards the club's address, checking the building numbers until she reached number seven. Her suspicion about being followed vanished at the sight of an iron door, raised from street level and set in the Victorian frontage of what had once been a textile warehouse. This was the place called 'Seasons in the Abyss'.

With the rain beginning to fall more steadily, and the black car having vanished into the evening gloom, Poppy skipped up the stone stairs to the door and pressed the buzzer. Almost immediately, an iron slot was pulled through its runners and a square beam of yellow light fell from the aperture. A pair of bright female eyes appeared and stared at Poppy.

Without a word, Poppy held her invitation before the opening. Fingers, clad in tight leather, probed forward and took the card. The slot slammed shut and Poppy stood alone in the dark again. In preparation, she tightened her French plait and checked her make-up in a small vanity mirror, guiding her ministrations under the pale glow from an overhead lantern. After applying another layer of crimson lipstick and smacking her lips in satisfaction, she heard the sound of a bolt being unlocked on the other side of the portal. When the hinges let forth a rusty screech and the door opened a fraction, she slipped inside.

The sight of the two uniformed guards left her lost for words. Dressed like the military officers she'd seen in old war footage, a tall man and a blonde woman greeted her with silence. Each pair of gloved hands had been crossed behind their backs and each pair of booted feet was set wide apart.

As if in a stalemate, the guards surveyed Poppy from head to toe as she in turn marvelled at their outfits – black for her and brown for him. Soon, her gaze began to linger upon the woman. Beneath the peaked cap, emblazoned with a silver insignia, the woman wore a white shirt, with an armband on her left bicep, a black tie, and a tight black skirt. The make-up on her stern but handsome face was minimal, and her blonde hair had been tucked under the cap. Only her footwear seemed irregular. Tight boots, made from patent leather, covered her legs to her knees, where the hem of her pencil-skirt ended. Despite the nasty attitude she intuited, there was something about the female guard she liked. In her imagination, since the *Loving Captive* period, she had often undressed women she found interesting. Especially those who put up barriers. 'It's customary for new guests to arrive early,' the woman said to break the silence, raising her eyebrow as she spoke.

'To acclimatise gradually. This prevents an adverse reaction,' the male guard added, standing tall as if on parade in his brown uniform, riding boots and leather braces.

'Things are well under way. We were close to locking the doors for the night,' the woman said, and Poppy thought she said 'night' with unusual relish.

'I won't faint,' Poppy replied.

The two guards looked at each other and the man shrugged.

The woman smiled, though not warmly. 'It's hard to judge an initiate's reaction, although Hector's guests have never disappointed us.'

'How do you know I'm Hector's guest?'

'Through the colour of your invitation,' the man answered, and seemed ready to smile until a sideward glance from his colleague killed the first sign of a welcome from either of them.

Poppy nodded. 'So who's the "us"?'

Stepping forward, the woman ignored her question and brusquely said, 'Let me take your coat. You won't be needing it because our premises are heated. And there is the slight matter of a search.'

Poppy nodded and began removing her coat. 'But you never answered –'

'You will know better than to pry into any member's

background,' the woman whispered as she relieved Poppy of her coat. 'Nothing from the outside is welcome here.'

'We leave our worldly selves at the door,' the man added. 'And for a very good reason.'

'My, what an outfit,' the woman added in a mocking tone, but Poppy suspected her eyes had paused on her leather-skirted backside and thigh-booted legs for longer than was necessary. 'Although it will have to be removed,' she added. 'Clothing impedes our submissives.'

'Though I wish, in your case, we could waive that regulation,' the male guard said, staring at Poppy's breasts, on display beneath the fine mesh of her transparent halter-neck blouse.

'Submissive?' Poppy queried, aiming to end any further presumptions. 'You're mistaken. I'm not here to serve you.'

The two guards exchanged glances.

'You're assertive?' the man asked, delighted. 'We can always use genuine female –'

'We'll see,' the woman said in a condescending tone, and adopted a facial expression that Poppy interpreted as disbelief. 'If you'd like to follow me, Miss . . .'

'Poppy. My name is Poppy,' she replied, irritated at both the woman's dismissive tone and her own susceptibility to the guard's stiff prettiness.

Following the woman out of the draughty reception, Poppy entered a small antechamber that seemed to serve as a changing facility. 'Chic,' she murmured, eyeing the plain wooden benches and the rows of dented metal lockers fixed to the walls.

'Please raise your arms and stand with your legs apart,' the woman said with impatience, and closed the door.

'What could I possibly hide under my arms?' Poppy answered with a sly smile, hoping to relax the woman now they were alone. 'See, nothing there, not even a bra-strap.'

'Do you want to be admitted or not?'

Poppy rolled her eyes and raised her arms.

Slowly, the woman paced around her, far enough away to inspect her garments, but close enough to make her feel uncomfortable. 'We often have kinky girls wandering down here in their high heels and PVC dresses. Amateurs, all of them. Run a mile when they witness real discipline. In my experience true dominants follow a less decorative dress code. We prefer something more formal here.'

'Well this is my first time, so I think you can overlook my amateur outfit.'

'To be honest, I don't approve of strangers just turning up. Even after an invitation, I think they should be vetted.'

'Can we get the search over with. I'd like to go in now,' she said, giving up on her attempt to placate the officer.

From behind, Poppy felt the woman's claws dig under her hemline.

'Watch what –' she cried out, but before she could finish there was a sound of ripping stitching and her skirt was yanked up around her waist.

Standing back, with her hands on her hips, the woman stared at Poppy's crotch and buttocks. Without panties, her sex was visible beneath the fine nylon of her dark tights that were sheer to her waist.

'If you've ruined this skirt –'

'You'll what?' the woman said with a smiling, though challenging, face.

'Do you treat all your new guests like this?' Poppy said, barely finding her voice.

'My way of sorting the wheat from the chaff.'

'Well, what am I?' she asked, struggling to speak for anger.

'Probably a thrill-seeker, masquerading as something she's not.'

Poppy threw her head back. 'And why is that – because I'm young with a nice little tush and firm breasts? Nothing but a good-time girl, curious about the perverts in an old warehouse? Don't assume anything about me.'

A flicker of apprehension passed through the guard's eyes, as if she'd realised that underestimating Poppy had been a mistake. 'I'm still trying to figure out why Hector invited you,' she added, to regain the high ground with an insult.

'What is your problem? Hector made me a preferred guest. Do you think he'll be pleased to hear how I was treated?'

'I'm on the central committee. He isn't.'

'Well, I let him have his way,' Poppy teased. 'And it was good. You know, really special. And because of that, maybe he decided I belong here.'

Poppy had seen frustration before – when the spoilt were unable to have their own way – and something about the guard suddenly reminded her of the baroness, and so many of the moneyed matrons she had encountered in the exclusive coffee houses. This woman desired her, but felt inadequate beside the height and beauty of a younger woman. She felt rejected before even making a pass and the only defence she maintained was that of the emotional bully. In the past, Poppy would always tolerate the attitude, but now she felt different – wilder and more confident. And tonight, she was prepared to offer a lesson.

Wanting to antagonise the woman further, because she liked the way the uniformed madam had begun to look when roused, she said, 'Sure you're not just being selfish?'

'What are you talking about?'

'Maybe you've gone all sour after realising you can't have the first turn with the new girl. Or do you feel threatened by me?'

The woman lashed out and struck Poppy's cheek with the back of her hand.

Raising her chin, Poppy let the sting die down to a pleasant warmth. She felt no shock, because she had wanted the blow. Instead, she relished the sensation of her anger mingling with what she recognised as a strange sexual charge. And when she felt ready, Poppy slapped the woman back, hard.

The guard's mouth opened, but she said nothing. When she touched her cheek in disbelief that a guest had actually retaliated, Poppy seized her by the shoulders and thrust her back against the table. But being of a flimsy construction, the table skidded across the floor and Poppy lost her balance, providing her opponent with an opportunity to snatch out a hand and grasp her hair. Wincing, Poppy knocked the cap off her opponent's head and dug her own talons into the immaculate blonde bun beneath.

Her world seemed to slow down, her actions felt sluggish; she felt sick with nervous excitement. Unable to see clearly or think straight, because of the sudden stream of adrenaline coursing through her, Poppy could do nothing but tug, lash, spit and wrestle with the woman until they fell to the floor. After breaking apart from the force of the fall on to the cold linoleum, the guard kicked at her with her sharp-toed boots. Her skirt, however, was far too tight for the manoeuvre and the kicks proved ineffectual. Unhampered by her own clothes, as her miniskirt was still ruffled around her waist, Poppy leapt upon the woman and clasped both of her wrists before forcing them down to the ground.

Hissing with rage, the guard thrashed about and almost succeeded in thrusting Poppy to one side. But, by quickly applying pressure with her own body weight, until both the tips of their noses and the points of their nipples were squashed together, she turned the woman's fury into an impotent wriggling.

Staring into her eyes, while she could feel every muscle and sinew straining in the body beneath her, Poppy began to smile. This increased the guard's rage to the point where there was no other option beside a call for help. She opened her mouth, took a deep breath and made ready to scream. But Poppy was too quick. She lowered her painted lips to the woman's mouth and kissed her, deeply.

There was a sudden resurgence of defiance from beneath her body, but as Poppy slipped her tongue beneath the guard's overbite, which gave her mouth a special beauty, she detected a loss of power in the arms she had pinned to the floor.

'You taste good,' Poppy murmured.

'Bitch,' the woman spat back.

With her tongue extended, Poppy licked the guard's pale throat and then tickled her ear while still managing to counter any attempts at escape by shifting her body or reasserting the pressure on the wrists she held tight.

Slowly, she moved her mouth back above the woman's lips and let it hover there, all moist and smudged. Her captive's eyes flickered up and down, but Poppy was pleased to see them linger on her mouth.

'Don't,' the woman whispered.

'But I want to suck your tongue. Let me.'

'No,' she replied in a quivering voice.

'Please, let me,' Poppy said, falling into the harsh green eyes and smooth skin beneath her; enjoying the sight of cruel features softening.

The woman closed her eyes, gulped noisily, and shook her head in a last act of defiance. But when Poppy extended her tongue and licked the smears of lipstick from the woman's mouth, her captive could hold back no longer. With a sudden renewal of strength, she twisted her hands free and seized the back of Poppy's head. After tangling her nails in Poppy's hair, she suddenly forced Poppy's face down so that her lips welded with those of the enemy who now wanted to be a lover. And never before had Poppy been kissed so passionately.

The fight was over, but a new struggle began; a struggle to taste, maul, fondle and touch each other as if an interruption was imminent.

Poppy groaned with delight when the woman's hands found her breasts. At first her touch was hurried and clumsy, but soon it subsided to a gentle caressing and tweaking of her nipples, made extra sensitive by the fine layer of fabric stretched across them.

As they kissed and rolled on the hard floor, they began to gasp quick instructions at each other in order to improve access to the choicest parts of their bodies.

'Your pussy,' Poppy murmured. 'I want your pussy.'

There was a scrabble and a change of positions before her request was granted. Lying on the rickety table, the guard hiked her tight skirt up to her thighs, which she then spread as wide as she was able in a tight skirt. While smoothing her hands down the outside of the woman's stocking-clad legs, Poppy forced her face between the softness of her lover's thighs.

The woman's underwear was black and old-fashioned, which Poppy thought beautiful, adoring the way it framed the woman's pale skin, peeking between her stocking tops and the red fringe of her directoire knickers. Clawing through suspender straps and shoving the panties aside, Poppy felt herself losing control in her haste to devour the woman's guarded intimacy. With the obstacles removed, she closed her eyes, inhaled the woman's strong aroma, and then inserted her tongue between bitter-tasting lips to find the warm and sweeter honey.

Purring through her nose, Poppy attended to the woman's pleasure bud and giggled with delight when she heard her lover's high-heeled boots begin to stamp and then scrape across the table surface. Taking a peek across the woman's uniformed body, she was pleased to see her lover had covered her face with both hands and seemed to be no longer in control of the lower half of her body.

Delighted by her conquest of the figure now sprawled before her, Poppy began flicking her tongue across the guard's clitoris until the familiar sounds of female excitement filled the changing room.

Her own arousal made her more assertive than she'd ever been with the Arab girl. Poppy began clawing the woman's hips and calling her a 'sexy bitch', and it appeared to be driving her lover wilder each time she repeated it. While lashing her tongue all over the woman's now sopping sex, until her chin and cheeks were smeared with an opaque stickiness, Poppy knew there was little she enjoyed more than the taste of a woman, and the harder sounds a girl would suddenly produce from the back of her throat when approaching climax.

Soon, the guard wept and began to buck her hips upward in an attempt to take even more of Poppy's mouth inside. Squashing her face into the wet softness between the guard's legs, while clawing upward for her breasts, Poppy responded with a long and concentrated ravishing of her opponent's most delicate skin, until she heard a loud groan erupt from the woman as if all the air had suddenly escaped from her body.

Moving from between the woman's legs, like a prizefighter viewing his combatant after the knockout punch, Poppy stood up, breathing hard, and watched the guard sink her nails into her own thighs, hard enough to leave marks. Her lover then turned her face towards the wall and began to sob.

Wiping her mouth, Poppy stared at the woman's defrocked legs, which were hanging off the table, and her tousled hair that trailed across her uniform in golden strands. A cold wave of shock passed through her. For the first time since she'd entered the changing room, she wondered how it started – how friction turned to passion so quickly, and how she had managed to overwhelm a woman who would have terrified her a few months before. But then, she realised she was thinking in the old way: feeling guilt and getting ready to run. But where had that got her in life? Looking down at the pointed toes of her shiny boots and her slender thighs wrapped in nylon and leather, she felt reassured. This is the way you are now, something seemed to be saying to her. From the time she left the hotel the day before until she dressed that evening in the severest heels and tightest skirt, it was as if a foreign spirit had taken possession of her body.

Am I dangerous? Have I worked too hard? Am I losing my mind? she thought, wondering if her addiction to this craziness was a symptom. One moment she was manipulating dangerous-looking men to take her, then she was dressing, inexplicably, like a fifties movie star, and now she wanted to slap, claw and bite her way to sexual satisfaction.

Still horrified, and mystified, but exhilarated by her behaviour, Poppy left both the room and another anonymous lover behind.

'A thorough search?' the male officer asked with a smile, as Poppy re-entered the reception and closed the changing-room door behind her.

Poppy nodded. 'Can I go in now?'

'Follow me,' the male guard replied and clicked his shiny heels together before leading her out of the reception to an elevator with a trellis door. 'Take it to the basement,' he said, and slammed the door shut.

Poppy pressed the correct button and disappeared down the elevator shaft into the dark.

Even through the metal slats of the door, after the elevator wheezed to a standstill on the basement floor, she could see the inferno she'd committed herself to entering. Suspended on anchor chains from the vaulted ceiling were a series of large mildewed globes, casting a sickly glow over what must have once been a vast storage facility in a working factory. Running down the middle of the gloomy space, between walls cast impenetrably in shadow, was a long banqueting table. Crammed around each side of its rectangular shape were the officers, and it immediately reminded her of the underground bunkers she had read of, from the days of blitzes and bombs, where the military elite would sit around maps waiting for their end or plotting someone else's.

On this table, however, stood flagons of frothing beer, loaded platters of meats and fruits, silver candelabras, and the solitary figure of a naked woman who danced for the amusement of the assembled elite. Whistles, catcalls, and drink-addled banter rose from around the table to echo throughout the stuffy hall that reeked of spilt beer, cigarettes and sex.

Without detection, Poppy was able to disengage herself from the elevator and approach the table. She stopped short of the gathering, not because she'd been seen, but because beneath the din of the officers' camaraderie she heard the unmistakable chink of a chain on stone. The sound had arisen from behind and away to her left and she turned to peer into the gloom. There was nothing to be seen as the lantern's dim illumination refused to pass much further than the centre table. Frowning, she slowly turned her attention back to the table and looked for Hector.

Beside a busty woman with short pigtails and a willowy blonde girl in her thirties, Hector sat and surveyed the dancer in silence. His comrades, however, slammed pewter beer tankards upon the oak table and roared encouragement up at the pretty redhead who had begun to gyrate her hips and sweep her pert breasts close to several flushed and eager faces.

Two men, uniformed in black, with their hats removed and creamed quiffs shining in the candlelight, noticed Poppy and nudged each other. Hector detected their sudden interest and followed their gaze to Poppy. Immediately, he stood up and bowed and Poppy noticed a remarkable change in not only his dress but also his demeanour. The alternative attitude and easy-moving athleticism had been forsaken for a formal and stiff facade. Smiling at the role he obviously favoured at his club, Poppy approached and took a space on the crammed bench beside him.

As she seated herself, the other officers turned their heads and surveyed her with an amorous interest.

'So pleased you came,' Hector whispered.

'It's a miracle I made it past the cloakroom,' she muttered into his ear. 'Your admirer upstairs was a handful.'

'Who, Helga?'

'Whoever,' Poppy said, smiling.

'She can be tough. Tries too hard, I think. What did she do to you?'

'Let's just say I reversed the roles.'

'You never. You were a parable of obedience when last we met.'

'My journey has taken another detour. Let's just say I'm seeing the world through different eyes now.'

Hector looked at her, smiled, and said, 'I'm a little disappointed, Poppy. I was rather looking forward to a sequel now I'm properly dressed, but I dare say my continuing curiosity about you will compensate.'

Before she could reply, Hector stood up and banged the table for everyone's attention. Immediately, the dancer dropped to a crouch and bowed her head. Around her left ankle, Poppy noticed a cuff and followed the attached chain with her eyes to the plump woman's hand, where it was fondled.

Hector introduced Poppy to the restless crowd, who all seemed dismayed the moment he boldly announced she had not attended for their pleasure, but as a guest officer. By the time he had resumed his seat, however, and the dancer had begun a fresh routine, lying on her back with her supple legs pointed at the ceiling, most of the officers had returned to their previous state of bawdy reverie.

'I'm not supposed to ask, but who are these people?'

'Individuals,' Hector replied, and touched the side of his nose. 'But let me drop a hint. The woman performing for us on the table is married to someone wealthy and terribly important who thinks she's playing bridge tonight. Discretion is everything.'

'Amen to that,' Poppy said, and lit a cigarette. From beside her, the thin-faced woman, who reminded Poppy of an elf, slopped beer into a tankard and offered it to her with frail hands. As she turned to thank her neighbour, however, her eyes were immediately drawn to the woman's lap. Despite the fact that she still wore a shirt, black tie and the jacket of her uniform, her skirt and slip had been removed and draped over the bench, leaving her slender legs, clad in nothing but sheer stockings, to disappear beneath the table. Detecting movement around the woman's feet, Poppy angled her head to peek beneath the table, but the woman leant forward, smiling, and obscured her view.

'Your uniforms and this club,' Poppy whispered to Hector, barely able to contain her growing excitement. 'Surely you can tell me about them. I want to know everything, Hector. This is the strangest thing I've ever seen.'

'The uniforms are the feathers of birds who flock together, and the factory is owned by a man none of us have met – someone sympathetic to our interests.'

'That's all?'

'You know all you need to.'

'Well, where's Chloë?'

'She's near.'

'But –'

125

He pointed at her tankard. 'Come on, drink up. Soon we turn the wall lights on.'

'The what?' she said, but the sensation of something brushing against her legs distracted her. Poppy leant back from the bench and screwed up her eyes to see under the table. Something white flashed through the shadows around her knees, and then it disappeared.

But there it was again. A pressure on her shins and the tops of her feet. When she moved her legs forward, she struck something soft and heard the slap of hands on stone, as if someone was scurrying away.

Amused at Poppy's curiosity, Hector pulled a candle from a stand and handed it to her. He winked and then turned back to converse with the plump woman who held the dancer's chain. Moving the candle to waist height, Poppy dipped its light beneath the table-top and followed the candle's pale illumination with her eyes.

Although it took a moment to make sense of the moving mass of flesh on the floor, when her eyes started to pick out individual limbs and faces the entire picture became clear. There must have been twenty naked people of varying ages beneath the table. All were anchored to either the bench or table legs by short silver chains that stretched no further than a few feet from their leather collars. And each individual was engrossed in the fastidious servicing of an officer, or in the receipt of a special kind of favour.

Between the open knees of the delicate blonde beside her, Poppy watched a man of retirement age sit and perspire as the woman's long feet pumped his erect penis. As if oblivious to the action of her feet, she smoked a cigarette and, with her heavily lidded eyes, stared at the naked dancer who had been seized by an overzealous male officer, intent on spanking her buttocks with woodcutter blows.

Elsewhere, beneath the long table, the display of mass submission was in full swing. At least three of the male officers on the left bench sat with their trousers gathered about their ankles. And between their pale knees, Poppy could see the rear of hooded heads moving up and down at differing speeds.

On the right bench, a matronly woman with coiffured hair and noble looks caught Poppy's eye. Although she kissed the neck of a male guard and shared a jug of ale with him, below the table her high-heeled feet were busy in spiking the back of a male slave who wrestled with another two men eager to fall beneath the dagger heels.

Close to the toes of her own boots, the handsome face of a young man presented itself to her with lowered eyes. His blonde hair was cut into a short, neat style, and although his body was slender he'd been blessed with a contoured musculature sealed within tanned skin.

'Can I please you, ma'am?' he asked in a soft, cultured voice.

'I should think so,' she muttered to the man in a maternal voice. 'Is it my boots you like?'

The youth nodded and blushed.

'How about what's inside them?'

'All of you is beautiful, ma'am.'

'Thank you,' Poppy replied and wiggled her tired feet before the rigidity between his legs. 'Now take my boots off and massage my feet and legs.'

For a second, the man closed his eyes and gave silent thanks.

'Poppy, the wall lights. Watch,' Hector hissed from beside her. She looked at him and his eyes were alight with the expectation of something profound.

A hush fell about the table and the plump woman who'd sat next to Hector waddled off into the darkness with her obedient dancer following on a chain. Beneath the table, Poppy could feel the subtle vibrations next to her calves as the pretty slave unzipped her boots. Air cooled her hot legs and she giggled a little when his delicate lips passed slowly along the tops of her feet and up her shinbones to her knees. When his hands were caressing the tops of her thighs, she was forced to close her eyes for a moment as her sex prickled with anticipation. Her bottom felt hot and a restless sensation began to burn in her stomach. She took a swig of beer to cool herself, but it was of little use. His touch thrilled her. It was good to feel a handsome man under her feet, worshipping her, even begging to serve, but something about his dotage irritated her.

Grinding her teeth, she knew she would have the pretty lad. She would do things to him. Make him squeal and moan and cry. Yes, she thought, I'll have my way, my own selfish and even nasty way with this one. I can do anything to him and I like that.

Poppy drank her frothy beer and in a sudden wave of gluttony swiped a leg of roast turkey from a large platter and tore through it with her teeth, until the grease shone on her chin. Beneath the table, the lad's face slipped between her inner thighs, and without glancing down she guessed he was inhaling her scent.

Suddenly, on every side of the officers' mess, large yellow lights caged in cast-iron frames spluttered into life and illuminated the walls of the abyss. Poppy nearly choked on a mouthful of turkey. Strung, chained, fastened, and tied to hooks, posts, beams and pillars were the slaves of the officers. All naked, save for the occasional hood, at least forty men and women had been waiting in the dark for this moment. They started to blink in the light and shift about as far as their bonds permitted.

From two large speakers, fixed into the ceiling rafters, Poppy heard a crackle as if a stylus had been placed into the grooves of an old vinyl record. Following the crackle and hiss came the thundering sound of string music, soon accompanied by wild drum flurries and the sultry tones of a woman singing in German. Slowly, the officers unlocked their slaves from under the table and peeled themselves away from the benches to seek the walls and the fresh lovers who waited there. Each officer's face, whether it were smooth and well shaven or painted to severity, revealed a lunatic passion. Poppy understood why the club was buried deep in a forsaken corner of the city. If she hadn't committed herself to a strange odyssey that took sensuality to an extreme, she would have run screaming from the eagerness sketched across the faces of the uniformed brutes and the smell of anxiety rising from the chained.

Hector unlocked a chain from a hook, positioned close to her thighs, and gently kissed her cheek before making his way to the nearest wall. Under the table she could feel the young man still lapping at her knees and rubbing his erection against her ankles. And around the perimeter of the room, the action began. Whips cracked in the air and then slapped home. Chains were dragged over flagstones. Grinning nudes were hoisted to their feet and escorted to the strange array of apparatus that resembled items of gymnastic equipment, made from wood and worn by decades of use.

Poppy drained her tankard, ripped her teeth through the side of a peach and flung the cup over her head. 'Are you ready for me?' she said quietly, and looked at the young man at her feet, engrossed by the beauty and length of her legs.

Carefully, she slipped the hand holding the peach beneath the table and ran the fingers of her other hand through the slave's soft hair, coaxing him with soft words to make him smile. The moment his excitement increased and he looked at her with adoring eyes, she clenched her fingers into a fist to pull his hair. She heard him gasp and watched his clear blue eyes blink in pain and surprise. When he removed his open mouth from her wet hose, she squeezed the peach until the juice ran all over his face.

He began to moan and lap at the sweet stickiness trickling around his mouth, but Poppy hauled him out from under the table by his hair. Overcome with a passion to be satisfied thoroughly and quickly, she tugged him over the bench and on to the flagstones.

'Eat me now,' she hissed at the hapless and naked man. 'Come on, I want to see what you've got. Serve me, you little shit. That's it, get on your knees. Look at me. No! Look up at me. Good boy.' With her toy in position, Poppy stood astride his head and lowered her sex on to his open mouth. Still gripping his hair, she began to rub the hard ridges of his face where she wanted to be touched, and smeared his cheekbones with the honey seeping through the fine mesh of her tights.

His eyes were closed and she heard him panting the phrase 'Yes, miss' over and over again as she serviced her need upon his face. By gripping the back of her thighs with his hands, he was able to press his mouth hard against her sex to trap the tenderest flesh against the bones beneath, making her dizzy with delight.

'Oh, you little fuck,' she groaned, happy to relinquish every shred of decency. 'That's it, do me with that sweet mouth, get your teeth in there. Up. Up. Up! Good, you sweet boy.'

Tremors spread up her legs and tingled around her anus until she was unable to remain standing. When she collapsed back upon the bench she brought the beautiful mouth with her, so the eager teeth never strayed more than an inch from her engorged fruit. Lying on her back, she draped her flushed face over the corner of the seat so the room turned upside down. Her lover's feast between her thighs increased its fervour and he began to gnaw through the transparent fabric of her tights, now sticking to her shaven sex. Employing his thumbs to peel her lips right back, he sucked at her clit until she ascended to a climax that made her spine shiver.

No one had even stopped to watch her passion. As the strange Prussian music swept to a crescendo, the officers had become engrossed in their own sport. Nearest to her prostrate body, she saw a tall raven-headed female officer bent double with her skirt ruffled around her waist. The long, scarlet nails on her fingers dug into the buttocks of the slave she was busily suckling while another young male slave thrust himself into her from behind with a startling rapidity. 'Oh that looks good,' Poppy murmured with a smile, and wrapped her legs around the shoulders of her own still-nuzzling slave.

Elsewhere, other officers indulged their needs and revealed their secrets. Two slave-girls had been arranged over wooden vaulting horses. Their slim bellies rested on the cushioned backs of the saddles and their slim wrists and ankles were tied together below. Stripped to the waist, with their braces hanging in large black loops round their knees, two male officers set upon the pert female backsides with short-tailed flails in perfect synchronisation. Loud, moist sounds joined the din in the cavernous room. Poppy could see the girls' pretty buttocks quivering in tiny ripples and could hear their squeals as the flails made contact. After the punishment had been delivered, the officers approached the girls' ruddy buttocks and promptly entered the slaves. A savage coupling began immediately, but as each deep lunge was forced home the officers still kept perfect time with each other.

It seemed that, everywhere in the chamber, hands, canes, straps and flails were tenderising the buttocks of the female slaves to ready them for penetrative conclusions. Young male slaves were ridden hard by the female officers, or simply flogged by the mistresses' frenzied outbursts, while the older male slaves could be seen lapping between the female officers' buttocks or cleaning the heels of their shoes with attentive mouths. The plump woman, who controlled the dancer, had dived upon a collection of male submissives who were scampering on all fours and fighting over one of her shoes. Lashing left and right with a riding crop, she scattered her devotees and made sure each backside was marked by at least one severe welt. After retrieving her shoe, she barked out a series of instructions, bidding them all to come back to heel. Dutifully, each man returned and apologised to the mistress, who stood above them with her hands perched, knuckle down, upon her broad hips. It struck Poppy that the officers had made sure the slaves outnumbered them, in case one of the elite required several servants to satisfy a scenario.

It was the sight, however, of the delicate woman who had sat beside her that reignited her desire for hard and immediate satisfaction. It seemed the fragile blonde enjoyed a special kind of nourishment from her men, whom she preferred silver haired. Two mature slaves, with their faces concealed by rubber masks, were bent over and touching their toes and she struck their backsides with a cane of an especially cruel design – the sight of its slender barrel and knotted joints alone sent shivers through

Poppy's body. Looking at the fragile girl, stripped to her corset and stockings, Poppy began to wonder if she had attended one of the notorious private schools when younger and now used the 'Abyss' to reverse the roles and relive a formative experience. When the caning had worn her out, the girl wiped her hair from her eyes and lay down upon a canvas mat, where she stretched out her arms and legs. Casually, she then invited the two older men to take her, closing her eyes and biting the fingers of one hand as they hurried to comply. And there they took her, one after the other, with an animal ferocity.

'Now,' Poppy demanded, sitting up to strip her tights off. 'I want your pretty cock inside me, boy. Do you hear? And it had better be hard.'

Complying instantly, the sticky-mouthed man arranged her legs so her ankles rested on his shoulders. When he shuffled forward, she felt the bulbous end of his penis nudge its way inside her.

'Good,' she said, and then moaned. 'That's it, right in. Oh! More! All of you, come on, push.'

When firmly inserted, Poppy noticed he had gritted his teeth in an effort not to ejaculate. 'Don't you dare come yet,' she hissed and clawed the underside of the bench as his glorious length settled inside her.

He paused for a moment, until the necessity to explode passed, before withdrawing to the tip of his phallus. 'Come on,' Poppy ordered, losing her patience as her desire for aggression increased.

'Yes, ma'am,' he muttered and began to build up his rhythm.

As he developed an even but quicker pace in which to rifle his solidity through her, Poppy relaxed, stretching her hands backward to seize the end of the bench.

'Fuck me, hard,' she whimpered. The exquisite slave complied. He was the best-looking man she had ever made love with, and the thought of him being under her control and about to pummel her sex on command made her shout obscenities into the swirling music of punishment, bombarding her from all around.

The force of his thrusts, delivered with all the power his hips could muster, pushed her body up and down the length of the bench. The muscles in her arms and shoulders knotted as she hung on to the bench for support, and she enjoyed a second climax of such intensity that although her mouth was wide open nothing but a silent breath passed across her tongue. She still retained enough presence of mind, though, to push her feet outwards and against her lover's jaw and face, denying him the satisfaction of seeing the results of his ruthless penetration.

The stamina of her slave was commendable and he continued to work his way in and out of Poppy for what seemed like an hour, helping her to maintain the sense of mindlessness she had grown to relish. Sometimes his loving would slow down, in order for him to regain his breath, and sometimes it would speed up as if he were in a hurry to expend himself after holding back for so long, but she never rewarded him with anything besides a curse or threat. And she understood that it was her disregard and endless demand for satisfaction that drove him on.

Only as the music died, which made the room feel even hotter, did her lover cry out and shoot his seed inside her. The dim sensation of his shaft, pulsing deep within her, and the warm trickle of his cream over her coccyx and between her buttocks, sent her mind and body over another precipice and into a pleasure which left her faint. When his organ had softened inside her, and her heart had slowed down from car-wreck speed, she became aware of her thirst and need for energy. She pushed the slave away with her feet and sat up to cram her mouth with fruit, sweetbread, and more of the refreshing beer. Sitting obediently beside her, her cast-off lover watched her feasting with adoration, until with a smile she turned to him and shared her fare.

Reclining on her back, amongst the candles, tankards, and platters of food, Poppy placed a selection of juicy morsels on her breasts and between her legs, and invited him to eat. And it was no surprise to her that he ate until his stomach was full.

133

After their supper, she bid her slave to sit at her feet and lap at her toes, while she continued to drink and watch the surrounding mêlée with heavy eyes. The sluggishness that began to overwhelm her had also encroached upon the party. Like a rabid fire, the fuel had been noisily and greedily consumed until only the embers were left smoking. Both slaves and masters were worn out. Here and there, a booted figure would stagger through the tallow smoke and yellow light in the pursuit of scurrying nakedness, or a scantily clad female officer would still be rising and falling on the flanks of a writhing slave, but many of the celebrants had fallen asleep. Like debauched aristocrats, fed to bursting point on the fruits and labours of others, the officers had caned and loved their way to exhaustion.

As her sight dimmed and her mind demanded sleep, she saw a lone burst of vigorous activity in a far corner. It was there she spotted Hector. Stripped to his dark trousers and riding boots, he sat on a wooden chair and puffed on a cigar. Before him, on a canvas mat, Chloë wrestled with a tall girl. Poppy watched the fight for a while and wasn't surprised to see Chloë win the duel. When the kicking and spitting opponent had been subdued, she was dragged on to all fours and ridden by the punky-haired victor, while Hector flexed a riding crop.

Immobilised by the toll her work and loves had wrought upon her body, Poppy experienced a thickening exhaustion pass through her body until she craved nothing but a sleep that would last for days. She beckoned the young slave to her and made him hold her tight, so she could drift to sleep on his chest. With a pleasant thumping sensation between her thighs, still pulsing like a second heart, and her head cradled in the arms of a beautiful submissive, Poppy fell asleep without a care.

Ten

'What are you doing?' Poppy murmured, propping herself up in bed on one elbow. Instinctively, she drew the thick duvet over her naked breasts, even though the figure crouched beside the bed had already averted his eyes.

'I'm sorry, miss. I didn't mean to wake you.'

'Who are you?' she said, recoiling against the headboard as the shock of awaking in a strange room swept away the last vestiges of sleep from her mind. 'Where am I?'

The figure stood upright. It was a young man, dressed in a dark suit, who looked oddly familiar. Had he been at the club?

'Please, don't worry. You're safe here,' he said, and then glanced over his shoulder at the open bedroom door. Slowly, he began backing away towards it.

'Wait!'

He paused, looked at the floor and then said something she didn't catch.

'What?'

'I – I can't . . .' he replied, and then scurried towards the door.

'You can't? You can't what?'

'She'll see you soon,' he muttered over his shoulder, and vanished from the room, closing the door behind him.

Stunned, Poppy sat still for a while, rewinding her memory back to the last time she had been awake. As if recalling a distant dream, she remembered the Abyss club and the night of depravity she'd witnessed and been a part of. She remembered falling asleep on the officers' table, and then . . . then there was nothing. Now she sat in a strange bed while her head throbbed and a desperate thirst raged inside her throat.

Glancing about her, she'd tried to make sense of her surroundings. The first thing she noticed were the bright colours. Sprays of flowers leapt from vases on every windowsill, dresser and table in the large bedroom. Behind the flowers, white walls stretched to a high ceiling bordered by a cornice. Oil paintings decorated the walls, and in each corner a marble pedestal had been placed to display a statue of classical design.

Amongst the heavy perfume of flowers and scented oils, she detected the aroma of hot toast and coffee. Beside the bed, where the strange man had crouched, Poppy spotted a large silver tray holding a tureen, several china plates, a coffee pot, milk jug and various silver containers holding marmalade, sugar, butter and so forth.

'Breakfast?' she queried, and kicked the bed linen from her legs. Poppy raised the tray to the bed and devoured the food.

Once the coffee had been drained, the bacon, eggs and toast demolished and the orange juice guzzled, she fell back against the pillows and wondered how long she had been asleep. Determining the time became her first priority. After clambering from the bed, she searched the furniture and ensuite bathroom for a clock. The search proved fruitless and her confusion deepened. She was lost – unaware of where she was or for how long she'd been imprisoned.

Weak grey light penetrated the curtains on either side of the imperial-sized bed. She ran across to them and peered outside. The first thing she saw were steel bars fixed like a cage on the outside of the windows. Stepping back, Poppy felt the first tremor of panic flutter in her stomach. She approached the window again and peered through the bars and into the leafy street below. At once, she recognised the four-storey buildings, with their iron railings, and the Victorian street lights bordering a wide, swept road. She had been here before; but only once, after the unveiling of her first sculpture, the *Loving Captive*.

The baroness had taken her. Now she remembered where she had seen the young servant with the nervous face. When she had dined with the baroness, he'd scurried about in the background with dishes and wine. 'Please, not her. Anyone but her,' she muttered, remembering the black sedan cruising past her in the street outside the Abyss club. She ran to the vast double doors guarding the room. Both brass handles turned in her grip, but neither would open. The bitch had locked her in from the outside.

But how did she get me? Poppy thought, slumping back on the bed. The baroness hadn't even been at the club. Cursing herself for drinking and playing so hard after her exhausting work on *Surgery*, Poppy clutched the sides of her face and scratched about for an idea. Despite her exhaustion, she wouldn't have remained asleep while someone moved her from the club. Her head still throbbed and at the back of her sinuses she detected a tang of something that smelt of ether. She'd been drugged and brought here unconscious.

'Bitch!' she cried out. Frustration burnt inside her. Regardless of how reckless she had been seeking erotic inspiration in Darkling Town, she had always felt in control. The baroness had taken more than a liberty: she had taken a captive.

Curiously, though, it was the thought of being prevented from starting another piece for the collection that rankled more than anything. And she was behind on posting her cast-off clothes back to Sheen Couture. It wasn't a case of her needing the money, but the thought of not receiving any more clothes in return for the old worried her.

Her clothes from the night before, where were they? Leaping off the bed, Poppy searched about for her boots, skirt, blouse and tights. Unable to see them on any of the surfaces, she began yanking the drawers of the dresser open. What she found there filled her with horror. Clothes in her size and taste lined every compartment. Slowly, she withdrew flimsy panties, transparent brassieres, chic skirts with tight fifties cuts, and antique hosiery. Although every item was expensive and made by a leading fashion house, nothing compared with the delights from Sheen Couture. These were imitations – not soft enough, not cut high enough, not revealing or concealing enough. Everything was wrong.

'She has no right,' Poppy murmured in exasperation. They had shared one time together. A significant and formative time for her, but she would not be the woman's captive. She was free: her imagination was unfettered, her spirit longing to roam and love where it chose. The vein she mined for her art was still bountiful and demanded so much from her. Time was more precious than anything – she would not stay.

After marching to the bedroom door, Poppy began hammering on the wooden panels and yelling for assistance. No one came and no one heard her cries – or at least they pretended not to. Pacing around the room, and thinking as fast as she was able, she decided in desperation to smash a window and call for help. She lifted a heavy marble statue, depicting two wreathed women making love. In a fit of rage Poppy raised it and took aim at the window. But the sight of the figures' faces, with their eyes closed in serenity as each mouth busied itself between the other's thighs, forced her to place it back on the pedestal and select a cushioned stool instead. With a cry she slung the heavy stool at the large bay window.

There was a booming sound when the stool struck the pane of glass. The window bent outward, shuddered within the frame, and then popped back as straight and flat as it had been originally. 'Bitch,' Poppy whispered, and sat on the floor in despair.

Hours passed and, despite her periodic attempts at beating the door with her hands and then the breakfast tray, no one came. Too angry and resentful to wear the garments supplied by her host, Poppy remained naked. It was only when she submitted to taking a bath, however, that she heard someone unlock the door. After gently raising herself from the steaming tub, so as not to make a sound, she slipped her legs over the side of the bath and crept to the bathroom door.

Dripping wet, with her face set in grim concentration, Poppy watched the main doors to her chamber open a few inches. The face of the young valet she had seen that morning appeared and peeked about. She presumed he'd been biding his time until an opportunity to discreetly enter the chamber presented itself, as he must have heard her run a bath.

Satisfied the room was clear, the young valet crept inside carrying a large tray that held a crystal bowl of fruit and another giant silver tureen. Slowly, he took several wary paces into the room before bending down to place the tray on the floor.

Poppy took a deep breath, tensed her muscles, and then struck. The valet had time to see her quick approach and straighten his back, but nothing else. Before he took a single step in retreat, Poppy was upon him. Flinching, he held his hands out and only managed to whimper the word 'Please' before being propelled backward from the force of her two-handed lunge. Winded, and lying on his front, he tried to raise himself to all fours, but Poppy launched herself across his shoulders and pressed his face into the carpet.

'No, don't,' he cried, clutching the rear of his head in protection.

Sitting on his back, she used a handful of his hair to pull his face off the floor. In the most aggressive voice she could summon, she asked him his name.

'Thomas,' he hissed. 'And don't shoot the messenger. Please, I'm only doing this under orders.'

She pressed her angry face close to his ear. 'If you don't let me out of here right away, I'll snap your neck like a twig. You hear?'

'Oh, I can't,' he whispered, sounding close to tears. 'You don't understand. She'd throw me out and I have nowhere to go.'

'You should have thought about that before kidnapping me.'

'We haven't. You're just a guest. I promise –'

'Liar! What about the bars on those windows? And what

about the lock on those fucking doors? You heard me trying to get out and you ignored me.'

He stayed quiet and closed his eyes, but there was a slight movement beneath her. The young valet was rubbing himself against the carpet. Climbing off his back, Poppy said, 'Turn over.'

When the young man rolled on to his back, still cowering, she spied the thick erection that raised his trousers like a big top.

'Well,' she said. 'It seems my predicament has turned you on.'

'Not at all,' he replied, far too quickly.

'Get it out,' Poppy ordered, intrigued by the pretty coward.

'But –'

'Get it the fuck out!' she yelled.

Without further delay, the young man unzipped his trousers and let his meat flop out. Bending down, she grasped the base of his shaft before smoothing her hand up and down its considerable length.

Thomas closed his eyes.

'I believe you,' she said, in a softer voice. 'I've met your boss once and I know she put you up to this. But you can help me escape.' Poppy continued to stroke his cock, enjoying the feel of the hard rod, covered in silky skin, that seemed to beat like a heart in the palm of her hand. 'And I like this cock. Recently, I've discovered quite an appetite for pretty boys with nice toys. In fact I took one last night. Hurt him a bit too. You know, played hard.'

Thomas began to pump his penis through her hand. Leaning across him, she traced her tongue around the moist tip of his phallus. 'Will you help me?' she asked.

'I'll try, miss.'

His cock began to feel too good and his pre-come had a clean taste. The servant was impossible to ignore and her anger began to subside. She still smarted, but if things went in her favour she could screw another male beauty and teach the baroness a lesson in the same morning. 'I'm all scrubbed and soft,' she cooed at the valet. 'And I do like to fuck first thing in the morning. What do you think?'

'Oh I want to, but my mistress could walk in at any moment.'

'Perfect,' Poppy whispered. Delighted at the opportunity for revenge, she spread her legs across his pole. Dipping her hips, she felt the dome of his phallus part her lips. Slowly, she lowered her body further and clenched her teeth. The moment of penetration was exquisite. It would hurt a little because his cock was so fat, but she craved the sensation of being stretched wide. Moaning, she slipped her body over his thickness. There was a sucking sound and she gripped his ribs with her thighs. Steadying herself, she slid the rest of her tight sex down to the base of his penis.

Poppy inhaled quickly. Impaled on the servant, she pinched her own nipples and began to envy the baroness's lifestyle. Maybe she would have a manservant. Were they hard to find? 'That's good, boy. Would the baroness let me buy you?'

This drove the hapless servant into a frenzy. He gripped her thighs, held her against his groin and began thrusting into her sex. 'Sometimes she loans me,' he said. 'To her friends.'

'I bet they take you all night,' she whispered.

'No, usually they just hurt me. But I don't mind.'

Poppy stopped mauling her breasts and scratched her nails down the firm and contoured surface of his chest. Hooking her feet beneath his knees, she began to thump her body up and down on his penis, forcing it right to the back of her sex. 'I'd like you in my arse,' she said, releasing herself into the decadent mode that had begun to rule her life. 'But I think you're too big.'

'Sometimes the baroness lets me.'

'If you can fit inside that scrawny bitch, you can take mine.'

'Oh, miss, I'm afraid if you keep talking like this I may have an accident inside you.'

Grasping his shoulders, Poppy pumped herself up and down, hard and fast, on his cock. Slamming her clit against his pelvis while thinking about his stiff hose rifling her

141

backside brought her close to climax. 'I'm coming,' she cried out. 'Don't you dare shoot until I'm done.'

Clenching his teeth, and clutching the rug with his hands, Poppy could see the servant restraining his desire to explode. 'I want it in my arse,' she said with a gasp. 'I'm going to walk out of here with a tender bum, you hear?'

He seized her by the waist and threw her beneath him, rolling over her body while keeping his cock rooted deep. Slamming his groin against her, the servant pumped her five times, filling her with his muscle until she began to shout.

'Still want me in your bottom, miss?' he stammered.

'Now,' she said with a hiss.

Reluctantly, he slipped his cock from her sex, and Poppy rolled on to her belly, eager to provide his penis with a new home.

It was as if a set of surgical forceps had been attached to her rectum. Pain scalded her. Sweet agonies choked her. It was like defecating in reverse, as he opened the vacuum of her back passage with his girth.

With two fingers she whipped her clit into a frenzy and crashed into the blissful semiconsciousness of climax. Behind her, Thomas heaved his cock in and out of her. 'Too tight, miss. Gonna come.'

'Fill me,' she said, and groaned into the rug.

Fingertips gouged her buttocks; she was pulled right on to his length, and deep inside she felt the throb of his muscles thumping hot cream into her rectum.

They lay in a heap, panting. Only when his cock had softened did he withdraw from her. He kissed her back and pulled himself to his knees between her thighs.

'What a way to start the day,' she said, and then giggled. 'Go and get my clothes, sweety, and open the door before that bitch comes home.'

'Bitch! Poppy, I am surprised at you,' the baroness said, announcing herself from the bedroom door.

Poppy leapt from the floor and turned to face her jailer. Dressed in a black dress that left her arms bare and her legs shimmering in silk to mid-thigh, the very presence of the woman seemed to fill the bedroom with ice. Poppy scurried back to the bed and searched for something with which to cover her nakedness.

'Ingratitude is not something I expected from a girl of your calibre,' the baroness added, and teetered across the room to open a wardrobe door. 'Neither is the rather carnal display I had the good fortune of walking in upon.'

'Well, you shouldn't leave your valuables just lying around,' she said, and winked at Thomas, who suddenly turned pale.

After whipping a black gown from its hanger, the baroness approached Poppy and offered the garment. 'French silk. I've spared no expense on welcoming you into my home.'

'Welcoming me?' Poppy queried. 'You had no right to take me from the club and lock me up. I'm not a toy.'

'Come now, it's not so bad.'

'But I want to go. Thanks for breakfast and lunch –' She blew a kiss at Thomas and watched the baroness stiffen. 'And your man here can drive me home.'

Trembling with rage, the baroness threw her manservant a look that promised trouble.

'I think a two-week loan of your valet,' Poppy added, 'might just prevent me from going to the police on account of being drugged and kidnapped.'

'Enough,' the baroness whispered. 'No more, please. If your refusal to return my calls was not enough of an insult, you speak to me now as if I'm a criminal.'

'You are,' Poppy said, unable to stop herself. 'But if you release me now, we can forget about this temporary loss of reason you seem to have suffered.'

'You are facing the greatest danger of your life, girl,' the baroness said in a thin voice. 'And I am not the threat you should fear. You understand nothing, but soon you will thank me with all your heart. I have put myself in jeopardy by acting as your protector.'

'Protector? What are you talking about?' she said, raising her voice, convinced the baroness was delusional. 'I'm in control of my life and in no danger from anyone but you.'

Smiling, the woman then moved towards her and attempted to take her hands. Poppy moved backward and rejected the gesture. 'Don't touch me,' she whispered. 'Just let me go.'

'Pardon?' the baroness replied, but her voice was nothing more than a frail version of its former self. 'Did you say, don't touch me? As if I'm the vilest sort of street pervert. After all I've done for you. For your art. For your safety. You say this, to me?'

'Oh, ma'am. Please let her go,' Thomas wailed.

'Silence!' the baroness bellowed, and Poppy felt herself flinch from the force of her outburst.

Finding his feet, the man began to plead, 'Ma'am, this is all wrong, she –'

'Be still, you little shite!'

Poppy gasped in shock at the baroness's language and was suddenly overwhelmed with pity for the soft-voiced youth who had brought her breakfast, lunch, and satisfaction.

'Get out!' the baroness bellowed at the figure who immediately flinched but refused to leave.

Rushing forward, her face a mask of rage, the baroness crossed the room and lashed out at the servant. Her long hand cuffed his ear and made him cry out in pain. 'Get out,' she repeated, her voice descending to an angry hiss. 'Go.'

The man fled from the room, dipping his head to hide the crimson blush that stretched from his face to the rear of his well-shorn neck. Patting her hair, the baroness raised her chin and turned to face Poppy. 'Forgive me. That boy is surly and has no right to question me, after –'

'I know, after all you've done for him. But he's right. I won't stay here, and you can't keep me here. I have work to do, and . . .' Her voice trailed off at the sight of the baroness's broad smile.

'Everything has been thought of, my dear. The rear conservatory has been converted to a studio that even Rodin would have approved of.'

Speechless, Poppy shook her head and sat back on the

bed. It was no use: the woman was obsessed. She had stalked her, abducted her, and now seemed to be justifying abduction with a wild fantasy about her being in danger and in need of a protector. She was left with no option other than force.

Suddenly, Poppy sprang to her feet, raced across the room and darted outside to the hallway. Across the landing, she saw a staircase with banisters descending to the lower storey and flew towards it. Taking three steps at a time, she leapt down the wide spiralling stairs to a marble-floored reception that housed the front entrance. Her eyes became frantic as they searched across the surface of the large white door for a handle or lock, but there seemed no way of manually opening it from the inside. To the left of the door was a keypad with tiny steel buttons marked with Roman numerals. Poppy slammed her fist against the console. There was a shrill beeping sound but the door remained closed. She beat one fist against the seam between the doors and would have continued the futile strokes against the heavy obstacle had the baroness not appeared at the top of the stairs and said, 'It only opens on remote. From a security code which you don't have.'

'Let me out, now,' Poppy said, her voice beginning to break up.

'It doesn't have to be like this, Poppy.'

'It will for as long as you hold me against my will.'

'It's for your own good, girl. Trust me.'

'No, I won't. I don't like you – I never will – and I demand to be released!'

Reaching out with her elegant hand, the baroness clasped the banister and steadied herself. She tried to speak, but stopped, and for a moment Poppy almost felt sorry for the woman whose face had become a mask of anguish. Without a word, the woman turned on her heel and scurried off into the gloom of the upper floor. In the distance there was the sound of a door slamming, and then there was silence. A deep and profound silence.

* * *

Thomas was in the kitchen when Poppy found him an hour later. He glanced over his shoulder as she entered, before quickly looking away. She moved closer, calmly smoking a cigarette and saying nothing. While continuing to baste a magnificent goose on the large wooden table, which was strewn with vegetables and steel cooking implements, he began to take furtive peeks at Poppy out of the corner of his eye. And she was pleased to observe this, after dressing for him.

Having finally conceded to dress in the baroness's finery, it was her high heels – a pair of elegant, thin-heeled mules, made in Italy and covered in fine black velvet – that seemed to interest him the most. Turning her ankle nonchalantly, she displayed her shapely calf muscle and pale ankle, visible beneath the fine nylon she had coated her legs with. She watched the servant, unable to prevent himself, glance down at her pretty leg and then blush. Staying silent, Poppy wandered around the vast kitchen and admired the copper pans and bundles of spices hanging from the ceiling. With every step upon the kitchen tiles, she made sure her heels struck the shiny blue surface with a resounding snap. Behind her, she felt the man's eyes following her legs and, without his knowing, she smiled to herself.

'You have a smart kitchen. I'm envious,' she said.

'I spend a lot of time here,' he muttered.

Poppy pouted her lips, knowing from the tone of his voice that his mouth had dried out with fear and excitement. 'I bet you do,' she said. 'The baroness is a demanding woman.'

Thomas raised his eyebrows and smiled, relaxing slightly.

'But then you like that, don't you?' she added brusquely, and swivelled around to look him in the eye.

He looked away, colouring instantly.

'Nothing to be ashamed of,' she said. 'But she treats you badly, I know.'

'She's been a good employer,' Thomas replied.

'Really,' Poppy said, drawing on her cigarette and

continuing her inspection of the kitchen. When she passed the kitchen entrance, she stretched out the leg he had been admiring and swung the door shut.

'Please don't ask, miss,' Thomas whispered, moving away from the goose, with his greasy hands hanging out in front of him. 'I'm going to pay for this morning.'

Poppy walked towards him. 'She's done a bad thing, young man. And you know it.'

'Yes, but she's very upset now. Please, let me talk to her, and in a few days I'm sure she'll relent.'

Smiling, Poppy shook her head. 'No, darling. That just won't do, will it?'

Thomas backed away from her.

'You have the code for the door,' she said. 'Which you'll provide shortly.'

'No, no. Absolutely not. I will not –'

'You think the baroness is hard with you, hmm? Treats you like a dog and makes your cock hard?'

There was a sudden intake of breath from the young man and Poppy laughed. She moved her lips close to his face. 'Getting tossed into the street by your employer will be worth what I'm about to do to you.'

'No,' he said, his voice barely a whisper.

'The door code,' she said.

Thomas shook his head and tried to move to one side, but Poppy was too quick and trapped him against the wooden table by placing her arms on either side of his waist, so her fingertips touched the table edge behind him. Thomas tried to push past her arms and escape.

'Touch my arm,' she said, 'and I'll break you.'

Thomas leant back against the table, turning his face to one side. When Poppy stood no more than a few inches away from his body, she felt the lump of his erect penis prod against her stomach. Slowly, she lowered a hand and gently scraped the tips of her lacquered nails against his bulge. 'Nice. Is that for me?' she whispered.

'Please, miss. I know what you're trying to do. But I can't help you just yet. She's so angry after what you said to her.'

'Angry!' Poppy shrieked and seized the servant by his shirt front. 'Want to see angry, shitbird?'

She spun him around and thrust him over the table, so his face ploughed through an assortment of chopped vegetables. When he raised his head, she cuffed him hard and then pressed his face down into a bowl of potato peelings. 'This could have been easy, tough guy. A little toe sucking, maybe my heels between your legs. I know how you like that, but now we have to do this the hard way. I've got to beat the code out of you.'

Working quickly, with her free hand, she untucked the servant's shirt, undid his belt by reaching around his front, so her forearm brushed his erection, and stripped his loose-fitting trousers down to his knees. He pushed back against her and begged for her to stop, but Poppy knew him incapable of either fighting back or ever saying no to an assertive woman. Since his teens, he had probably been dreaming of a humiliating debagging and thrashing in a kitchen.

'Little shit,' she cried out, and belted his naked buttocks with a wooden spoon, giving him the broad, flat head at full speed. 'Think you're going to mess me around?' She slapped him again, hard, and then again, and over and over again, until his buttocks were bright red. 'What's this then?' she said through her teeth, and gripped his thick erection. 'Why does a pussy like you need such a big cock?'

'Oh,' he moaned, and clenched his buttocks.

She wrenched his head from the potato peelings, before dragging him across to a large ceramic bowl where leeks were soaking. With all her strength she pressed forward and dunked his face into the bowl. When she pulled him back by his hair and heard him spitting and wheezing, Poppy slid her slippery knee between his legs until it nudged against his scrotum. Again, he groaned deeply, but this time he gripped his manhood with his greasy hands and began to perform a quick jerking motion in front of his body.

'Dirty shit,' she said, smiling, and dunked him again. While she held him under water for a few seconds, she thrust her other hand out and grasped a yellow rubber glove the servant used for washing up. After pulling his face back out of the bowl, she spun him round so that when the salted water cleared from his eyes he could watch her pulling on the rubber glove.

'Bend over,' she hissed.

Thomas hesitated, so Poppy flung her hand back as if to strike his face. Immediately, Thomas bent double, with his red buttocks pressed back towards her. Calmly, Poppy strolled to a work surface and covered the fingers of the glove with olive oil, making the rubber squeak and snap.

In full view of the servant, who peered back at her from between his legs, Poppy then licked three of her fingers, tinting them with her lipstick and saliva. 'Stand still,' she said, and stood behind him with her heels planted wide apart.

He made nothing more than a muffled groaning sound as she widened his tight ring with one finger, and then a second. When the third slipped up inside him, he fell forward, snatching at the table edge with his fingertips to stay on his feet.

'The code,' she said, easing her hand in and out.

'Please,' he whispered, his voice rising a few octaves.

'Code, shitbird.'

'Seventy-seven, nineteen, sixty-nine,' he croaked.

'Good,' she said, memorising the number and withdrawing her hand.

'Sit on the table,' she demanded.

Stumbling, with his trousers stretched between his ankles, Thomas raised himself off the floor and sat on the table surface. Poppy ripped her glove off and cast it away before approaching Thomas with an eyebrow half-cocked. 'If she tosses you, darling, tell her you're going to come and cook for the sculptress. I love a heel who knows his place, *comprende*?'

He nodded enthusiastically and Poppy sank between his legs. Stretching her lips wide, she embraced his large phallus and let it pass deep into her mouth. Relishing the salty tang, she lapped at the rippled underside of his shaft, and Thomas shuddered as if he'd been hurled into icy water. Deflating her cheeks, Poppy began sucking him, sliding her lips up and down his shaft, slowly, while breathing heavily through her nose. She thought herself a glutton but couldn't help dreaming of the young man's generous dimensions sinking through her sex for the second time in one day. How much cream can he produce second time around? she thought, and then started to hum in expectation of the large deposit soon to arrive on her tongue.

Groaning and clawing the table-top, Thomas leant back into his cooking preparations. Working the base of his thick wood with her hand, Poppy felt herself swept away with the joy of conquest. She lapped the fleshy treasure with more enthusiasm than she could remember lavishing on a cock in the past. When the servant's moans broke into a garbled begging and he began calling her 'beautiful', Poppy released his penis from her mouth to beat it harder with her hand. Thomas looked down at her with glazed eyes and Poppy winked at him before stretching her tongue out to flick it around the curves of his phallus. A large drop of dew appeared at the end of his penis.

'Nearly there,' she said, and began whipping her hand up and down his stem. Over the hard muscles of his shaft, the soft skin of his penis grew hot in her palm, and Thomas began to squirm on the table. 'I want your cream again, Tom,' she whispered. 'All of it.'

He moaned and stared at her lips.

'Where shall I have it?' she said. 'In my mouth? You know I'd like to swallow you. Or in my pussy? Would you like to shoot it into me? What do you think? How about my bottom? A top-up?'

Fisting his hands on the table, Thomas whispered, 'Your feet.'

'My feet?' she asked, smiling. 'You want to come on my high heels?'

There was a quick throb from the stiffness in the palm of her hand.

'Kneel on the floor,' she said, sensing the end. 'And put

150

your cream on my feet. Pump it on to my toes if you like, where they peek through the end of my mules.'

With a look on his face that reminded her of the rapture she had seen in portraits of the saints, the baroness's servant groaned and chopped several thick dollops of his seed on to her feet, ankles and shins, where it hung like pearls from her stockings.

'Good. That was so good,' Thomas mumbled, and gripped her calf muscles with his hands.

Kneeling down, Poppy leant forward and kissed his forehead. 'Where's the bitch?' she asked.

'Sulking, upstairs.'

Poppy lifted the servant's chin so she could look him in the eye. 'Being captured has turned me on.'

'Really?' he asked.

'Umm. Will you give me a little suck?'

Thomas nodded, still wary of her temper, which pleased Poppy.

'I should get going, so we'll have to be quick.'

He nodded and she stood up with her knees close to his face. With her feet pulled together, Poppy pulled her skirt up to her waist and then stepped on to his mouth. Needing no prompt, Thomas arranged himself for the task and slipped her panties down to her knees.

'Oh, she's trained you well,' Poppy said, feeling dizzy at the first touch of his mouth between her legs. His jaws stretched wide, surrounding her sex. Thomas's tongue poked forward and pressed against her clit. Poppy felt faint but he held her steady by gripping the rear of her thighs. Rising to his knees, he pressed his face against her sex, pushing her on to the tips of her toes.

'Oh, you taste good,' he whispered, after pulling his mouth away to take a breath.

Poppy growled and pressed her sex back on to his lips. Bending her knees and leaning forward, she closed her body around his head, smothering his mouth and nose. The young man between her thighs was trapped, but he continued to worship her sex. It was as if he could sense when she wanted his tongue to move faster, or to dip inside her.

'Will you take me again?' she asked, breathless and not far from climax.

Thomas cupped her buttocks and raised her from the floor. Gently, he laid her on the table behind them. Smiling, he parted her thighs and pulled her buttocks down the table until her body was in place. 'Are you comfortable, miss?' he whispered.

Poppy giggled. 'Just get that fat cock inside me, quick.'

Thomas guided himself inside her sex and pressed his length forward.

'Oh that's good.' Poppy raised her feet and placed them on his shoulders. 'Now put it all in. Right to the back of me.'

Closing his eyes, the young man turned his head to the side and began to kiss and suck at her heels. As his tongue glided over her instep and across her sticky toes, he began to bang his groin against her. His thick girth stretched through her, forcing Poppy to bite her fingers to prevent herself from crying out.

There was something about the young man that made a woman want to abuse him, Poppy decided. Be it teasing or flogging, the boy just made a girl aggressive. The baroness had an eye for detail, she thought. Perhaps it was his boyish good looks and slender body, combined with his polite and timid nature. He made a girl feel strong and gave her the desire to lash out before taking a quick satisfaction.

'Oh, I could just slap your face,' she said, before he forced her to groan by pumping her harder, pushing her body up and down the table surface.

'I'd like that,' he replied, and then lapped her slender ankles with his tongue.

'Come on, do it harder. Just throw –'

Poppy never finished. His hands folded round her thighs; his fingers sank though her stockings to indent her thighs; and he raised her bottom an inch from the table. With his hips, Thomas thrust himself in and out of her at a speed and depth to remove every thought from her mind. There was no pause in his stroke; it just seemed to get faster until she no longer cared what she whispered at him.

'Oh miss, oh miss, can I come in you?' he pleaded, blinking his eyes against the stream of sweat that fell from his forehead.

Unable to speak, Poppy nodded her head.

Rolling through her in successive waves, the climax left her faint. Driven to his peak, Thomas squashed himself against her and filled her sex with a river of something hot.

'You sweet boy,' Poppy murmured with her eyes still shut. 'You probably know where I live, so remember, if she tosses you out, you can crash with me for a while.'

'Thanks,' he said, blushing.

Poppy rose from the table and gave Thomas a hug. He held her against his chest and kissed her mouth, tentatively.

'It's all right,' she whispered. 'You're allowed to kiss me.'

His mouth explored hers and Poppy drew his tongue inside.

'I like that,' he said.

Poppy pulled her face back. 'You're not allowed to kiss her, are you?'

He shook his head and looked away.

'Why don't you come home with me now?' she asked.

'I can't. But I do want to. It's just –'

'I know,' she said, and pressed a finger against his lips. 'But you know where I am.'

He nodded, smiling.

It was time she moved. After rearranging her clothes, she blew Thomas a kiss and skipped towards the kitchen door.

'Miss,' he said.

'Yes.'

'What my mistress said about . . .'

'Go on.'

'About you being in danger.'

'Yes.'

'It's not a lie.'

'Sorry?'

'I can't say any more now, but I'll be in touch. You'd better go, before she starts wondering why the evening meal is late.' There was something in his expression that warned of sincerity. 'Forget my mistress,' he added. 'The baroness is harmless. She means well, but is so clumsy and childish. But the danger does exist. There is someone –'

Before he could say another word, a small bell began ringing on the kitchen wall. Immediately, a look of anxiety spread across Thomas's face. 'The baroness, she wants me. Go, miss, and quickly, before she comes looking.'

Poppy nodded and fled from the kitchen, removing her sticky heels as she sped away. Instead of feeling elation, however, at having escaped the baroness, she experienced nothing but a deep sense of unease.

Eleven

Surrounded by his wall-mounted treasures, Eliot sipped his vodka and gazed across the icy vault of his study to where the musicians played. The four pretty girls, who sat on stools with their violins raised by fragile arms, or their cellos slung between elegant legs, never looked him in the face. They knew better. Their role was clearly defined: they were to dress for him and play for him. This had been the arrangement for years. He would make his selection once the ensemble had concluded its performance – when the cold stiffened their delicate fingers and toes.

Alice, Imogen, Marisha, and Pepper: the very best the Darkling Academy for Performing Arts could offer. And they were lucky girls. Not only were their studies maintained by his generous scholarships; he also provided them with the most beautiful gowns in which to perform, privately.

Smiling, Eliot reminisced on their interviews for the scholarships two years earlier. Amongst the innocent, the poor, the over-keen, the ambitious, and the dozens of other young ladies who vied for his maintenance, only this quartet had captured his attention. It had been their intelligence, style, and the odd glimmer of something indefinable to the untrained eye that he favoured. He had deciphered the hidden signals in their eyes – eyes already open to a different kind of loving. Eyes that asked for and then forgave cruelty. Seductive and clever eyes, but also shy eyes that watched and accepted the rising and the falling of his right arm.

When their rendition of *The Magic Flute* approached its conclusion, Eliot squeezed his hands together. It was the last piece he had requested them to play, and soon one of their long and agile bodies would twist in his arms. Would it be Alice, dressed in emerald and cushioned by fur? Or Marisha in black, so he could see how her eyes matched the undergarments she wore beneath the floor-length gown? Maybe Imogen in scarlet would placate the prowling beast beneath his blue flesh. Or Pepper, who had screamed in soprano the last time they performed. Who would it be?

Eliot drained his glass and enjoyed the taste of quinine on his palate. Tonic was good: it killed things in warm climates.

'Wonderful,' he said, and began to applaud when the last bow was allowed to rest and the final whispers of Mozart died in his ears. 'Marvellous, girls. You spoil me. If my schedule wasn't so full, I'd allow myself the indulgence of hearing you play every week. But then,' he said, rising from his chair, 'I suppose that might spoil the delightful brevity of our pleasure.'

Even though Marisha's face was angled towards the floor, he saw her smile and something knotted in his belly.

'At ease, girls. Relax. In the dining room you will find refreshments and an envelope addressed to each of you. A little something extra to help your studies.' And then he paused and looked at each pretty face. None of the girls had moved. They were waiting for his selection. 'There is wine in the dining room,' he added, enjoying the pause before his sentence was delivered. 'And the cake you like. So go and enjoy the fare. All of you except for –' four pairs of eyes flashed wide open and from amongst them he heard a sharp intake of breath '– except for Marisha.'

Without looking at Marisha or bidding her farewell, the other three musicians cased their instruments and left the room. Blushing, Marisha smiled through the glossy black locks that fell about her face.

'My sweet,' Eliot whispered as he approached her chair. 'Are you cold?'

'A little,' she murmured, raising her hazel eyes to soften him inside.

Cupping her chin, he felt her swallow, which passed a little vibration through his fingers as if a butterfly were beating its wings against his hand. 'There will be warmth soon enough, Marisha.'

'Yes, sir,' she said, and he heard her breathing quicken.

Eliot raised his face to stare at the huge photograph of Poppy with its gigantic eyes.

'Are we going to your chamber?' Marisha asked.

'Yes,' he answered, without removing his eyes from the smile on Poppy's mouth.

'She's very pretty. Can she play?' Marisha asked, leaning close to him so he could hear the rustles from beneath her gown.

'She's a solo act,' Eliot said with a smile, before reaching for Marisha's proffered hand.

'Will you ever let us wear these clothes?' the inquisitive girl asked as they walked past his treasures on the way to his bedchamber.

'No. It's best not to disturb ghosts,' he said softly, reminding himself about the history of the garments he sent to Poppy, and the warning of the French tailor who made them. For a moment, Eliot closed his eyes to banish such thoughts. Tragedy struck those who wore or bought the garments in the interest of seeking power. The clothes were sacred, the elderly tailor had said. They were to be worn on special occasions and not allowed to become part of an obsession. It had happened so many times before. The Jean Ray family had been hand-crafting the lingerie for generations, and it had taken much persuasion for them to allow Eliot to buy in bulk.

But there was no such thing as the supernatural, and magic was dead. Still, it was uncanny how so many lovers had met unfortunate ends while enchanted by the world's most expensive clothing. 'Just a coincidence,' he whispered, and tightened his grip on Marisha's hand.

'Sorry?'

'Nothing but a thought,' he said, and led her towards the huge canopied bed in his chamber.

157

Without prompt or command, Marisha left his side and stood beside a large dressing mirror. Slowly, she removed her gloves and stole, and then slipped the black velvet gown from her creamy shoulders. Torrents of her luxuriant curls dropped across her pale skin and swung about the handsome swell of her bosom. With her eyes closed, she dropped the gown from her waist and stepped out of it.

'Bravo,' Eliot whispered, but he wondered what he enjoyed more – the final display of the lingerie he hand-picked for each girl to wear during a performance, or the mere knowledge of what each girl concealed beneath her gown as she played.

Marisha straightened her back and raised her chin as her master approached.

When his nose hovered no more than an inch from her throat, Eliot inhaled and drank her fragrance. Barely touching her, he traced the palms of his hands around her silhouette. From her shoulders to her wrists he grazed the roughness of his fingertips over her goose bumps. Dipping his face, until his nose tickled the flesh of her cleavage, he savoured a draft of the perfume she had sprayed on her sternum. He cupped his hands and felt the weight of her breasts. Cradling them in his palms and stroking her nipples with his thumbs, he pondered on how her brassière was like a dark fog – transparent and yet adding a tint to the softness it covered. Lowering himself to his knees, Eliot caressed her narrow waist and kissed the small mound of her belly, both above and below the delicate fabric of her garter belt. With one finger he gently stroked the dark triangle of her sex that slipped about and whispered beneath the gauze of her panties.

While he ran his hands up and down the rear of her silk-clad legs, the girl closed her eyes.

'Marisha,' he called to her.

'Yes, sir.'

'Go to the bed and arrange yourself.'

The beautiful legs disappeared from his hands and the girl walked to the base of his bed-frame. She bent her upper body over and fisted her hands on the embroidered covers, planting her legs together so they descended into the points of her high heels.

Standing behind the immaculate curvature of her buttocks, Eliot rolled his sleeves up and thought on which tool would serve his need. A simple paddle, made from seasoned wood? Yes, one of the Victorians would do. They made such delightful sounds: a symphony all of their own.

From a rack on the wall, Eliot removed several sturdy examples of the antique correctional implements he collected. After rotating his shoulders to limber up, he made graceful backhand motions with the selected paddle before turning and making downward swipes at the air, creating a whooshing sound that made Marisha's body stiffen.

Eliot walked back to where she shivered and admired her in silence. It was as if an ice-flow roared between his ears and a frost had settled to stiffen his groin. 'Are you ready for me, Marisha?'

'Be tough,' she gasped, and raised herself to her tiptoes, longing for his stroke.

Whap!

Her entire body shook. She gasped and a cloud of foggy breath gathered around her mouth.

Whap! The sound rang out again and echoed around the tomb of his bedchamber.

For the third stroke, Eliot stood sideways and pulled the paddle right back before swinging it forward and upward until it exploded across her lower buttocks. Her flesh shuddered and Marisha raised her head to whimper.

'Again?' he asked.

'Again,' she said with a sob.

By swaying from side to side and moving his weight from one hip to the other, Eliot launched a flurry of blows against each buttock in turn. Moaning, stamping her heels, and throwing her head about, Marisha managed to remain standing throughout the entire delivery.

A twinge in his shoulder, and the bright-red flesh of her buttocks, warned him to stop. Eliot stood back, breathing hard, and ran his fingers through his hair. Slowly, Marisha straightened her body with all the poise and care of a woman lowering herself into a steaming bath. Only Marisha was pulling herself upright, slowly ascending until she stood and looked over her shoulders at her punished bottom, with pride.

'Was I hard?' he whispered, his voice hoarse with excitement.

'Ever so.'

Eliot tugged her around to face him. 'Too hard?' he asked, lowering his mouth to her lips.

'Never too hard,' she managed to say before his tongue filled her mouth and stopped her breath.

She tensed when he clasped her warm backside, but with his elbows he held her steady and then raped her mouth with his own.

'I could devour you, girl,' he said, when her lipstick was smeared from her chin to her cheekbones and her eyes blinked with wonder.

'Ruin me,' she whispered.

Raising her breasts and pushing her head back, she invited him to eat. Eliot plastered his face against the warmth of her neck before slowly moving into a crouch so his mouth was level with her breasts.

Marisha clawed the back of his head and tried to pull his long, white teeth forward until they would touch her nipples; the sleek fabric of her bra would offer no defence against his canines when they became busy.

'Be hard with my tits,' she gasped.

Eliot paused, stunned. He had never heard one of his musicians use such a word. But the way it was uttered – full of longing in a cultured accent – and the manner in which her lips curled thuggishly as she spoke made him want her with a passion he rarely experienced.

He tore through the fabric of her brassière with his front teeth before gorging himself on the plump fruit beneath. Sucking hard, he pulled the soft flesh around her nipple into his mouth, grating his teeth against the tender skin until her claws nearly drew blood on the back of his head. Standing up, Eliot moved his mouth to her other breast.

As he chewed, he clamped a hand between her legs. By rubbing her sex hard, to squash the little ridges of her lips flat against her bones, he could feel the warmth of her dew gathering in the palm of his hand and the impatience of her body as it trembled for satisfaction.

'I'm ready,' she said, and tried to climb on to his hand, chasing it as he withdrew it from between her warm thighs. 'Don't tease me. Hurt me or fuck me, but don't play with me.'

'Marisha, you will always be my favourite.'

Eliot felt his body suddenly suffuse with an even greater power. A desire that would forbid any interruption until it had escaped and been splashed all over the young woman's body. Death was preferable to stopping at this point.

He carried her across the floor rugs and threw her on the bed, where her body bounced on the enormous stage of his mattress. Before she had time to pull her hair from her eyes, the master was upon her. There was no time to undress. His belt was whipped free of its loops and bound around her wrists. Her panties were ripped from her waist and left hanging like a rag from around the top of one leg. With his knee he intimated that her thighs should part, and they did.

Curling her feet under his shins, she steadied herself against the eruption she had coaxed forth in this dangerous man. After a final deep breath, she dipped her head and bit into the sheets as something long, and tipped with ice, slipped between her thighs.

Reaching beneath her, Marisha guided him through her lips and into the softness beyond. Eliot entered her sex evenly, slowing down when his phallus could probe no further. Stroking her back, hips and waist, he paused until she became restless. A grin spread across his lips as she began to press her buttocks against him.

'Don't tease, it's not fair,' she said.

Eliot slapped her backside hard.

'You bastard,' she said with a hiss, and took a swipe at him with one hand. Catching her wrist, he pulled her off the bed and grabbed her other arm. Marisha began to purr when he had both of her wrists trapped against the small of her back. She knew what was coming.

Tensing her arms and back to make herself rigid, she said, 'Do me, sir.'

'Do you?' he asked, smiling, and then pushed her away from his body until only the end of his penis nestled inside her. Gasping, Marisha prepared herself for the return journey along the length of his icy cock. With a tug, Eliot pulled her backward, so her bottom slapped against his groin. Before she was able to catch her breath, he had pushed her out again and yanked her back, using her wrists like the reins of a horse.

'Who was in here last?' he demanded.

'No one,' she whimpered.

'Don't lie –'

'I'm not. No one has taken my pussy, sir. I promise. Not since the last time you selected me.'

'Good, but what of the other place.'

'That's not fair,' she said. 'You know I need it there.'

'Will any man tame you?' he said, smiling and feeling dizzy.

'Not unless he butchers me in that place.'

'There are bruises on your back. Where did they come from?'

'Not telling unless . . .' She peered over her shoulder. 'Unless you feed me properly.'

Unable to contain himself, Eliot squeezed her wrists and slammed himself against her buttocks, sending his cock through her at a hasty and barbaric speed.

'I like to feel your softness first, Marisha,' he said.

'That's for boyfriends, sir. When they lie on top of me and think they're in love.' She turned her face away from him and in a deeper voice said, 'But I want it like a dog.'

Eliot whipped his penis from her sex and impatiently fed it between her buttocks. She shrieked as her muscles resisted his shaft, but with an insistent drilling action Eliot broke into the supple beauty and pressed her down to the bed. Grunting, with his teeth clamped shut, he ground himself inside Marisha until the resistance around his rigidity turned to warmth and his face was buried deep within the perfumed locks of her hair.

'Hard,' she gasped.

Holding her hipbones, he complied, thumping against her red backside until she reached out and began slapping the bed with her hands.

'You still favour this?' he asked.

Marisha nodded but stayed quiet.

'Don't be coy, girl. Have you been bad again?'

She nodded. 'I couldn't help it. He reminded me of you.'

'Who was he?'

'I don't know. A man in a car park.'

'How did he take you?'

'In my arse,' she replied, and turned her head to give him an evil smile.

Closing his eyes, Eliot thought on what she had said. Marisha never lied. She took her pleasure swiftly, recklessly, and usually with strangers.

'Was it good?'

'Yes,' she said, but then her voice broke up as he held her buttocks tight against his groin, so all of him was buried in her succulent rear. 'Same as before, sir. Couldn't get the car started. He came to help.'

'What did you wear?' Eliot said, struggling to breathe.

'No panties, a short skirt and the stockings you gave me. He watched me bend over the engine and couldn't resist my creamy arse.'

'No,' Eliot cried out.

'Yes,' she said through clenched teeth. 'I let him fuck me in the open and then on the back seat, under the symphony hall. And he was so big.'

Eliot lay across her back and hammered himself inside her, as if he were trying to dig through her body. For a moment, Marisha stopped speaking. She had closed her eyes and emitted a series of deep and satisfying groans when his shaft reached the end of this precious and sinful cavity.

Then it struck him. If he closed his eyes, it could be her. Yes, it could be Poppy. She was this tall, her legs this long, her hair as thick and sweet. She would writhe as Marisha did, and grunt, and make demands of his mastery. Her skin too would feel like satin, her breasts would demand his teeth and her legs would slide around his body as he fed. The comparison was too much to bear.

'Poppy.' He mouthed the word into Marisha's hair.

'Fuck me,' Marisha cried into the mattress across which her body was strewn.

'Poppy,' he whispered.

'Use me up,' Marisha whimpered, and squeezed his thighs against her own by looping her feet around his legs to draw him in.

He had never heard the sculptress's voice, but it would call out to him in the same way.

'Fuck me,' she cried out. 'Hurt me.'

Eliot's vision broke up; a burning spasm shot through his groin; his mouth hung slack; his rectum squeezed itself shut; and the thick gush of his seed filled the rocklike muscle he'd planted inside his lover. From the pit of his stomach, he unleashed a groan as every contraction emptied his shaft of its scalding offering.

Marisha pushed her buttocks back, so the velvety pipe of her anus could collect and not lose a drop of her master's gift.

'I love you,' he murmured, unconcerned whether Marisha heard him or not.

'Even when I'm married, I'll be yours,' the young musician whispered from where she lay.

The decision had been made and it was irreversible: the baroness would disappear. How had she failed to understand the importance of the venture? He had warned her, but she had continued to defy him. He was left with no choice.

It had been hard work to ready his plan for its approach to the final, crucial stage. So many rivals had bid for Poppy's work. So many plots had to be balanced against others to keep the sculptress's journey on course. A journey he charted towards the reinforced front door of his metropolitan retreat.

And yet, through Nin's greed and pride, his prize was nearly lost. And through her rebellion one outfit had not been returned. Yes, Nin had kept the boots, skirt, and the pretty blouse that must have covered Poppy like a second skin. She kept them from him, knowing how the very thought of her theft would rankle.

If only Poppy knew the trouble she'd caused. How she had made him tighten the screws on debtors, raise the rates on property rentals, and develop new methods of generating quick capital. The price of this bride was high, but she was worth every penny spent and risk taken. And when she was delivered – the only living, breathing work of art amongst her collection – he would tell her how she had made him suffer.

After Henry had driven Marisha home, Eliot summoned his valet to the study.

With a grave face, Eliot asked Henry to take a seat. An invitation he rarely made. 'Henry, there is something you must do for me. A task you have both the vision and skill for.'

Leaning back into his seat, Eliot slammed the remainder of his drink down his gullet and winced. 'I have given the situation much thought and there is no other alternative. Our friend, Baroness Nin, must vanish.'

Emotion made few appearances on his valet's face, but Eliot thought he noticed a tightening of the man's lips.

'Same caution and style as before. When you see fit, rid me of her.'

There was no nod or 'Yes, sir', just a searching stare from Henry.

'It comes as a shock to you?' Eliot asked.

'It does.'

'But you understand that, for as long as she and I live in the same city, my designs on Poppy will fail. I cannot tolerate her interference and an example must be set.'

'What of her valet?' Henry asked.

'They take the same trip together,' Eliot said. 'The ship must go down with the full complement of her crew. It shouldn't be difficult to arrange. Perhaps you could make it look like a lover's tiff.'

165

'May I be candid, sir?'

'Of course.'

'Is she worth it? Poppy, I mean?'

Smiling, Eliot spoke in a paternal tone: 'Come now, you know better than to question me on that account.'

'But we take such risks and there is no guarantee . . .' Henry's voice trailed off as Eliot flashed him a warning with his eyes. 'There is no guarantee,' he continued, 'that she will be yours.'

'In time, she will love me like no other. I feel it, Henry. The long wait is over.'

'I just wish we could go back to the way things were, sir, with the collection.'

'It was easy then, wasn't it, compared to this? But I'm tired of holding nothing but the shadows of extraordinary women. They're no longer enough. I need a companion.'

'Even if she destroys you.'

Eliot closed his eyes. 'I never heard you say that. This is no fixation, Henry. She is fate.'

'Yes, sir.'

'And after the baroness has left the stage, you will bring Poppy to me.'

'I am to take her?'

'Yes, and you are to deliver her here.'

'When?'

'When the Sheen Couture contract is complete, you will invite her to join us. If necessary she can complete her collection here. It'll prevent those foreign vultures from throwing their money at that fat toad of a gallery manager. *Surgery* has fallen to Persian oil money, and I will not be stolen from.'

'Yes, sir.'

'Now go, you have work to do.'

When Henry left him alone, Eliot turned his attention back to the large photograph of Poppy and knew his dreams would be full of her again, now that she was so close.

Twelve

Something smashed in the bag – a bottle of milk or a jar of sauce. No sooner had Poppy entered her apartment than her bag of groceries slipped from her arms and hit the floor. But the breakage was of no concern. Not when a strange man sat on the solitary wooden chair in her studio.

For a while they watched each other in silence. She had never seen the man before; he stared at her without a trace of emotion on his face. He continued to smoke a cigarette and only spoke when she turned to flee her rooms. 'No point running, miss. I'll only turn up again.'

She stopped on the doorstep and turned around. 'Who are you?'

'A messenger.'

'Really. And your name is?'

'Not important. Please, move away from the door and come in.'

'How kind,' she said, and took several careful steps inside, neglecting to close the front door. 'How did you get in?'

'Easily, and there's no damage. Please sit down.'

Anger replaced her initial fright. 'Look, who are you? You sit there on my chair after breaking and entering, scaring me half to death, and –'

The man raised one gloved hand. 'I apologise, but I mean no harm.'

'Is that right –'

'There isn't much time, and I came here to help you.'

'This is becoming a recurrent nightmare. What are you, one of the baroness's gimps?'

167

'Hardly, but the man you met at the baroness's –' He paused at the sound of the toilet flushing. From the bathroom door, Thomas appeared and offered a weak smile. 'Sorry, miss. I tried to wait until you came home before using the toilet, but I just couldn't hang on any longer. I'm a little nervous.'

'I bet,' she said, relieved at the arrival of the sweet-faced valet.

'Henry means well, and we're only here to talk,' Thomas said, and Poppy noticed the stranger flinch at the sound of his name.

Poppy moved into her studio and leant against the kitchen bench.

'You're in danger,' Henry said, before lighting another cigarette.

'Is that a threat?' she said, narrowing her eyes, but it was an effort to keep her voice steady.

'Oh it's such a mess,' Thomas moaned, and flopped down on the corner of her bed.

'I'm not here to make threats,' Henry continued, unflustered by either her challenge or his companion's despair. 'I have no quarrel with you, but I am here to deliver a warning. It's warning number one and there won't be another. This morning, you received a package from a clothing company that calls itself Sheen Couture. Inside the parcel were a selection of undergarments and certain items of evening wear. You are to wear these before posting them back to the company for dermatological testing. Am I right?'

Poppy caught her breath. 'How did you know? Bastard, you've been opening my post.'

'No,' Henry said, shaking his head. 'But we are fully aware of the process, and I am even a part of the conspiracy against you.'

'Conspiracy?' Poppy cried out in disbelief. 'What conspiracy?'

'Please, Poppy,' Thomas muttered. 'It sounds preposterous, but listen to Henry. He's risked everything by coming here.'

Still a long way from being convinced, Poppy began to laugh. 'Perverts, they never cease to amaze me. The pair of you are unbelievable.'

'Even so, you will be best advised to shut up and listen.' Henry's tone had changed; patience had disappeared from his voice and Poppy didn't like what had replaced it. 'Take a seat and try not to interrupt.'

Despite an urge to hurl something at his head, Poppy obeyed.

'Thank you,' Henry murmured, staring at the wall behind her in concentration. 'My employer is behind the scam. A very wealthy individual, but also a sick man who has become rather fond of you. You have never met him and you don't want to. He is a collector and what he collects he keeps. He is prepared to pay anything for what he desires. His unusual tastes have led him to purchase a certain type of artefact from all over the world.'

'You're not making sense. What does he collect? Art? Antiques? What?'

'I've never said this much to anyone before –' He paused and doused his cigarette. 'What I say will sound crazy, but it's important you understand. My employer is unwell. Unable to ever leave his home on account of an illness, a rare blood virus, which is only kept in remission for as long as he lives in a refrigerated environment. He has never been able to live as a normal man, and so he has adapted to his condition. His pleasures are brought to him. Pleasures that would seem bizarre, or unsavoury, and even dangerous. Thomas, will you?'

'Poppy,' Thomas said, softly. 'He has been sending you the clothes. So that you wear them for him. They are now a part of his collection – his collection of underwear.'

'He collects my dirty laundry?'

Both men nodded.

'They are unique,' Henry said, looking at the floor. 'Each item is handmade by a family of tailors. For generations, centuries even, or so the story has it, these tailors have made clothes for women of beauty or power, changing the styles to suit the age in which they are

169

manufactured. You have been wearing these clothes, and my master believes your sculptures are a direct result of their influence. He sees you as an ultimate work of art – your life and creations have become an obsession. And once his collection of your clothing and sculptures is complete, he intends to add you to the gallery.'

Stunned into silence, Poppy found it hard to even think straight. But the men continued to talk, telling her the weird tale of the master with his collection of antique lingerie, the coven of dominants who served him and the submissives they hunted and then used.

'There isn't much time,' Thomas said, when his friend finished speaking. 'Henry has orders to abduct you and to kill my mistress.'

'The baroness?' she said, beginning to wonder if her life could sink any deeper into the realms of the bizarre.

'For interfering and trying to take you for herself,' Thomas added.

'My meeting with her was no coincidence then?' Poppy queried.

'No. She disobeyed a command and made the master – Henry's employer – very angry. When she made me take you from the Abyss club, the master lost his mind.'

'I'd never seen him like it,' Henry added.

'You must leave Darkling Town,' Thomas said. 'And we intend to stage the baroness's disappearance. To make it look like Henry has carried out the execution the master has ordered.'

'Slow down. Just wait one minute,' she said, trying to recover her wits. 'I have work to do. Three sculptures to complete –'

'Forget them,' Henry said, turning his pale face towards her. 'Leave town –'

'No, you forget it. I'm not about to let some panty sniffer –' She stopped at the sight of the long pistol Henry had withdrawn from his dark overcoat.

'When my master asks me to do something, I do it. If it wasn't for the fact that I no longer trust his reason, that he could destroy everyone – me, Thomas, his followers, his business interests – I would have already carried out his command, and you would be somewhere else, miss.'

As if her mind was now disassociated from her numb body, Poppy found herself sitting next to Thomas on the bed, unable to remember walking across the room. Gently, she touched the long black skirt she wore and breathed in to feel the grip of the corset on her stomach. 'Would he kill me?'

'No,' Henry said. 'He adores you. But he wants you to become his companion.'

'His prisoner,' Poppy answered.

'If you like. You'd be held against your will and there would be no chance of release. You'd be kept in the cold, for ever.'

'The baroness wasn't too hard to slip,' Poppy said, with a sudden spurt of defiance.

'She's a fool. A clumsy, emotional fool,' Henry said, and then turned and offered an apologetic nod to Thomas.

'So what's your story?' Poppy cried out. 'Why warn me? What do you gain from this act of mercy?'

'With luck, I get my master back from obsession.'

'And my baroness lives,' Thomas added, before releasing a tired sigh.

There was a long silence in the apartment until Poppy lit a cigarette and said, 'OK.'

Both men seemed to jump and stared at her in disbelief.

'OK?' Thomas asked.

'Sure. I'll leave. When my collection is finished.'

Thomas shook his head, and the man called Henry seemed to collapse into the chair.

'Don't despair,' she said. 'The baroness is a bitch, but I don't want her hurt. Take her away as you plan, and as for the other guy, the collector, well, we shall see.'

'Don't think about being clever,' Henry said, leaning forward in his chair. 'I won't let you harm him.'

'Come on,' Poppy said, pushing herself off the bed to stroll around the lounge. 'That is hardly my style. But I want you to stall things a little, until the collection is complete.'

'How long?' Henry said.

'Couple more months.'

'Impossible.'

'Take it or leave it. I've come too far to quit.'

There was a silence, and despite her cocky attitude Poppy held her breath until Henry spoke again. 'OK, but take more time returning the clothes. As soon as the contract is up, he wants me to grab you.'

Poppy nodded. Although frightened, she experienced a curious thrill. She had sensed there would be a price for her success and for wearing the beautiful clothing. And she had always suspected the lingerie had a spirit of its own, but, if the garments had given her freedom, then why couldn't they help her keep it? A man's obsession had unwittingly influenced her life. But an obsession was a weakness only a fool would reveal. 'It's a deal,' she said. 'I'll need two months to finish my next exhibit. After that, I stay at my own risk.'

Henry stood up and gave her a swift nod before advancing across the studio towards the door.

'I hope it works out, miss,' Thomas said, appearing beside her. 'I really do.'

'Are you coming?' Henry asked Thomas from the door.

'Not yet,' Poppy answered, and curled one finger inside the belt of his overcoat. Not only was the memory of what he had done to her in the baroness's kitchen still fresh, but the new crisis in her life had begun to excite her. 'I don't suppose you have any idea how you're going to persuade the baroness to leave?' she asked the valet.

'I am considering several options.'

'Just what I thought: you haven't a clue. I got her into this, so it's only fair I give you some advice, despite what she tried to do to me.'

'Thank you, miss,' Thomas said, smiling.

'Don't thank me yet,' she whispered. 'Danger gets me high. You have no idea what my advice entails.'

'The baroness is expecting me home within the hour,' he pleaded.

Poppy shrugged. 'I doubt your colleague will mind

waiting –' Poppy stopped herself. When she turned to direct her sarcasm at Henry, he'd gone.

Poppy took Thomas's hand and led him to the bed. 'I never thought anything in this town would surprise me, but you two have me stumped. But . . .'

'What?'

'I knew.'

'Knew what?' Thomas queried, sitting beside her.

'I knew something wasn't right. The clothes, I mean. It's hard to explain, but I always thought they had a life of their own. And in my dreams, I saw things, people, places. There was something cold about it all. Something obsessive.'

'Henry told me about the women who've worn them,' Thomas added. 'Actresses, spies, women who disappeared, or who destroyed powerful men. He said Catherine the Great and the Medici princesses wore them.'

As if suddenly awaking to find herself bedecked by the crown jewels, Poppy slid up her skirt to the tops of her knees and stared at her boots and stockings. 'No,' she whispered, and shook her head. Suddenly afraid, she unzipped a boot and yanked it off her foot. When she prepared to remove the second, Thomas moved off the bed. She paused to watch him begin pacing up and down the room, while stealing surreptitious glances at her uncovered legs.

'Are they that beautiful?' she asked him.

'You know what I am,' he said.

'Are they so important that this man you live in fear of and call a master should kidnap me? Answer me,' she said, and unhooked her long skirt, so it could no longer cling about her thighs and knees.

'Don't, please, miss. I must go, my mistress will be suspicious.'

'Damn her!'

Thomas paused and swallowed.

'Look at me,' she insisted. 'And tell me what it is I'm wearing.'

Slowly, she dropped her fur coat and began unbuttoning her blouse.

'Oh, no,' Thomas whispered, and stooped into a crouch at the sight of her corset, and the shimmering panels that provided a dark sheen across the pink of her nipples and the cream of her flesh.

'Can a man risk everything for these?' she demanded, feeling something rise inside her – like anger, or desperation, or excitement, or a combination of every powerful emotion. It was as if she suddenly understood the delight of the cold voyeur who had sent these gifts to bewitch her. A man who immediately intrigued her.

Poppy walked around Thomas so her long and shiny legs seized his attention. 'I always thought men were such strange creatures –' she pulled her transparent French knickers out from her hips '– tormenting themselves with their fetishes. But you know, Thomas, we're not that different. You see, I enjoyed wearing these and being loved in them. Can you understand that?'

Thomas nodded but stayed quiet. He seemed to be both cowering away from her and experiencing an urge to reach out and seize her.

'But are they worth everything now at stake, Thomas?' she asked, stroking her legs.

'They are only as lovely as the woman who wears them. They are only as intelligent and seductive, as innocent or cruel, as the girl who slips inside them. And you, miss, are extraordinary. I can see why a dangerous man must have you.'

'But he shan't,' she whispered, and bent down before him. She placed a crimson nail beneath his chin and raised his face, so their lips were close. 'No one shall keep me, Thomas. Some things have to be fought for, like my freedom and the respect you deserve from your mistress.'

He nodded.

She moved her mouth to his ear and said, 'Let me show you how to love her.'

It was the last act of tenderness he received from Poppy that morning. Like an irritable window dresser, trying to guide a heavy manikin into position, Poppy manoeuvred him across the room and pushed him on to the bed. As she walked across the apartment to close the door, she said, 'Poverty chased me out of London, Thomas. And now, for the first time in my life, I've done something special, with my own talent. Can I give everything up, because of one man who has become accustomed to using people as tools and devices? Like your mistress?'

'But, miss, you have to leave. You're in danger.'

'Defiance, Thomas. Sometimes you have to be defiant. To do something unexpected. To think for yourself.'

'Please, you're worrying me.'

'No, I'm helping you. You love your mistress?'

'Yes.'

'And you enjoy your subservience?'

Thomas looked at the floor.

'But there must still be a limit – a basic understanding that guarantees your future. Am I right?'

'It's impossible with her.'

'Not so. She doesn't realise just how lucky she is. Like a spoilt child she expects to have her own way. You said so yourself. Well, it's time for a revolution, Thomas.'

She stood before him, in her corset and stockings, and on his face she could see the uncertainty, fear, and indecision – a lifetime's worth of surrender. 'Sometimes it's good to surrender, Thomas. Even the baroness needs to surrender a little. And you will choose your moment and make her aware of her taste for surrender.'

'What –' He started to speak, but Poppy never allowed him to finish.

'Lie on your stomach. Go on, stretch out on the bed. Lie on your stomach,' she repeated, adding a tone of insistence to her voice.

Looking uncomfortable, but unable to deny his nature, Thomas arranged himself as she had ordered, but propped himself up with both hands as if unwilling to completely concede. With a quick and unexpected blow, she knocked his arms forward so he fell face down. 'When I ask you to do something, you do it. There isn't much time. Now, I need to think, and hurting you helps. I am sorry.'

Poppy sat beside him on the bed. 'You like to serve your

175

beautiful bitch, don't you?' she said, and watched the back of his neck colour. 'And she'd be lost without you. So be tough.'

'Oh, I can't. It's not in my nature,' he whined.

'Crap!' she spat at him and seized his wrists. After whipping his tie from around his neck, she lashed it around his hands. 'For the first time in your life, take control, like this.'

'But I can't.'

Poppy unbuckled his trousers and yanked them, and his pants, down to the top of his thighs. 'Master her,' she said to the back of his head, giving in to her delight at the man's vulnerability. 'She's waiting to meet her match, but is scared of losing control with a lowly valet.'

'You don't know how tough she is,' he cried out.

'Look at that soft white arse,' Poppy sang to herself. 'I know damn well why she has you installed in that penthouse.'

She ran to her workbench to retrieve a strap of leather. 'Imagine what she'll think when you take her, firmly. When, for once, you assert yourself. Your begging infuriates her. There are times when a woman needs strength.'

'She's too strong. She'll talk rings around me.'

Slap! Poppy's strap fell heavily against his buttocks and the end of the leather strip curled around his hips to add an extra sting. 'Be forceful. Just tell her to pack her bags.'

Slap. Slap. Slap! The strap fell in a flurry of blows and Thomas tore at the bed sheets with his teeth and began shuffling his behind from side to side. *Slap!* 'When she bawls you out, show her how you love her.' *Slap!* 'Kiss her firmly on the lips and then take her.' *Slap!*

'She'd struggle,' he moaned. 'Knock me down and throw me out.'

Slap, slap, slap! 'But you're her protector,' Poppy whispered sweetly. 'Your devotion will save her. Tell her she's a beautiful demanding bitch who you won't leave in danger.' *Slap! Slap! Slap!*

'Miss, that's so hard.'

Slap! 'It'll get harder before I take your cock.'

Overcome by the sight of the handsome and youthful body sprawled before her, now red as beet from knees to waist, Poppy had to pause and squeeze her thighs together to contain the urge to shove Thomas on his back and ride the thick member she knew he'd pressed into the bed linen.

'Will she have me?' he murmured.

'Oh yes, darling. She'll see your beauty, and loyalty, and sweetness. She'll see your passion. A mistress is nothing without a good slave. But even slaves have limits. Show her yours.'

Poppy rolled Thomas on to his back and quickly backhanded his left cheek. Then she clambered on top of him, with her long legs bent behind her, and raised her sex to hover above the tip of his phallus.

'You'll have to plant your pretty cock deep inside her,' she said as her hair fell across her pouting, sinful lips, and she lowered her sex to nuzzle his penis.

'I'll come,' Thomas gasped, and began writhing his buttocks about on the bed.

'Umm,' she purred. 'A man of your age can come over and over again, until the baroness feels faint. So how must you take her?'

'Hard,' he said with a sigh.

'Show me,' she demanded.

With a powerful thrust Thomas sheathed his penis inside her, catching her off guard and making her bite her hand from the exquisite pain. He continued to press upward with his hips until he raised her from the bed.

'Good, that's it,' she said, gasping. 'If you can make a girl feel that good with your hands tied behind your back, think what you can do when you're on top.'

Straining and panting, while every muscle on his stomach defined itself, Thomas continued to push her up and down on the bed, rifling her with a pleasure that seared and stretched her sex until she thought she would choke.

'Yes!' Poppy cried out, and dug her scarlet fingernails into his pectorals to press him down to the bed. 'Your cock is so fat,' she murmured, and blinked a tear from her eyes. 'Does your mistress like it?'

177

'She does.'

'When there's no alternative.'

Thomas said nothing but managed a groan that mystified her. Was it a result of his pleasure or agony as she reminded him of his employer's deceit? She smiled to herself and ground her hips down and across his pelvis until the lips of her sex sucked at the broad root of his phallus. 'We've got to be quick and clever, Thomas. We both do, to survive.'

'Yes.'

'Can you do it?'

'Oh yes.'

'Then fuck me,' she growled and pulled herself free of his rigidity. Thomas opened his eyes and looked at her in confusion, trying to understand why she had left him. But when she seized his hair and tugged him to the floor, he knew their pleasures were only advancing to the next stage.

'Fuck me, hard and quick. Like you did in the kitchen. Come on,' she insisted, lying on her back on a thick rug while guiding him between her thighs, steering him with feet she had clamped on either side of his waist.

Losing balance, with sweat dripping off his chin, Thomas moved into position and reinserted himself inside her sex. Poppy pulled her legs into the air and clamped her thighs together to squeeze his thickness into providing the maximum level of friction against her lips.

'That's so tight,' she gasped, and he slipped out of her twice before finding a method of pumping her while his hands were restrained. 'In,' she said with a moan. Thomas sank through her and parted her legs with his face.

Gripping her toes with her fingertips and spreading her legs, Poppy opened her lower body up to his ferocity, so he was able to lean into a thrust and then rotate his pelvis against her sex. 'Oh, harder,' she said in a high-pitched voice that dissolved into a hiss the moment he had thrust himself to the neck of her womb.

'This is what you'll do to her,' Poppy urged, closing her eyes to focus on the brutish thrusts the servant's penis made into her.

'I will,' Thomas whispered.

'And she'll love your cock like I do.'

'She'll be mine,' he said.

'Oh, this is good,' Poppy whispered. 'Sure you don't need a new mistress?'

Slowing down, the valet moved his hips in small circles, teasing the mouth to her sex. 'You'd have me?' he whispered.

'Me and a thousand others. Put it in me, Thomas. Deeper, like before.'

He slipped his shaft back and bit at her Achilles tendon. With a series of licks, he worked his mouth down her legs, tasting her stockings and the perfume she sprayed down her shins.

'You can cook, Thomas,' Poppy said, as she writhed beneath him. 'You're pretty. You have a fat cock and you always do as you're told. You're just what a modern girl needs.'

'Thank you, miss,' he said, and increased the power of his lunges.

'Now come on, fuck me, hard. Serve me, Thomas. Give me what I want, right now.'

She felt his body tense. Ejaculation was imminent and the thought of his cream spurting against her inner softness was all Poppy needed to release her grip on the world. Grunting, Thomas hammered his groin against her buttocks and the back of her thighs, sending ripples through her sex to lap around the pip of her clit.

'I'm going to come, miss,' he whispered.

Poppy fell into a climax that made her limbs feel suddenly weightless.

She felt the valet press his face against her calves and in the background, beyond her hot pleasure, she heard him whisper, 'Every last drop.'

Deep inside her, something throbbed and left a fluid warmth behind.

Poppy opened her eyes and smiled. The baroness didn't know how fortunate she was. But soon, maybe she would.

Thirteen

Little did the guests know, but they had already succumbed to the bait.

On this night, Poppy had decided to be ready for her critics; her party was to be like no other the art world had ever attended. By the time the sculptures called *Compression*, *Fraulein*, and *Highway* had been unveiled at the Daemonic Gallery, at just after eight in the evening, the spirit of Poppy's new exhibition had already infiltrated every guest's imagination. The gallery had become her chrysalis which, when allowed to mature under special conditions, would transform itself into something far more colourful.

Preparations for the new exhibition of Poppy's work had taken the gallery staff weeks to complete because of her exacting instructions for what she called the 'Carnival Party'. In time for the premier display of her three new pieces, she had wanted the largest studio on the ground floor to become an extension of her bizarre vision.

In corners, deliberately left in shadow, several couples had retired to become more intimate. Just outside the range of the spotlights well-dressed men and women began to whisper into each other's ears. Here and there, Poppy even saw the uninvited hands of certain men reach out to probe tight-skirted bottoms, or to brush across breasts uplifted and proffered by underwired corsetry.

The guest-list had been exclusive: collectors, agents, reporters, and fashion correspondents had flown in from New York, Paris, and Milan to witness the unveiling of the new exhibits from Darkling Town's unknown genius. Each female guest had dressed in a manner suiting the occasion. Leather skirts, latex dresses, dark furs, patent heels and elbow-length gloves were on parade, while the male guests appeared resplendent in tuxedos. They had arrived in a fleet of taxis and limousines and within minutes of entering the gallery a sense of wonder was etched across every face.

Champagne had been flowing since the beginning. Hors d'oeuvres, carried on trays by the nude models, hired to cater the occasion, were being greedily wolfed down. From powerful speakers a curious industrial music spanked the air and made the wine glasses shudder. A mist of dry ice, tinged with the fragrance of opium, covered the entire floor and lapped around the knees of the guests. Random red and indigo lights, attached to a lighting rig, offered spots of illumination. Ceiling-high banners of black silk covered every wall and built trenches of shadow around the studio. And placed upon the three floodlit stages, in the centre of the studio, were Poppy's new works.

This was to be a time for the dark and its secret perfumes, of unforeseen reactions and careless hands, of quick, shameful thrills and impetuous words. From her new desire to coax and control, she had lured them here and now she wanted to set them free. She wanted these pretentious, powerful, moneyed, and opinionated people to perform on the stage she'd built for them.

Compression was the first of the sculptures she had finished and it featured what appeared to be another woman experiencing an extreme of bondage, her posture frozen as if time had suddenly stopped at the moment of her climax.

With *Compression*, although the manikin's head had been covered by a veil of pink silk through which only the outline of her features were visible, most of her flesh remained naked. Even under the closest inspection, the guests were mystified by how the artist had managed to detail goose bumps on the pale flesh, while also giving the appearance of tiny hairs standing on end as if a giant shiver had passed through the submissive's body. Her breasts, featuring succulent cinnamon-brown nipples in the centre of wide aureolae, seemed to have been thrust forward in defiance. Or perhaps the strictures of her corset, reducing her waist like the centre of an hourglass to an unfeasible sixteen inches, had shifted her posture to add weight and substance to her bust. The corset had been made by black leather of a smooth texture and a shiny finish. Laces were featured at the back, and through the evil-looking eyes the stays appeared taut enough to snap. Her sex was pretty and blonde, closely cropped, and proud of its shrimp-pink lips and their slight protuberance. But what appealed to the never declining crowd of critics and fashion journalists were the figure's legs and shoes. Both of the sculpture's lower limbs had been exquisitely presented in dark stockings of such a fine denier that it was impossible to see the knit of the nylon without a magnifying glass. The eyes were drawn to the length and contour of her thighs before sweeping down her long shins to her braceleted ankles, below which her slender feet were manacled into possibly the most impractical shoes ever manufactured. The thin heels of the shoes were so high that each foot was presented in the vertical position leaving the tips of her toes poised like those of a ballerina.

Standing close to the crowd who jostled around *Compression*, Poppy heard a tall and distinguished man whisper, 'I want to make love to her,' angling his head in the direction of the statue. Beside him stood a younger red-headed girl, dressed in a smart leather suit, whom Poppy presumed was his assistant. The woman smiled and stared into the man's eyes with a look that informed Poppy their relationship went beyond the profession that brought them to the show. In a voice made richer by cigarettes and good wine, she whispered, 'But, darling, won't I do?'

He then dipped his head and whispered something Poppy didn't catch, but in response she said, 'Of course I brought them. They're in my bag.' At which he massaged one of her buttocks and angled his head towards the restrooms. Quietly, they disentangled themselves from the audience and walked hurriedly towards the adjoining annex holding the toilet facilities.

Smiling and relishing her role as voyeur, Poppy followed. Like the dreams that came and left her restless for a certain kind of touch, discomfort, or caress, her guests were proving themselves susceptible to the party that encouraged the forbidden.

After escaping the baroness, she had worked in solitude for two months to prepare the new exhibit, the very idea of which had forbade sleep and relaxation until it was complete. Desire had raged through her for the entire period as she shaped her new manikins and their props to capture her dreams and relate her experience, but not once did she venture beyond the four walls of the gallery. Food had been delivered, and her agent had arranged security from the most exclusive firm in town. Two ex-special forces soldiers had patrolled the gallery since Henry had delivered his warning. The gallery owner suspected she was suffering from extreme paranoia on account of her isolation, but Poppy was not prepared to take chances with her own freedom until the time was right.

Removing her dark glasses, she paused for a moment by the arch that led to the restrooms, looking away when the grey-haired man peeked about to assure his fiery-headed amour the coast was clear. When the onyx door to the ladies swung shut with a dulled *whump* sound, and the lovers were safely ensconced in the toilet, Poppy approached the door.

Assuming their need for each other was desperate and would require an instant satisfaction, she only waited for a minute before slipping inside the bathroom. Taking care to prevent any sound, she inched the door open, entered, and then pressed it closed behind her. Inside the bathroom were eight gleaming sinks and ten black toilet stalls separated down the middle by a tiled and reflective floor. To her satisfaction, the room was empty besides her and the lovers. Immediately, she noticed the door of one cubicle was not only locked but vibrating. Walking on the balls of her feet, so the tipped heels of her boots didn't catch the tiles, Poppy slipped inside the neighbouring stall and listened to her neighbours.

The tastes of the gentleman were savage and seemed to match those of his lover. On the other side of the black divide, above the grunts and bumping sounds, Poppy could hear the man muttering a series of strange questions. 'What are you?' he asked in a soft voice. 'Go on, tell me. Tell me.'

'A slut,' she answered, before resuming a soft and rhythmic panting sound.

'Are you sure?'

'Uh huh.'

'And is this what you like?'

'Ummm,' she moaned.

'More than anything?' he said, pressing for the extra detail he required.

'Yes, but harder. I want you to do it harder.'

'Like this,' he said, and the wall of the cubicle, which Poppy had her ear pressed against, began to shake violently.

'Oh yeah. That's it, you bastard,' the woman cried out, and there was the sudden sound of her high heels stamping on the ceramic tiles.

'You beautiful slut,' he shouted, no longer caring about the volume of his voice.

Then her cries came more quickly, became deeper, and what sounded like a set of long fingernails scraping on cold porcelain was added to the sound of their voices. 'Fuck me. Come on, fuck me. Fuck me. That's it, throw it right in, hard,' she demanded before her voice descended into a series of barking sounds. Listening intently, Poppy detected another sound: that of a chain dragging itself across a metal pipe as the woman's weight lurched and shuddered over the cistern. Smiling, she remembered the woman's hushed words about bringing 'something' in her bag.

The main door to the ladies then swung open and Poppy heard the sound of a woman's heels enter the bathroom. Immediately, the footsteps came to a stop when the visitor realised a couple were having sex over a toilet. Leaving her stall, Poppy smiled at a matronly woman who stared in

184

disbelief at the shuddering door of the cubicle containing the lovers.

'I don't believe they're actually doing it in there. This is going too far,' the woman whispered, unable to remove her eyes from the door. But Poppy just passed by, winked at her, and left the room.

Back in the exhibition studio, the situation was developing beyond the control of the guests. Their behaviour, they may have kidded themselves, was in the spirit of the unusual party, but Poppy knew those invited had already travelled some way down a slippery slope. All around her, people were pairing off and even dancing with their bodies pressed close together. Those who preferred to sit in the dark, at the sides, had done so to conceal the explorations of their hands, or the passage of their lips over the choicest parts of a partner's body. The shy and the coy stood alone, or were huddled together, nervously smoking cigarettes while glancing about at the other guests who stalked about looking for the unattached.

Before gauging the reactions of the critics around the other two sculptures, Poppy inspected the relaxation lounge. Accessible from the exhibition, a darkened room had been filled with the black leather benches from other parts of the gallery. After the furnishings had been added, the room was heated and the discreet music of female moans, procured from an erotic movie house, were filtered through the gallery announcement system. Earlier in the evening, the guests had peered inside, turned their noses up at the sounds of sex, and skittered back to the sculptures and refreshments. Now, however, the relaxation lounge had several occupants. And it was no accident that Poppy had chosen an outfit in black for the evening, while concealing her ice-blonde hair with a Jackie O-style scarf. If things went according to plan and her guests loosened up, it was unlikely that anyone in the relaxation lounge would see her drifting about.

Amongst the recorded sounds, inside the womb-like lounge, she could now detect the sounds of real and vital passion. In a far corner, she could just see the outline of a pair of white thighs, almost luminous between stocking tops and a ruffled skirt-hem, rising and falling across the unzipped lap of a man. Huddled at the end of the bench, the couple would remain anonymous because of the dark, and it appeared to Poppy that their love-making, like that of the pair who sought refuge in the restrooms, was being taken in a hurry. The woman had begun to slam and grind her backside into her lover's lap, while biting her hand to muffle her cries.

The man cried out when her nails pinched the skin of his shoulders through his dinner jacket, but his partner continued to claw him and make her strangled sobbing sounds as she was overwhelmed by the exquisite pleasure coursing through her. Determined to see more, Poppy carefully sat down on the couch and peered towards the couple. By staring hard at their movements and listening to the noises they made, she realised the man had buried his face in his partner's cleavage, where the woman's blouse had been opened and her brassière unclipped. In each of his hands, he grasped and squeezed her thighs, and succeeded in unhooking one of her suspenders so her stocking slipped down the skin of her thigh.

'Quickly,' he murmured. 'In case he comes in.'

'Shut up,' she whispered, and continued to thump herself up and down on his lap, increasing the volume of the squelches their coupling created.

'I can't get in far enough,' he said. 'The seat's too soft. Let's use the floor.'

The woman allowed herself to be lowered to the carpet, where she stretched her legs upward and placed them on her lover's shoulders.

'That's better,' he muttered, and stroked his hands down her silken legs.

'Oh yes, that's good,' she murmured. 'I can feel you right at the back of me.'

Grunting, the man began to thrust wildly between the woman's thighs, and she released a little yelp every time his pelvis squashed against her sex. They rutted, noisily, like animals on the floor, tangled in their expensive clothes, and

Poppy drank their every sound inside herself, where the noises swirled about and fanned her heat.

'I want you on all fours,' he muttered, and Poppy crossed her legs on the bench to stifle the little spasm she felt.

Turning over in the dark, the woman rearranged herself on her hands and knees. With her eyes more accustomed to the dark, Poppy could see the woman's pale back, revealed as the man's hands slipped inside her blouse. His hands gripped her shoulders and she dipped her head when he entered her.

'Got to be quick,' the man whispered.

'Fuck me thoroughly. I don't care if he comes in. It'll serve him right. You don't know what I have to put up with.'

Pumping his naked buttocks, the man began thumping against her behind and they moved forward across the floor into deeper shadow. Leaning down, Poppy continued to watch and was delighted to see the woman thrusting herself backward, determined to reach satisfaction before they were discovered.

'Harder,' she insisted. 'You don't know when we'll get another chance.'

Breathing heavily, the man began working the lower half of his body like a machine, pounding against the white softness of someone else's wife.

'Coming,' he began to gasp, and she released a little shriek of delight.

'Oh,' he moaned. 'I'm going to cream all over your panties.'

'Put your spunk on me,' she shouted, and Poppy clapped her hand across her smiling mouth.

The musk of their sex laced the air, and Poppy savoured it for a moment before moving off to watch another couple, propped against the rear wall. From their position, Poppy detected the unmistakable sounds of a woman's mouth, busy in the application of a thorough suckling.

'You – you have such a beautiful mouth,' the man stammered, and rubbed his back against the wall, as the

187

blonde bob between his thighs moved back and forth at an ever increasing speed. 'Can I come in your mouth?' he whispered.

'No,' she answered, removing her mouth from his slick tool. 'Do it in a tissue, darling. You might spill it. This dress cost two grand.'

'Fuck it,' he swore and grasped the back of her immaculate bob. 'Open your throat and I won't spill a drop.'

'George,' she shrieked, with her mouth half-full, and then tried not to laugh.

The man continued to stuff himself into her mouth and she began to purr and claw his stomach. When Poppy heard him sigh, she knew it was over. The woman's head remained between his thighs and Poppy heard the sound of her swallowing something in the dark.

Pleased, Poppy left the lounge and passed a bald man wearing a cravat, who asked passers-by if they had seen his wife. 'I'm sure she was over here,' he murmured, with a puzzled expression on his face. 'Getting a refill.'

Smoking a black Russian cigarette that sat comfortably in the long holder she held between two fingers, Poppy teetered back towards the sculptures and the thinning crowd, who had either looked at them for too long or were unable to stop staring at the strange creations.

Fraulein had been the second sculpture she'd created, using a throne entwined with thorned black vines. Upon the throne sat the figure of a woman dressed in a magnificent, floor-length mourning gown. Poppy had embellished the dress with a series of veils that stopped just above the figure's pale chin and blood-red mouth. The bosom, waist, and hips of the gown she had made from leather, and each of the woman's hands were concealed by opera-length gloves. At the front of her many skirts there were two partings which her legs poked through. At first glance there seemed to be something incongruous about the legs. The position of them, spread wide apart and thrust through an elegant gown, made a suggestion that something illicit was about to happen to the figure in the cruel chair, or it had just occurred. But under closer examination, the viewer would become aware that only one of the legs was real. One leg was tightly booted to the knee and stocking-clad to the mid-thigh area, and appeared as lifelike as a real limb, due to the refinements of the latex dummies Poppy had cast and then adapted for her sculptures. But the other leg – the right leg – was cast from a paler latex skin and, just above the knee, a discreet harness could be observed attaching the calf to the figure's thigh. The artificial leg was presented exquisitely in a black Cuban-heeled shoe. By walking around to the back of the *Fraulein*'s throne, a rack came into view, containing another four artificial legs, each shod in a beautiful shoe to suit an occasion that called for cruel heels and extra height.

There were no clues as to the identity of the individual in the chair, how she came to be an amputee, or why she had adapted her false leg to suit these shoes. A sepia-toned photograph, placed between the finger and thumb of the figure's left hand, added to the enigma. As people bent down and squinted at the photograph, they saw an image of a young Rudolph Valentino.

Before *Fraulein*, two women with matching raven-coloured bobs and clad in short latex dresses stood side by side and sipped champagne from crystal flutes pinched between their long, black nails. There names were Alicia and Kate and Poppy knew them only by reputation as the editors for a leading adult title called *Stroke* that never ceased in praising her work. Dithering beside them was a young male photographer from a leading fashion magazine who had taken a special interest in all of Poppy's sculptures to date, though none with the obvious fascination he held for *Fraulein*.

Standing back and watching the trio intently, Poppy became amused at the young man's inability to speak to the tall girls. His attraction to them was obvious, but Poppy suspected the girls frightened him. But his fear, she also knew, provided its own thrill.

After knocking back his glass of wine, the man took a deep breath and then bleated something in their direction.

Either the girls didn't hear him or they remained indifferent to his presence. He cleared his throat and spoke again. Without looking at him, the two women laughed raucously and then began whispering to each other. Grinning, the young photographer approached them and handed over what appeared to be his card. Soon all three were talking quite happily, hands were shaken, and the girls' long eyelashes fluttered before his face.

It all seemed innocent enough, but Poppy continued her observation. She was waiting for something to happen. The girls, she had heard, had extraordinary tastes. There seemed to be a bond or telepathy between the long-legged vixens that the young man failed to detect. There was something odd about their beautiful faces – something irreverent and cold. But the photographer continued to chat away, keen to impress, failing to notice the curious signals exchanged by the heavily lidded eyes before him. Slowly, the girls drew closer to the man, to encircle him and invade his space.

Walking to the other side of the sculpture, Poppy glanced past the *Fraulein* throne and lowered her eyes to the young photographer's groin. As expected, a noticeable lump pressed his dark trousers outward and each of his hands fidgeted inside his pockets. One of the girls draped her arm around his shoulder, and the other drew his attention down to her small, pale breasts, where she revealed the golden hoops hanging from each pink nipple.

Unable to contain his excitement, the man tried to kiss one of the girls who immediately pulled away. Before his embarrassment took hold, however, her partner pressed herself against him from the other side, and slung her arm about his waist where she flexed her dark talons under the red studio lights. Confused, but eager to retain their attentions, he allowed himself to be led away to a shadowy corner of the studio.

The girls worked quickly and a struggle commenced the moment the gullible photographer had been shepherded to a patch of unoccupied floor.

'No, come on. Alicia, cut it out. Someone could see us,' the man said, trying to fend the girls off with the palms of his hands. They succeeded, however, with a discreet blow to the back of his knees, in dropping him to all fours in the aromatic smoke. Each of the pretty tormentors laughed with glee, and Alicia climbed across his back and held the collar of his shirt like a horse's reins. Kate crouched down and seized his ankles.

He looked over his shoulder, past Alicia's long legs, clutching his ribcage, and had enough time to see Kate blow a kiss before she yanked his ankles backward, flattening him face down on the floor. By the time he had raised his torso into a press-up position, the fight was lost. In a sudden frenzy of activity, the two girls darted around him. They pulled his shoes off, stripped his jacket down his back to trap his arms at his sides and unbuckled his belt so his trousers hung slack around his waist.

Casually, Poppy teetered around the ambush and lit another cigarette. The young man peered up at her with a look of horror on his face, before one high-heeled foot was planted before his eyes. Breathing quickly and excitedly, the two girls continued to scurry around the photographer, kicking smoke up in long tendrils that began to resemble arms clawing for handholds.

A crowd gathered on either side of Poppy, tittering and remarking on the spectacle before them. 'The Daemonic really knows how to promote an event,' one woman said, her words slurred by drink. 'This must be an S and M sideshow.'

'But isn't that Peter from *Catwalk*?' someone added.

'Can't be,' the woman said. 'They're just actors.'

Peter was unable to plead any more, as Alicia had gagged his mouth with the velvet gloves she'd stripped from her long, pale arms, while Kate proceeded to tug his trousers off his feet. Stripped to his vest, the young man was yanked up to his knees, and his hands were securely knotted behind his back with a fishnet stocking.

While he was held fast by Alicia, who prevented him from crawling away to safety, Kate stood behind him and raised her hand to the delight of the audience. For the crime of pestering two notorious dominants, the sentence

191

was harsh. The sound produced by Kate's hand connecting with his buttocks sent shudders through the onlookers. Losing control, Kate then lapsed into a spanking frenzy and delivered a flurry of slaps to the photographer's rear end.

'Harder,' Alicia prompted. 'Give the little shit what he deserves.'

Kate complied, and bombarded his twitching rear until she was worn out.

Alicia held his red and tear-soaked face above the mist to reveal his identity to the crowd, before spreading her thighs on either side of his face and dipping her sex to hover no more than an inch from his lips. Every pair of female eyes in the audience latched on to the erection between the captive's legs.

When Alicia's unveiled sex pressed against his face, the young photographer gave up the struggle and closed his eyes. Pleased with the spanking she had meted out to the humiliated photographer, Kate reached beneath the belly of her captive and began a methodical milking of his penis.

While supping from Alicia's shaven sex, their captive responded to Kate's hand by thrusting his penis through her pale fingers. Sighing, Poppy thought the sight of the lacquered nails on an exposed phallus to be wonderful. But the beautiful image disappeared when the captive's cock became buried to the hilt inside Alicia. The giantess dropped to the floor and wriggled beneath the captive. Hooking her legs around his waist and swinging from his neck, she opened her body to his prepared and succulent meat. Immediately, the man nudged himself inside the dominatrix. Pleased with his length, she rolled her eyes back and pulled him on top of her body. Her claws raked his back and she moved her hips up and down to accommodate his frantic strokes.

Kate lowered herself and stretched her body across the man's back, crushing him against her friend. Sandwiched between the two Amazons, the captive continued to thrust until, over his shoulder, he saw the girls kissing each other. At that moment he uttered a cry and released his fluid inside Alicia.

Several of the onlookers feigned disgust but did nothing to break up the spectacle and seemed unable to remove their eyes from the enforced submission in progress. Others disappeared to the leather couches of the relaxation lounge, with people they had only just met close at heel.

As Poppy moved off to check her third sculpture, she became aware of an older man in pursuit of her. She had seen him earlier, taking excited puffs on his cigar near the third piece. Now, while remaining a few feet behind her, and taking quick sips from his drink, the man followed her back to the place where she had first seen him.

Perhaps it was her long booted legs, or the simple black silk dress she wore that caught his eye. Or maybe her dark glasses and headscarf appealed to his curiosity. But whatever struck a chord in the eager pursuer, Poppy wanted to make him perform. Once again, she felt irritated by the adoration and became aroused at the prospect of punishing a man made weak by his lust.

The sight of the ever increasing number of kissing couples in the gallery, and the glimpses of persistent hands groping their way along slender legs or inside tight dresses, served to further ignite Poppy's need for satisfaction. Flushed faces continued to flee in and out of the darkened cave-like entrance to the lounge, and the ever-present scent of arousal and consummation bombarded her from all points of the gallery's compass. Even her detractors – the critics who attempted to stem the hype surrounding her work – could be seen cornering the models who served refreshments, or made clumsy passes at their rivals. Everyone was losing control. The sights and sounds teased Poppy. It had been months since she had received the special kind of nourishment required when attired by Sheen Couture.

She had waited and watched for long enough – it was time to take a lover.

Pretending to be a curious guest, Poppy wandered over to the sculpture she'd called *Highway*. With a casual air, she walked around the long body of the black Cadillac while her admirer stayed close. Pausing by the driver's window, Poppy peered through the tinted windows at the shapes of two blonde women, wearing sunglasses and headscarves, who occupied the wide front seat. Each effigy stared forward through the windscreen. Each pretty face was calm, although perhaps a little melancholy, and the cast of their faces made it difficult for observers to guess what they were thinking. What they had tied up on the back seat of the car added another dimension of suspense to the scene.

'I could see you driving that car,' her male admirer said.

Poppy said nothing and continued to smoke.

'I mean,' he added, smiling cheekily. 'The young ladies are very stylish, like yourself, but obviously dangerous – judging by what they've done to the poor chap in the back. Who do you think he is?'

Poppy shrugged her shoulders. After a drag on her cigarette, she said, 'You think me dangerous?'

'It's an impression I had the moment I saw you.'

'And you've been looking at me for a long time,' she replied, without looking at him. Immediately, she sensed his discomfort.

'Sorry,' he said, quietly. 'I – I couldn't help myself.'

'Because you like the women driving this car.'

'I suppose.'

'And you were too afraid to speak to me?'

'Well, a little reticent. You look so cold.'

'Cold? But at the very least you had to try your luck. Because if you hadn't, you'd never have known.'

Unable to contain his excitement, the man asked, 'Known what?'

'Don't try and lead me.'

'Sorry,' he replied quickly, desperate for the conversation to continue.

Poppy turned her back on him and began to walk away.

'Wait, please. What's your name? Are you a model?'

Casually, she walked around to the other side of the car and glanced at the shape of the hooded head on the back seat. The man followed her. 'Can I get you a drink?'

'No,' she said.

'Oh,' he replied, and Poppy noticed his hands were shaking.

Her eyes were drawn down to her handiwork on the back seat of the Cadillac: the figure of a man in a black suit, contained by nylon bindings on his wrists and ankles, while his head had been concealed inside a US mail sack. It seemed that the fight had left his body. He had accepted the unknown fate the duo of icy beauties drove him towards.

'I'll leave you to it then,' her admirer said, and turned to gaze at the noisy party he seemed to have missed.

'Don't go,' she said, firmly.

'Oh,' the man said, turning on his heel and looking at her with expectation.

'Not until I've found out why you dream of being on this back seat. And others like it.'

'I don't follow,' he said, looking perturbed.

'Don't fuck with me. You know exactly what I mean. Being the captive of dangerous women. Women who'll betray you and punish you, but who you would forgive the moment they smiled in your direction. And then they'd betray you again, destroy you inside, and make you long for them until the longing becomes a pain. The most exquisite pain you ever felt.'

Speechless, the man beside her made swallowing noises and blinked his kind eyes quickly.

'Knowing all this,' Poppy said to him in a quiet and soothing voice, 'would you still accept a ride from these two girls?'

The man nodded his head and sniffed a little. 'Who are you?' he asked.

'Your driver for the evening. Now give me your hand,' she said, and took the man's hand. She liked his small round head and unassuming nature, and his inability to display himself like the others at the party. But Poppy instinctively knew he kept hidden inside him one of the most bizarre secrets in the gallery. Most of the other guests, she presumed, were trying something new – flirting with the unknown or allowing themselves a new experience

195

– but this man was here because he couldn't escape himself or the images inside his soul that her sculptures reflected back at him. It was for this man that she had made every sculpture. For those individuals who hid and nurtured the most illicit stories inside themselves, only playing these fantasies out behind closed eyes, each night when the lights went down. For his devotion to his own secrets, she would be good to him. She would be brutal.

'Come with me,' she whispered in a sweet voice and led the man to the lounge.

He began to fidget and his smile weakened. 'Perhaps we can go somewhere else. You see, I have something of a position. If people were to see us –'

'Sssh,' Poppy hissed, holding one finger to her lips as they stood outside the lounge. 'You crave the risk of exposure.'

In the dark, his forehead glistened with pebbles of moisture.

'The other guests won't see all of you,' she murmured. 'They may never be sure it was you.'

'I don't understand,' he whispered, tortured by his desire for her but terrified of the risk.

Pressed against the roundness of his belly, Poppy raised her skirt inch by inch to the peaks of her thighs. When he gasped, she smiled. 'This will be your hood,' she whispered in his ear, making sure her lips touched his skin. Then, she slithered her black French knickers down her legs. They dropped from her knees to the floor, where she stepped out of them, lowered her skirt, and then stooped down to retrieve the flimsy satin shorts.

'Wait, please,' he said.

'No. Bow your head.'

'Look here, miss, I really don't know –'

'Quick,' she hissed. 'Before they go cold.'

There was a noisy swallow from the man, a short mutter that sounded like the first line of a prayer, and then he bowed his head to receive the hood.

'That's a good fit,' she said, and shaped the waistband under his chin. 'I like the way it's tight around your face.'

His whole body seemed to be quivering as Poppy led him into the lounge. Amongst the shadows of swaying couples, the sudden flurries of drunken laughter and the occasional bursts of slapping sounds, Poppy unbuttoned the man's shirt.

'My clothes, leave them on,' he said, his voice nothing more than a whisper now.

'Quiet, or somebody will recognise your voice.'

'Can they see me?'

'It's dark, who knows,' she replied, and tugged his trousers to the ground.

'No!' he hissed into the darkness above her.

Standing up sharply, Poppy yanked him about and lashed his backside with her hand. The sound of the blow cracked through the air and several people turned to stare at the two fresh silhouettes.

'Another word will be the end of you,' she said, pressing her lips against his cheek before she encircled his erection with her hands. With the tip of his phallus touching her soft belly, she pumped his rigidity, massaging the stiffened muscles with her fingers.

'Now be smart and listen to me carefully,' she said. 'Take your shirt off now, because I want you naked, except for the hood. That's it, lift your arms up. Good. Now relax and enjoy that feeling. You're naked in a room full of people, some of whom you probably know well.'

The man sighed and moved his hips in circles to increase the friction between her long fingers and the velvet of his cock. Circling it with a tighter grip, Poppy began to spank his shaft vigorously, wondering how it would feel inside her.

'Don't come,' she whispered. 'If you do just what I say, I have a special place for your seed.'

The man gasped and his penis pulsed in the palm of her hand. Immediately, she released his erection and heard him moan with disappointment.

'Not yet,' she whispered, and then sucked his phallus clean of spillage.

'Is that chap naked?' someone said from behind Poppy, and she felt her captive's body tense.

A woman began to laugh, so Poppy licked the captive's cheek to calm his tremors.

'Oh, this is good,' he muttered.

'Then it's time for your cuffs.'

'What?'

'Sit down on the couch behind you. When I put my boots in your lap, you are to unzip them immediately and remove my stockings.'

'But –'

'Do it!'

The man dropped to the couch and she placed her first boot in position. Blinded by both the dark and his fragrant hood, the man reached up her leg and fumbled about until he found the zip. Each boot was removed clumsily while Poppy listened to his wounded breath in the dark. Slowly, each of her stockings was peeled off and she snapped them from his fingers. Then she demanded he stand.

Around them, the audience maintained a curious silence. The man complied and she turned him around and bound his wrists.

'Who are they?' someone eventually whispered, and Poppy felt a shiver pass through her captive's clammy arms.

'Now,' she said loud enough for people to hear. 'Your wrists are tied and you're naked.' She paused and waited for the whispers and sighs to die around them. 'You've done well. There's a wall nearby where I want you to do something for me.'

Poppy slipped through the lounge to the darkest corner, tugging her stumbling captive in tow. From behind them, there was a sudden sound of confusion as people tried to follow. Someone ignited a cigarette lighter to guide the way, suddenly illuminating the sight of a mature woman, on all fours, whose face bobbed in the lap of a waiter.

The distraction offered Poppy enough time to secrete her captive away in the corner.

'Did they see me?' he gasped.

'Maybe,' she answered, and found his penis to have maintained its solidity.

'Now, before I leave you –'

'What?'

'Silence, damn you.'

'Sorry.'

'Before I leave, you will perform a small favour. When I'm satisfied, I'll be gone and you'd better dress in a hurry. Your clothes will be at your feet.'

The man tried to argue but Poppy clamped her gloved hand across his mouth. Pressing her mouth to his ear, she whispered, 'I have a need for your mouth. Put it between my legs. Eat me for all you're worth.'

The man almost choked.

'If you do well,' she added, 'I may offer another favour. A special place for your cock.'

In the dark, she sensed the figure nodding his head.

'On your knees.'

The man complied and with her fingers she found and then positioned his head. After raising her skirt, Poppy stepped on to his face. Without delay, his tongue and teeth worked through the gauze of his hood. Shifting slightly, Poppy positioned her tingling clit on his top lip and front teeth. The man breathed heavily through his nose and the attentions of his plump mouth thrilled her. She threw her head back and let the heat burn through her body.

In the dark beside them, she watched the glow of a cigarette end and smelt the aroma of burning tobacco. Someone had found them, and through the dark they reached out their hands to explore. The slave between her legs tried to pull away when a strange pair of hands trailed across his snuffling head, but Poppy held him still.

Long fingernails trailed down Poppy's back and, as the mysterious figure stood no more than a few inches away from her, Poppy could smell perfume. It was a woman near them in the dark. A woman who said nothing, but who now crouched down and shaped her hands over their silhouettes to discover the exact nature of their sin.

Excited by the presence of the stranger, Poppy bucked her crotch all over the captive's hooded face, clamping her teeth shut to dampen her own squeals. Pushing down with her hips, she ground her sex against the man's face and then closed her thighs against his ears to keep his tongue working in the right place. His sucking was fastidious. Back and forth, up and down – his tongue leapt across the wet furrows of her sex. As he used the tip of his tongue to beat her clit, her breath shortened and she experienced the urge to cry out aloud.

With a gasp Poppy came and clenched her fists on his hood to maintain her balance. When the dizziness passed, she hoisted the captive to his feet and seized his shaft. 'Now, stand still and only push when I give the word.'

'OK,' he murmured, through the sticky fabric of her panties stuck to his face.

Poppy bent over before her slave. In order to satiate her need for something quick and sharp that would hurt her in a pleasing manner, she pressed her buttocks backward so his penis passed between her cheeks and touched the outside of her anus.

'Now,' she said, and took a deep breath.

She felt her eyes popping and her knees buckling as the penis sank into her. But the anonymous woman, who had been studying and stroking them in the dark, seized Poppy's shoulders so she could keep her feet.

Her captive grunted and thrust wildly, filling the air with his noisy snorts and gasps, while Poppy clutched the legs of the unknown woman, who stood before her, clawing her stockings into ladders and scratching her skin.

The captive thrust at her with all his might, reaming his shaft in and out of the spiteful madam who had taken him to heaven. She needed this violence in the most illicit entrance to her body to take the edge off her appetite. There was fire in her rectum, and a glorious sense of being stretched too far apart. Dipping a hand between her legs, she whipped her fingertips across the pip of her delight.

The slave had endured his exquisite torment for long enough. After thrusting into Poppy, until his heart was ready to give out, she let his penis slip from her anus. While he gulped at the hot air, she felt the fountain of his seed splatter across her buttocks – a warm flood she had grown to adore.

Climbing with her hands, and using the woman's dress for handholds, Poppy pulled herself upright and said 'Thank you' to the stranger, who said nothing in reply. Poppy then turned around and removed the hood and stockings from the body of the man she had vanquished. He could do little besides lean back against the wall, struggling to breathe and comprehend what Poppy had done to him. Clutching her knickers and hose in a fist, Poppy tried to sidestep the woman in order to leave the lounge. A pair of gentle hands held her still and a voice said, 'Leave him for me, please.'

Smiling in the direction of the stranger, of whom she could see no more than a faint outline, Poppy said, 'Will you be discreet?'

'Yes,' the woman said, and her tone betrayed her eagerness.

'And will you be tough?'

'For sure.'

'Then take him,' she said finally, before turning back to the man whose cream was now sticking her dress to her thighs. 'Listen,' she whispered to him, fingering his damp face in the dark. 'This is the night of your dreams. I may be done with you, but there is another woman here who wants you. Maybe she knows you. Maybe she's a rival, because I think she followed us in here.'

'Who?' he stammered.

'I have no idea, but I've offered you to her and she's accepted.'

'But can I see you again?'

'No,' she replied, and left him questioning the dark as a new shadow approached his corner.

Poppy left the lounge with a broad smile on her face. Around her the shadows continued to stumble, whisper, giggle, and clasp at each other.

'Poppy!' the gallery owner shrieked, racing towards her. 'They're having sex!'

'Who?' she said, calmly.

'The guests. What shall we do?'

'Let them decide in the morning. After all, they are the media.'

'The scandal could work in our favour. I mean some of these people are award winners and look at them.'

'The only things I'll ever expose will be in sculpture. You know my rules. Stick to them.'

The gallery owner continued to babble at her, but Poppy no longer heard him. From across the room, the sudden appearance of Henry had captured her attention.

He stood watching her – his face impassive, his hands sunk within the pockets of a long overcoat – waiting for her to move towards him. She followed him to the corridor outside the main gallery.

'Already?' she asked.

The man nodded his head, and his well-groomed hair shone even beneath the dim lights.

'There's nothing I can do?' she said.

'Nope. Leaving is the only option. If you stay, I'll follow my orders.'

It was the end for her if she didn't run. But her work wasn't finished. There had to be one final portrait for the gallery – something to reach further than its predecessors.

'How much time do I have?'

'Tomorrow, you'll receive the last package from Sheen Couture. Then the contract is up and you're free for as long as it takes me to find you. If I delay for more than a week, he'll become suspicious. I'm sorry.'

'I should be impressed by your loyalty to this man, but I'm just finding it inconvenient.'

For the first time since she had met the strange messenger, he smiled.

Her art was the key, then. If her assailant thought it belonged to him, and she was merely the key to his vision – a tool or pet he could keep – then through her art there must be a way to defeat him.

'I may be insane,' she said. 'But I'm going to need every hour of my last week to work.'

Pulling on his cigarette, the man thought on what she'd said. 'I like you, kid, but one week after the last package is delivered to you, I'll be back. Have a good, long think before attempting to try anything funny. Nobody has ever gone one better than my boss, and I don't expect they ever shall. Especially when it comes to his collection.'

Henry dropped his cigarette on the floor, ground it out beneath his boot, and walked away.

Poppy leant back against the wall and a smile crept across her face. This was a good feeling inside her: the feeling she got when standing close to the edge.

Fourteen

The baroness was home, and the moment of reconciliation or farewell had arrived. He could hear the sound of her high heels on the marble floor downstairs. She would be irritable, no doubt, after taking a risky excursion outside the apartment.

Thomas stood with his eyes closed in the baroness's bedchamber, mentally preparing himself for the confrontation. On the bed, behind him, were her cases. The moment she'd left the apartment that morning, he'd begun packing. His own belongings had fitted neatly into one box and, even though he had been ruthless with what he would allow her to take in the car, two large cases and one steamer trunk were full of her 'necessities' and stacked beside the bed.

He took several deep breaths and assured himself he could be firm. Poppy was right: pleading would be of no use. When the baroness saw the baggage there would be fireworks and then, for the first time in his life, he would have to be assertive.

Out in the vastness of the apartment, Thomas could hear the footsteps of his mistress drawing closer. Since he had allowed Poppy to go free, relations between him and the baroness had been restricted to that of the silent servant and the indifferent employer. It was as if she was no longer even aware of his existence. But tonight she would be.

Click, clack, click, clack! The snap of her heels on the wooden floor out in the hallway, like the sound of approaching gunfire, tightened every muscle along his spine, and he felt dizzy as the blood seemed to suddenly evacuate the top half of his body.

'Incoming,' he muttered, and then swallowed.

There was a glimpse of her shadow and then she appeared in the doorway of her chamber. Behind the lenses of her sunglasses he was aware of her eyes moving from the cases to the steamer trunk. It was hard to read her face because her crimson lips remained stiff. Perhaps the fine lines at the side of her mouth deepened. To his delight, she had failed to erase the creases with surgery. They made her face colder and he liked that.

A long silence followed between them and it was only broken when he cleared his throat and said, 'We're leaving today.'

And it was all he said; all he was capable of saying.

She angled her head towards him but said nothing and the silence resumed. She walked into the room and began a casual inspection of her portraits and sculptures. While he watched her, the layer of perspiration covering his back began to feel uncomfortable.

'Leaving, you say?' she asked distractedly, while fingering a marble bust of a young poet she once knew in the days of the circuit, with its horse races, parties, and summers, before the politics of the world had changed.

'Yes, ma'am.'

'Today?' she murmured, keeping her back to him.

'Yes.'

'Know why I hired you?' she asked, after a pause.

Thomas swallowed and the baroness turned to face him.

'Because you reminded me of Rupert,' she said, and rapped her lacquered nails on the head of the bust. 'And of all the other young men who adored me. But I suppose even you, my favourite, had to change and disappoint me. It will be hard to find a suitable replacement.' She paused and removed her sunglasses. 'I want you gone by the time I've finished afternoon tea.'

'No,' he replied. 'No, we leave together or not at all.'

Slowly, she raised her face. 'Have you been at the

brandy? It's a bit of a cliché for hired help, don't you think? Do you forget to whom it is you speak?'

'Enough,' he said, and then listened to the echo his voice made in his ears. It didn't sound like him – it was forceful.

'I'll have you removed,' she said, and marched to the telephone beside her bed.

Thomas followed her, gripped the wire and then yanked it free from the wall socket.

Her hands began to shake. 'Then I shall remove you myself.' Her voice was low, hard, and seemed to press against something inside him, a weakness he'd have to fight.

'There is a price on your head,' he said quickly. 'Soon, Rilke's valet will enter the apartment and take you on a little journey. A car ride you will not return from. So listen carefully. Yesterday I received intelligence from a reliable source that you are to be removed –'

'You lie,' she snapped at him.

'Take a peek through the chink in the curtains and tell me who owns the car parked outside. It's been there all morning. Ever since your cab pulled up, I'd guess the driver has been making his final preparations. Putting on his gloves and loading your one-way ticket.'

Walking quickly, the baroness crossed the room and glanced through the curtains. He watched her shoulders stiffen and then she stepped away from the window. 'He wouldn't dare,' she muttered.

'He already has. We'll go to my parents' cottage on the coast until this mess has cleared up. It will be resolved – and soon, I hope. You see, the sculptress has become an ally.'

'Poppy?' the baroness asked, turning quickly.

'I think she has a plan for the master.'

'I must help her then; it's time that frozen bastard thawed out. Get the car.'

'No!'

The baroness stopped and her body stiffened. 'Raise your voice to me again, boy, and –'

'And what? You'll sling me out, or thrash me raw? I

think not. I'll get the car ready and when we leave we head in the opposite direction from another of your futile fancies. Poppy would rather you stayed away.'

'Bastard!' she screamed, and covered the ground between them in a heartbeat. Her blows fell from the left and right and his world slowed down. Instinctively, he wanted to revel in the assault. The slaps from her gloved hands stung his cheeks; he was thrilled at the sight of her raven hair pulling free from the tight bun on the back of her small head, and at hearing the soft grunts she made as she swung her hands. But this was not a time for self-indulgence; he had to protect the spiteful, cruel, and beautiful woman he loved.

By snatching a hand out, he managed to catch her right wrist. He pulled her towards him and spun her around, clamping his arms around her chest to trap her arms at her side. Then, for a moment, he paused, dumbfounded by the realisation that he had touched the baroness without permission. This is your mistress! the voice of panic shrieked inside him.

His momentary hesitation was all she needed. A sharp pain razored down the length of his left shin. She had scraped the heel of her slingback down the front of his leg. Crying out in pain, he felt his grip loosen. With a triumphant squeal, she broke his arms apart and, before he could react, snatched a hand out, seized his ear and then twisted her fingers. Wincing from the pain, he was manoeuvred down to the floor where the baroness made sure his eyes could not avoid a close view of her stocking-clad legs. 'Look, boy,' he heard her say in a voice trembling with emotion. 'Did you forget how good these heels feel on your spineless back? Kiss them. Kiss them now. Kiss them for the last time before I throw you in the street.'

Thomas kissed her long shins and slender ankles. He passed his tongue along the top of her feet and, inside his neatly pressed trousers, he felt his erection thicken and pulse. Breathing out hard, he fought the desire to submit – to submit beneath her blows and frightening voice. He fought the desire to surrender to her power.

Uninvited, he slid his hands up the rear of her calves before gripping the warm cleft behind her knees. For a moment he buried his face in the soft nylon-covered flesh of her lower thighs and vowed never to stop his worship of this woman.

'Did you forget how good it was? How much it hurts? How the fever starts, boy?' she said, smiling down at him.

'I'll never forget, ma'am. I'll never stop needing you and loving you, cooking for you, cleaning for you, and obeying you.' Through his tears he saw her smile, and above the rushing sound in his ears he heard her sigh. 'But,' he continued, 'you will have to forgive this role reversal, ma'am. For once, you'll do as I say because we really should leave very soon.'

'You shit,' she said through closed teeth, and drew one leg back to deliver a kick. Thomas twisted his ear free of her pinch, seized her around the back of her thighs and hoisted her from the floor. She rained a flurry of blows on his shoulders and the top of his head, but he continued walking in a straight line until he reached the bed.

'Now,' he said, glowering down at her after depositing her on the mattress. 'Will you come freely, or must I restrain you for the duration of the journey, ma'am?'

'Restrain me?' she roared, and with the speed of a cornered animal she stabbed the heel of one shoe out towards his stomach. But this time, Thomas was ready. He countered the lunge by seizing her ankle and turning it in his hands until she was forced to roll on to her front where she began an undignified floundering on her belly.

'Stop this madness!' she screamed over her shoulder, but Thomas just pulled her tight-fitting shoes off her feet in order to disarm her. Without the high heels, her stature seemed to diminish and he felt stronger – strong enough to whip two binding cords from his trouser pockets and wrap one around her ankles.

Realising it was his intention to tie her down, the baroness began to squirm her body about and to thrash her fists back at him. When her slippery ankles were about to pull free of his moist grip, Thomas compensated by

208

sitting on her behind, with his back to her horrified face, and tugged her feet towards him in order to bind them together.

'Stop!' she bawled, and the stream of insults that followed only served to caress and arouse him to the point when he was sure he would faint if relief didn't arrive soon. Working quickly he bound her legs together by circling the cord around her ankles until there were two short ends left over for the knot. Soon, the powerful weapons of her kicking legs were made safe.

Leaping off her body, Thomas then clambered up the bed holding the remaining cord for her hands. When he readied himself to snatch her wrists, their eyes met and they stared at each other in silence – as if each of them struggled to comprehend the turn of events.

'How dare you?' she said.

'It's for your own good, ma'am, so you'll live to strike me another day. I'm sure you'll make me pay for this, and I can assure you I'll be ready to pay penance for what I've done. But in the meantime, please stop struggling. We have to be out the moment it gets dark. It'll be harder for them to follow us then.'

Thomas approached the baroness and was surprised when she allowed him to take one of her hands. When he reached for the other, however, she twisted on to her back and fisted a hand into his hair. In a flash, his tear-soaked face was buried in the duvet. Behind, on the bed, he heard her struggle to her knees. While holding his head down with one hand, he guessed she was desperately picking at the cord around her ankles with her free hand. The mattress kept dipping around his face and she was swearing under her breath in between the little hissing noises that rose from the back of her throat.

Thomas felt his patience run dry.

Thrusting his arms forward, he seized her waist and pulled her down to the bed where a desperate wrestle ensued. They rolled the length of the bed as she scratched, clawed and spat at him. He was able to do little other than deflect some of her blows, and ended up beneath her

209

amongst the mountain of pillows. When the fight came to a halt, their fingers were intertwined and his body had been pressed into the mattress by her tight shape. Her lips were no more than an inch from his and he could smell the quick minty gusts of her breath as she used all her strength to hold him still.

Thomas pressed his groin forward. Unable to keep his powerful rigidity still, he began to rub his erection against her stomach. From beneath the pale skin of her throat, he heard her swallow, and in her ocean-blue eyes he saw the signs of another struggle – a conflict between anger and desire.

'No,' she muttered. 'I won't.' But her words were futile and she offered no resistance when his lips welded with hers.

For a while she fought his gentle kisses and the swishes of his tongue by keeping her lips shut, but then she opened her mouth and called him a 'bastard' before losing control. While her long nails clawed at his face and her thin teeth bit into his mouth, she began to pant and thrust her corseted belly against his crotch.

Thomas slid his hands around her waist and began massaging her buttocks. From her tightly packaged backside, his fingers fumbled up her body to her breasts. And there, after so many years in servitude, he took this pleasure without permission or prompt. And if he wasn't mistaken, his touch was delighting her. She purred through her long nose, swept her tongue through his mouth and continued to rub the tight triangle of her sex against the lump in his crumpled trousers.

'Don't,' she whispered when he ran his hands up and down the silky, black blouse she wore. 'No, stop it,' she murmured as he kissed her neck and gently sucked her earlobes.

'I won't stop,' he said, and rolled over so her body was squashed beneath him. 'I will have you. And then I will save you.'

'Have me?' she murmured, and her eyes seemed to have misted over, as if the magnitude of his disobedience and the force of her own arousal had rendered her powerless.

Thomas could no longer hold back; he had to confess everything. 'I must have you, ma'am. You're destroying me,' he said, and ripped her blouse open to uncover the treasure of her pale skin and silk brassière. 'I think of no one but you,' he added, and rolled her on to her side to unzip the side of her pencil-skirt. 'And without you I am nothing. I won't let anyone take you away.'

The baroness bit one of her fingers and closed her eyes as he slipped her skirt and slip over her bound ankles.

'I worship you; I adore you, and I want to preserve everything we have.' He sat back on his heels and stared at her scarcely clothed body, lying still before him. 'But if you don't want my help, I'll leave now. I can't force you to want me.'

'No,' she said quickly, and turned her face away from him. 'Stay.'

Smiling, he began to stroke her legs and work his way up her slender limbs until he was able to dip his face and lap the inside of her thighs. Her stiff body became soft beneath him and he felt her fingers slip, and not tear, through his hair.

'Am I really in danger?' she asked in a childlike voice.

'Yes,' he said, and felt her skin shiver when he kissed the softness of her navel.

'You care that much?' she whispered, and her words were spoken with difficulty.

Thomas murmured his assent and began an assertive sucking on each of her hard nipples.

'But what of my affairs?' she whispered.

'I love you for them.'

'Boy?' she whispered, and stretched out her legs between his thighs so she could rub his erection with her thighs.

'Yes, ma'am.'

'Untie me then.'

'No.'

'But you love me.'

'I do, but you're a snake. An evil, black snake.'

'You bastard,' she hissed, but never struck out at him or did anything other than stroke his head as he tugged at her nipples with his teeth.

211

'What will you do to me?' she asked.

Thomas looked up at her and saw that her eyes were closed, and her beautiful head had begun to move from side to side in the thick folds of the bed linen.

'It is my intention to pleasure myself thoroughly,' he said, and his throat tightened and threatened to kill his voice. This was the strongest desire he had ever experienced for anyone – a lust that made him feel dizzy and desperate to bury his manhood, quickly and savagely, inside the beauty beneath him.

'You have the impertinence to use me?' she asked, with her eyes still closed, while she pressed and rubbed at her breasts.

'Yes, I need to take you. I'm going to lift your legs in the air. And then . . . and then I will fuck you.'

She bit her fingers and screwed up her eyes even tighter. Thomas smiled, raised her legs and placed her bound ankles on one of his shoulders. She trembled and he shuffled his crotch against her buttocks. Slowly, he pulled her sheer panties to one side and unzipped himself.

'Look how wet you are,' he whispered.

'No,' she whispered.

'Yes,' he said, and caressed her hips and buttocks while licking at her ankles – wanting to taste and then devour every part of the woman who had made him a slave. 'I'd like to spend an age with my mouth between your legs, ma'am, but there just isn't time. It'll have to be fast and deep.'

'Do it,' she whispered.

Without further delay, he slipped his shaft completely inside her tight sex in one motion. Immediately, her red claws seized the bed linen and her cold face became a portrait of insatiable lasciviousness. 'Take me,' she demanded, and pushed herself down the bed as if there were more of him to take inside her body. Thomas pressed his face against the rear of her calves and withdrew his shaft back to her shallows before plunging it through her depths.

'Feels so good,' she said, and her voice trembled as if she were on the verge of tears. 'I don't deserve this.'

'You do,' he said with a gasp. 'In my own way, I'm as corrupt as you. And that's why we belong together.'

Groaning, the baroness rolled her eyes back and raised her body off the bed to accommodate the rhythm of his quickening thrusts. It must have been a long time, he realised, since she had indulged herself. The time for his coup was perfect. Since Poppy's escape, the endless procession of younger lovers from her circuit had stopped. There had been no more invitations to private gatherings, and she had been forsaken by the cult she'd founded. Now, at last, she might realise who had always been there for her.

'Yes,' he repeated with every pump, delighting in the moist and yet tight glove his employer had at last provided. 'Yes, my beautiful bitch.'

'Say it again, louder,' she ordered, raising her buttocks even higher off the bed to feel a fuller impact from his groin jabs.

'My beautiful bitch, I'll do anything for you. I want to fuck you for ever,' he said, breathless, and pressed the long and bound legs down to her face.

'Oh, I like that. Be a brute, boy.'

'Yes, my bitch, my beautiful, demanding bitch.'

'But my appetites,' she said, her face flushed, her mouth willing to go further than ever before. 'What of my appetite for other men?'

Thomas clenched the muscles at the back of his cock to prevent the climax he desperately wanted to unleash. 'You'll always come back to me. Always. Because if you don't I'll have to assert my rights.'

The baroness began to claw the back of her own legs, starting a running ladder close to the seam of her stockings. 'Take me then. Make me yours, boy. Make me all yours.'

Her lips stretched back across her teeth and he heard her mouth begin to issue a series of strangled sounds. She was coming. She was coming because he had made her his own. Thomas roared the word 'Yes!' into the warm bedroom air and experienced an orgasm that blinded him for a few seconds.

213

'All of it,' his mistress squealed. 'Put all of it in me.'

And he obeyed. Planting his groin hard against her sex, while gripping her thighs until his fingertips left bruises on her skin, he held her against him until every last drop was sealed inside his lover's sex.

'Quiet,' he whispered, as he crept through the unlit carport buried beneath the baroness's apartment. 'They could be outside,' he warned, and swallowed his desire to shout with triumph at having secured the prize of his life. But the pretence of danger had to be maintained. He was late for his rendezvous with Henry and there was still a fight to be staged.

She wriggled against his back and complained about the pointed bones in the shoulder he had thrown her over. In response he slapped her soft backside, still covered in nothing but her damp panties. He had told her there wasn't time for her to dress and threw an overcoat over her scantily clad body to keep her warm for the journey.

His mistress was bound hand and foot. After they had made love, she never asked him again to remove the bonds from her ankles, and she even willingly offered her wrists for the second restraint. It was the adventure, he knew, that excited her. Something new and thrilling for his insatiable mistress to experience. She had never been mastered by one of her own servants, let alone rescued from an assassination attempt, and despite her complaints, as he carried her down through the apartment to the car, there had been many signs from her that she was delighted by the whole evening. Never had she been the centre of such dramatic attention, and he made a resolution to surprise her in the future with similar escapades.

Carefully, he lowered his mistress on to the wide rear seat of the car, so her head rested against the cases he had been unable to fit in the boot, or on the roof. 'There,' he whispered. 'Now be still and do not move or speak until I say so. We're most vulnerable once the garage door is open. If Rilke's men see us trying to escape, there'll be trouble.'

'They have guns,' she said. 'I don't want us hurt.'

Thomas looked away to kill the grin that crept about the corners of his mouth. 'No one will risk a shot. It could draw the attention of the neighbours or one of the private security patrols. We'll be OK. Trust me.'

'Thomas!' she hissed. 'Be careful.'

'Sssh,' he said, before leaning down to kiss her. Her lips responded to his kiss, and before he pulled his face away she slipped her tongue inside his mouth.

He covered her face with the fur coat and eased the rear door of the car shut before creeping to the control panel on the garage door. Beside the panel he flicked the outside security light on and off to alert Henry. Peering through a small observation window, he saw Henry appear at the top of the driveway and extinguish his cigarette underfoot. He was ready. Thomas punched the code into the keypad and the garage doors began to open.

'She's sitting up on the back seat,' Henry whispered, as he trotted down the drive towards Thomas. 'Better make this look good.'

Something hard connected with the bone of Thomas's forehead, and his world turned dark red. When Thomas regained his senses, he was staring at the garage ceiling. Henry crouched down beside him and made the pretence of slapping a magazine inside his pistol handle.

'Why so bloody hard?' Thomas whispered.

'Barely touched you,' Henry murmured through a smile. 'Now remember, when I start walking towards the car, you jump up and hit me over the back of the head. Got the cosh stashed?'

'Yeah, and it'd serve you right if I filled it with billiard balls.'

Henry smiled and then stood up to begin his slow approach to the car, with his gun clasped against his side. Imagining the paroxysm of terror the baroness must be enduring as the silent killer approached, Thomas covered his mouth and pulled his lips down to halt another smile. Maybe it could look like a demoniac grin, he thought, and rose to a crouch behind Henry's back. From the inside of his jacket, he pulled out a sock filled with a handful of small cooking onions and followed Henry.

The moment his friend leant over to squint through one of the rear side windows of the car, Thomas slapped the sock down hard, across the back of Henry's skull.

'Shit,' he heard his friend whisper, as he fell, rolled to the side and fired off one round, as planned, into a wooden skirting board. The sound of the pistol shot, however, was deafening in the confined space and Thomas clapped both hands over his ears. From inside the car, he heard the baroness shriek.

Wasting no time, Thomas ran to the driver's door, yanked it open and clambered inside. He gunned the motor, and the car tore out of the garage and on to the street.

'Are you shot?' the baroness whimpered from the back seat.

'Stay down,' he muttered, as his jaw began to ache from the effort of suppressing yet another grin. 'We've done it, ma'am.'

She began to sob with relief. 'Thomas, you could have been killed. I don't deserve you.'

'You can pay me back in your own good time, ma'am.'

'I will, I will. I promise you,' she urged and he heard her begin to sniff.

As he joined a carriageway that would take them to the city limits and the motorway beyond, Thomas began to dream of her Italian stiletto sandals, and the wonderful marks they left on his stomach.

She stayed silent in the rear of the car for at least an hour, which surprised him; he could only suppose she had much to consider about their future. But, as a testament to their bizarre relationship, she did something that made him suspect her of clairvoyance.

He heard the baroness say, 'Enjoy them while you drive.' Before he could turn and question her meaning, she had passed her feet, clad in patent, slingback heels, over the front seat to rest beside his cheek. Smiling, with one hand on the wheel, Thomas unzipped his trousers and took a heel into his mouth.

Fifteen

There was something final about the day. Everything around Poppy suggested a conclusion to her journey. The last parcel from Sheen Couture lay on the bed, still unopened one week after its delivery, and in the centre of her studio the last sculpture for her collection was cushioned within a long wooden crate, open-topped and awaiting the pine lid and steel nails.

Sipping her coffee and smoking the first exhilarating cigarette of the day, she sat by her window and watched the pale yellow sun rise above the black and spiky buildings of Darkling Town. Very soon, she would leave the cobbles, eerie monuments and dark lanes of this town. Where she would go was a mystery, but somewhere, beyond the city, she would start again. But before she left there was one final lover and one last destination she felt compelled to visit.

And this time, she would direct the last scene herself. She would take control of the strange adventure and finish what the cold stranger had begun when he selected her to be the object of his desire. Desperation had forced her to apply for the Sheen Couture test and now desperation would force her to end it. Someone had changed her life and art by sending her the most beautiful but dangerous flowers through the post – dark flowers with see-through petals to adorn her body. Now, the time had come to meet this mentor and master. One last adventure and then the odyssey would be over.

Since Henry's final warning at the Carnival party, she

had slept for less than a few hours a night and stayed indoors the whole time to finish the final piece. It was a sculpture she had spent seven nights and days working on. Something she hoped the world would see, but there were no guarantees. It might end up trapped in a place she had been told was very cold – locked away with her in a private collection.

This model was not to be delivered to the Daemonic Gallery but to a private address. A place she had followed Henry to after he'd visited the PO Box, to collect what was to be her last package – the final set of garments she should have worn for the cold voyeur. But she had sealed something else in a plastic wallet, designed to preserve the freshness of her cast-offs. There would be a surprise at the other end when the last package was given by Henry to his employer. There would probably be a great deal of mystification too, and then disappointment when the clothing was seen to be missing. But the master wouldn't have to wait long for the last set of garments. She would deliver them in person, later, on this final day.

Crossing her room carrying a scalpel, Poppy sat on the bed beside the last component in the Sheen Couture fraud. She cut the string and tape and opened the top of the box. A cheque, rewarding her for the completion of the contract, sat on the top of the box's contents. Ignoring the money, Poppy dug through layers of pink tissue paper and found the last set of clothes.

Besides the hosiery – one pair of sheer and seamed stockings – the underwear differed from anything delivered in the past. Leather, silk, gossamer and satin were no longer in evidence. Instead, she was to wear fur. Both the panties and the bra had been made from fur – the softest and most delicate black fur, crafted seamlessly around a fine leather framework. The knee-length boots had been manufactured from a heavier leather that proved exceptionally supple and shiny despite the sturdiness of their manufacture. Here were the portents to remind her of the final act: fur to keep her warm and strong boots to protect her feet. It was as if she were close to something cold enough to freeze her life.

Poppy showered quickly and relished the thick streams of hot water for as long as time permitted, before she fixed her hair and coated her face with a lavish make-over. Over her new underwear, she wore a black woollen dress that hugged her body from knee to throat, and completed her outfit with a headscarf and black fur coat.

Once dressed and scented, she picked up her phone and called the courier firm who usually delivered her work to the Gallery. Only this time, she gave the operator instructions for a crate to be picked up from inside her unlocked apartment. No, she wouldn't be at home, she told the operator, but the delivery men were to pull the door shut behind them. Then she gave the operator the name of the street and the number of the apartment to which the crate must be delivered.

When she had finished imparting the instructions, and after the operator read them back to her, Poppy hung up the phone, lit a cigarette and turned about to smile at the rectangular crate that housed the last masterpiece in her collection.

'Fetch her,' Eliot said. 'Bring her here. Don't delay, Henry. Get her for me.'

Standing in the doorway of his study, dressed in nothing but his green silk robe, Eliot appeared to have suffered a shock.

'Sir?' Henry asked.

'Look,' Eliot said, pointing at the surface of his desk. 'She knows.'

Holding his breath, Henry approached his master. Shredded all over the smooth surface of his desk was Poppy's last parcel – the one he had just collected that should have been filled with her last set of Sheen Couture garments. But this time, the package had been returned from the sculptress with an alternative content. There were no ripped panties or crumpled bras or satin slips enlivened by pearly stains. Instead, she had sent a bunch of dried roses – black, thorn-encrusted roses with brittle petals.

'How?' Eliot asked as he stared down at his open hands.

'The baroness must have warned Poppy, before I dealt with her.'

'But why flowers? Dead flowers. No note, or angry letter about being duped. She never went to the authorities. Why?'

Henry stayed quiet and silently prayed Poppy was well beyond the city limits.

'If this gets out, we're ruined,' Eliot said, and began running his fingers through his hair. 'Get her, Henry. Right away. I need to think, to be alone. Please go now, and take the boys.'

'Yes, sir,' Henry replied, and sped towards the front door, while the two excited Dobermans leapt after his ankles.

At the sound of a mighty bell chime, Eliot stopped his incessant pacing around his study. There was someone at the front door of the apartment.

It wouldn't be his followers; they would never disturb him without an appointment, and the commissionaire, stationed in the lobby of the building, knew better than to allow a salesman access to the apartment. And it couldn't be Henry – he was still searching for Poppy.

Still clutching the dead roses, Eliot made his way through the apartment to the front door and peered through the spyhole. Two men, accompanied by the chubby commissionaire, stood in the corridor outside. Eliot felt his throat dry. Could they be police? Had Nin divulged his intentions to kidnap Poppy before Henry put an end to her? After a second look through the spyhole, however, he realised the men weren't wearing police uniforms. Instead they wore the blue shirts and peaked caps of the manual worker.

Eliot pressed the intercom buzzer. 'Yes,' he said. The sound of his voice buzzed loudly in the corridor outside, startling all three men, who stepped away from the door.

The commissionaire approached the receiver on the panel outside the door. 'Mr Rilke, forgive the intrusion, but these men have a delivery for you. Only Henry didn't tell me to expect anything, and this thing is huge and must have your signature. I had no other option. It's from a Ms Poppy Stanton.'

Eliot's agitated mind and body became immediately still. How could this be? After returning flowers instead of the lingerie, she had now sent a gift, a large gift, to his home. Which meant she knew where he lived. Eliot swallowed and wiped at his brow.

'What shall I do, sir?' the commissionaire asked.

Despite his immediate vulnerability, he had no choice. Without Henry to go outside and inspect for traps, the door would have to be opened for a short time – with the danger of temperature contamination – but Eliot's curiosity about anything connected to Poppy allayed his anxiety. 'I'll open the door. You must bring the delivery inside and then go. Do you understand?'

With his eye still pressed to the spyhole, Eliot watched the men wheel a large rectangular packing crate, made from pine, before the door. A sculpture! He began to feel dizzy with excitement. What could it mean? She approved of the experiment?

As quick as he was able, Eliot released the seals on the airtight door with a wheel lever. 'Quickly!' he implored the delivery men, as he reeled away from the gust of warm air hovering at the entrance of his retreat. The delivery men wheeled the crate indoors and then released it from the trolley.

'Go!' Eliot roared at them, and the commissionaire ushered the delivery men back outside by pushing at them with his hands. 'Sorry, sir,' he muttered over his shoulder, but the sudden slamming of the door killed his apologetic cries. Eliot then resealed the apartment against the wretched warmth of the outside world.

For a while, he did nothing but walk around the crate, fingering the wood. It was bigger than a wardrobe. A free gift, perhaps, offered to the mysterious benefactor who had changed her life. Unable to wait for Henry's return, Eliot rushed to the utility room and seized a crowbar.

After a deep breath, he levered the top of the crate free

and peered at a sea of straw. Casting it aside, his hand passed across something hard and smooth. Peering through the dry packing, he could see something black and reflective buried deep in the crate, like onyx or a laminated ceramic. In a sudden frenzy of destruction, he wrenched the sides and end pieces of the crate to the floor and watched the straw packing spill over the splintered wood.

It seemed to be some kind of sarcophagus or coffin, mounted on four small feet shaped like claws and made from brass. Without a visible seal between top and bottom halves, he began to wonder how to gain access to the strange man-sized capsule. It was a sinister-looking thing, but not without its own morbid appeal. After walking around the curious lozenge-shaped creation, he began to find it quite beautiful. The finish was smooth and mirrored, and every corner had been rounded. Eliot ran his long fingers over the lid, searching for a catch or lock. At the side, a few inches down from the top, he found a tiny keyhole. But where was the key? He had to have it immediately. The real prize must be inside.

Taped to the underside of the strange container he saw a pink envelope, which he ripped free and tore open, catching a small golden key before it fell to the floor. Restraining the shakes in his hands, Eliot thrust the key into the lock.

The key turned silently and he stood back at the sound of a click inside. Before his eyes, the lid began to rise. There must have been a motor inside, because he heard a muted whining sound as the lid rose to a vertical position.

There was no further sound or suggestion of movement from within. Leaning forward, he took a quick glance inside the casket and then stepped back in a hurry. It had been filled to the brim with something black.

Eliot crept back towards his strange gift and touched its soft contents. A distinctive fragrance reached his nose. It was her scent – Poppy's perfume – an aroma he had briefly sampled from her other postal offerings. Dipping his fingers deeper inside the casket, he scooped up a flimsy brassière and inspected it as it hung from his middle finger.

Eliot slipped his fingers back inside to find more treasure. Another exploratory search unearthed a wispy pair of black panties. Something rejoiced inside him as the realisation hit home: Poppy had sent him a beautiful sarcophagus filled with a sea of black and fragile nothingness for his pleasure. She had not just sanctioned his private passion but blessed it with the most wonderful gift. This was a sculpture made in honour of his desire.

Suddenly, something within the casket clutched three of his fingers. With a yell, Eliot tried to free his hand, but his fingers were held fast. The surface began to ripple with movement and something white and spider-like broke through, attached to the fingers he was unable to pull free.

It was a hand. A long, elegant hand with blood-red fingernails.

Before he was able to react, a tall girl sat upright in the casket. Dripping with lace and nylon, she turned her head and smiled at him. Eliot fell against the wall.

'Are you the man they call master?' she asked, and plucked a garter belt from the side of her headscarf, as if it were a small, annoying jellyfish.

He stayed mute with shock.

'Are you the man from my dreams? Who enchanted my life?'

'Can't be true,' he muttered.

'Well, are you?' she asked in a coquettish voice, and removed her dark glasses.

'Poppy,' he whispered, recognising her eyes in a heartbeat. He slid down the wall until he sat on the floor, like a poet before his darkest muse. 'Poppy,' he repeated.

'Are you surprised to see me? It was my destiny after all,' she said, and her beautiful lips parted to reveal the perfect teeth he had never seen before.

Stunned to silence, Eliot watched Poppy ease herself to her feet, stretch, and then climb out of the casket. 'The guinea pig is here to confront the scientist,' she said, still smiling.

Once on the floor of the reception, she moved gracefully towards him wearing the last pair of leather boots. As she

223

bent down to offer him a hand, her long dress parted and the lure of a shapely kneecap flashed before his eyes.

Slowly, Eliot rose to his own magnificent height. 'Why,' he said at last, 'have you come to me like this?'

'Is it not what we both wanted?' she said, still smiling. 'You coaxed me out of the shadows and have studied every one of the indiscretions your gifts encouraged. And I guessed it wouldn't be long before you began to hunt me too, so I saved you the trouble. Your spy is very good, but I have seen him from time to time, watching me. I realised Sheen Couture, the spy and the anonymous bidder for my work must all have been connected to someone – you.'

'But the casket. You could have suffocated.'

'No, there is ventilation. Besides,' she added as an afterthought, 'haven't I learnt to pleasure myself in times of crisis?'

Eliot smiled, still clutching the hand she had offered in support. 'The cold? You're freezing already.'

'No,' she replied. 'I refrigerated the sarcophagus to acclimatise to your world.'

Overwhelmed by how much she knew, Eliot was lost for words.

'I dreamt about you,' she said, softly. 'I knew about the cold, and I knew there was a connoisseur behind Sheen Couture. A collector.'

'Dreams,' he stammered. 'Dreams . . . But how?'

The smile on Poppy's face died. 'You have no idea what these clothes have done to me. They told me all about you when I slept. When I slept the sleep of the exhausted.'

It's impossible, Eliot thought. But the *Fraulein* piece had been an image of the widow – the most loyal member of the cult. 'The *Fraulein*,' he whispered. 'You saw her too.'

'Yes, she is also a part of your world.'

She walked up to him and kissed his cheek. Close to his ear, she began to whisper words from his own dreams. A strange dialogue he had always imagined flowing from between her lips. 'Show me your world,' the girl said. 'Now that you've opened my eyes, I want to know why they call you the master.'

* * *

Stripped to her boots and underwear, Poppy forced all thoughts of the freezing temperature from her mind. She did not expect to be cold for long.

She had deliberately goaded Eliot straight away – deciding to work fast in case Henry came home. And the master had been unable to resist her. Despite her fear, she had to play the submissive for him. It was the only role he would accept.

She had found herself led into the sinister mirrored annex where she disrobed on command. Then his massive hands had manacled her limbs into a quartet of steel cuffs that hung from a wall hook. Now, she awaited his next move.

Behind her, she heard him re-enter the chamber after leaving her to 'attend to something important'. She could hear the squeak of his shoes as he crept back and forth, admiring the prize, perhaps still disbelieving his eyes at the sight of her, prepared to his taste and willing to submit. A silk bandanna had been wrapped around her mouth, but the rest of her had been left uncovered and stretched into a large starshape, to open her up and reveal her in her entirety. In the fogged mirror panel a few feet in front of her eyes she could see the outline of his black shape, crouching down to study every inch of her skin – its texture and colour – before it became hidden by the sheen of her stockings, the shine of her boots and the pelt of her underwear.

'You are so beautiful,' he whispered, and she turned her head to look at him. Immediately, she caught her breath.

He had covered his tall and rangy physique with a smart dinner jacket and trousers, white shirt and bow tie, as if he were about to attend the opera, but the sight of his face made the hair stand upright on the back of her neck. A skintight rubber mask clung to his face and head. Of his real features, only his eyes and whipping tongue were visible through the shiny skin. There was something both unnerving and exciting about his hood. It was the rubber moving over his mouth when he grinned, the red rims of his staring eyes, and the continual flicking of the long tongue, that made Poppy shiver with an obscene pleasure.

225

In one hand he carried a case which he laid on the floor and then unlatched the lid. Carefully, he withdrew a black rod and unwrapped several long straps from it. By moving her limbs as much as she was able and clenching her fists over the steel cuffs, Poppy braced herself for the passion of this fiend whom she had tortured for every minute of every day, month after month.

She relished the anguish of anticipation. This was how it had been in the beginning when she dressed for brutal strangers. She remembered it with a glorious sense of shame. She would assume the role again and completely surrender, and he would see she had learnt to fear no limit or danger. He was a tyrant – a manipulator and a destroyer of lives – but her curiosity, and her appetite, and the plan she brought with her, demanded she experience him. His love would be fierce. Perhaps harder than any other lover in the city, but after their bodies became entwined both of their long and dangerous journeys would be over. He didn't know it yet, but this was the end – an end to their experiments, and their collections, and the adventures they learnt to love. Maybe he suspected her arrival to be a final struggle for power: a battle of wills that would leave one victor. Or maybe he thought he had already won.

His rubber-slicked face brushed across her naked shoulders, kissed her pale back and sniffed at her hair – like an animal enjoying the exquisite moment before it fed and tasted the salt and rust of fresh blood.

When her neck suffered a series of small bites, she dropped her head back so her long hair fell across him, exposing her throat for the kill. Never had he found such a perfect sacrifice. His quick breaths, washing across her collar-bone, warned her of his eagerness, which pleased her.

Cold fingers gripped her backside. Hard fingertips dug into the flesh beneath her furs, and an incredible strength raised her from the floor until the chains around her ankles became taut.

'I want to eat every piece of you,' he whispered, and

gently lowered her back down to the floor, as if he were only flexing his muscles to fight the urge to explode. That wouldn't be his style; he would be thorough and would prolong his pleasure for hours before collapsing into ejaculation. And Poppy was ready for him. It was just a matter of who mastered who first.

The pain came quickly.

There seemed to be a crack of streak lightning behind her which ricocheted off every wall. It stung across the back of her thighs and licked inside her legs to touch the skin beneath her fur panties. The next two lashes struck no more than an inch above and below the first hot ribbon of pain. Poppy flew forward in her restraints, her thoughts dissolving until she existed in a realm of pure feeling. Cold air numbed the edge of the thin welts, while fresh lines were drawn across the whiteness of her buttocks as the lash continued to fall with precision. The chains on her ankles pulled her legs apart, and her sex moistened in readiness for a length she wished to enclose inside her body.

The master danced behind her and struck from near and far – mapping her vulnerability and softness with his wicked instrument, exploring the shudder of each buttock, the bend of each knee, the stamp of each high heel upon the wet tiles. Each tensed muscle and thrust of her head, every gasp and sigh, every single moment of her willing immersion into torment delighted him. With the tip of the whip, he nicked and licked her body from every angle, electrifying her with a pain that soon became a warm lather over her smooth complexion.

His breathing had become ragged and his voice desperate. 'I have to show you my pain,' he said. 'The longing to inflict my love on you hurts, Poppy. It is love. Understand . . . the strongest love you will ever feel.'

'Then take me,' she said, her voice strong.

She sensed him hesitate. He was mystified by such a request so soon after the flogging. But she knew he was too aroused to question her further or to prevent his hands from gliding between her buttocks, to ready her.

'Pleasure after pain?' he asked.

'Rough pleasure,' she said, smiling through her tears. 'To make me sleep on my side.'

'Beside me?' he said, with a harder tone to his voice.

'Maybe.'

'You have someone else?'

Poppy never answered, but made sure her eyes were full of deceit.

'I'll make you mine,' he whispered, and the whip was forsaken for the skill of his touch. Her panties were pulled down to stretch wide around her thighs, and the dew on her outer lips became frost. His fingers found her sex and his red tongue slipped through the mask to probe her anus. From torture, he melted her body into pleasure. Wave after wave of ecstasy rippled through her as expert fingers massaged the delights inside her honey-blonde thatch.

Moaning, Poppy stood on tiptoe, trying to escape the exquisite sensation of a pointed tongue exploring the rim of her anus while deft fingers rubbed her clitoral bud, creating a shower of sparks on her lips and a tremor through the roots of her womb.

'You made me suffer, girl,' he said.

'Good. I wanted you to be desperate for me.'

'I would have waited for this,' he whispered, and slipped three fingers inside to tickle the walls of her sex. 'Once you were here, I was prepared to wait.'

'I've learnt to be an opportunist. I work fast and take my pleasure quickly.'

'I know,' he replied, before scurrying around her to suck the moisture from the lips of her sex.

Feeling faint, she called him a 'bastard' and climaxed.

After her sobs subsided, he freed her from the chains and carried her to the centre of the chamber. She was laid upon the cold floor, where she watched him rustle with a fresh set of chains above her head. He picked her up from the tiles and slipped her chest and arms into a leather harness. There was the sound of a chain creaking through a pulley and her arms were pulled together and upward. Slowly, she was raised from the floor, until her heels dangled several inches from the tiles.

Through the leather struts of the harness, the rubber face

228

of this devil kissed the fur of her brassière. Then he hummed and the sound vibrated against the pebbles of her nipples before he unhooked her bra and his red mouth fed with a bestial appetite on the sweetness of her breasts.

'Be hard with them,' she moaned, and tried to squeeze her thighs together. Without further prompt, his feeding became savage. He crammed his mouth and hands with her breasts, biting, sucking and pinching the sensitive skin. She felt herself passing into a swoon as he stretched her nipples from each breast to grind them between his incisors.

'So many have passed through here,' she said with difficulty. 'But you've never found the right one.'

'No,' he muttered and fell to his knees to smother her tattooed navel with kisses and licks.

'But isn't perfection a mirage?' she asked. 'Isn't the greatest force in life a burning dissatisfaction that can move mountains but never find perfection?'

'But I have heaven now,' the hooded giant said, and then slipped his face between her thighs. Unable to control herself, Poppy raised her legs and draped them over his shoulders. His tongue immediately busied itself with the most tender regions of her sex. For an age, he performed miracles between her legs, sustaining the gentle beat of his tongue against her clit, before offering a hint of penetration by stabbing his long tongue inside her. His mouth guided her to release, and Poppy began to sob from the delight of being taken in this cold and dangerous place. When he fell back, his rubber face was wet around the lips.

From pleasure to pain, the cycle continued.

With a flat paddle, he belaboured her striped buttocks with even strokes to tenderise it a little further, until she could no longer feel any pain, only warmth. Poppy felt faint and it seemed like hours were passing, measured by the methodical strokes of his weapon against her softness. He clamped her nipples and left a circlet of love bites around her waist – one inch above her garter belt. But every bite thrilled her, and every whack from the paddle sent a vibration through her womb to lap around the desperate hunger that lived there. A hunger for conquest.

It was as if he wanted to devour her all at once. She could see the lust and greed shining in his eyes. Unable to control his gluttony, he wanted to completely consume her, digest her, understand her, demystify the woman who had filled his cold life with longing.

When the black figure next appeared before her, he unleashed a long and pale erection. Her thighs were gripped and she found herself poised at the right level for penetration. 'At last,' he said. 'At last our affair will be consummated.'

'It's been a long time since you seduced me into all this,' she replied, in a whisper.

'And now you have a true master?'

Poppy growled, and threw her head back saying neither yes nor no. As if to coax a confession from her, he made sure his entry inside her was slow. Immediately, his cold clashed with her warmth, but something inside her ached for his pillar of ice to reach into her furthest extremes. She felt dizzy from the pleasure of capture, punishment and enforced entry, silently vowing to show him her own talents for this kind of loving.

He began to withdraw and then slip back inside her – each thrust quicker than its predecessor – and Poppy prepared herself for the crescendo. Go on, pleasure yourself, give me pain and love, she wanted to say. Stretch my nerves and thresholds until they snap. And then I'll stretch you until you feel the most exquisite ache, for ever.

Soon his noisy thrusts made her swing back and forth in the harness, and through the slits in his mask she could see his eyes misting over, as he adored her body and admired the contortions his lovemaking had brought to her face. While her body shook in the harness, Poppy heard her own moans turn into croaks. She kicked and then pedalled her legs in the air as the master continued to plunder her sex, harder and harder with every thrust. The sounds of passion filled the air, and the heat they produced erupted into clouds of steam from each of their mouths.

His thrusts became more ruthless, and she thought the size of his shaft moving at such a speed would make her pass out. She began to shriek, unable to form words with her mouth. But, with her animal sounds, she unveiled the basest of her own desires and pushed him to his limit. After three deep, slower lunges, the master's body stiffened. Something thick and cold erupted inside her sex and triggered a climax so strong that when it subsided nothing but fatigue remained inside her.

A part of Poppy that had once perspired beneath so many lovers now cried out and swore fidelity to his savagery. It was as if, for this climactic moment, she would not and could not wish for anything more from a lover. This was an endurance test in hell, but also a glimpse of something divine.

'For ever, Poppy,' he whispered, through the long and ragged breaths he sucked into his body. 'These pleasures are for ever.'

Remaining still and compliant in his arms, she was freed from the harness. Unable to feel her legs from the cold, he carried her from the tiled annex and through long corridors to a lavish bedroom. She felt his large hands wrap her in a thick, fur robe and then lay her on a warm bed.

'Hayworth wore these furs,' he whispered. 'And now they are yours. Rest now and I shall come for you again, very soon.'

After he had kissed her forehead and tucked the robe beneath her chin, she watched him leave the chamber, unsteady on his feet from the exertion and heat of their coupling. Once out of the room, he closed the doors and locked them.

Did he think it was her destiny to be kept like a rare bird in a gilded cage? Like the baroness, the master had tried to disguise a prison cell. The bed dwarfed her long proportions. The walls had been papered with silk. Tables and dressers had been covered with liqueurs and French scents. Roses filled gigantic vases, and thick rugs the colour of blood were laid from east to west in order to conceal the icy marble floor.

Wrapped in Hayworth's furs, Poppy climbed from the bed and began to admire the furnishings and gifts. It came as no surprise when she uncovered an exotic array of undergarments that not even a princess would have been able to wear in one lifetime. And then there were the dresses – beautiful evening gowns in emerald, ruby, sapphire, and onyx, fashioned from satins, silks and leather. One entire walk-in wardrobe was dedicated to high-heeled footwear, housing every style of boot and stiletto and sandal from Europe's most exclusive designers. Stocked carefully and exhaustively with every luxury she could want, this was the royal bedchamber of a queen – his queen, the woman of his dreams and future. It was here he hoped to install a companion to thaw the cold and solitude.

Some things could not be bought. Now it was her turn to show him what she had learnt on the outside of his freezing cave. She wanted to leave a lasting mark on the warlord. It was time to end her journey.

Despite the cold, she stripped quickly and showered, soothing a pine soap over the marks his lust had left upon her body. Then she repaired her hair and repainted her face before selecting a long fur-fringed gown. Knowing he hadn't stopped thinking about the final set of Sheen Couture garments, she placed the black furs and stockings in her handbag, understanding her presentation of them would have to be made at a crucial moment. They were still the key to defeating the master.

Although excited by this final adventure, she knew it was vital to maintain some level of indifference towards him. What she had learnt as a seductress, in both submissive and dominant roles, would have to be used tactically. If she continued to appear too willing then he would be suspicious, and if she became too contrary he would probably resort to using confinement and punishment until she offered obedience. Balance was everything.

As if she were under observation, the door to her chamber opened the moment she'd finished dressing. Eliot entered her room and offered Poppy his arm. 'Dinner is ready when you want to eat. You must keep your strength up. Until you're used to the cold, the low temperatures can be debilitating to the constitution.'

'The room is beautiful,' she said. 'For whom was it prepared?'

'The woman of my dreams,' Eliot replied, and he led her through a long corridor where the walls were adorned with a collection of lingerie, all presented behind glass.

'So this is your collection?' she asked.

'Part of it. It's expanded into the dining room and I began to worry about space, but now I don't need to.'

'You have everything you want?'

'Yes, thanks to you.'

'Are my clothes to go up there?'

Eliot chuckled. 'No. I have no intention of displaying those to anyone but us.'

'Why?'

Eliot cleared his throat, and she could see he wanted to speak, or perhaps confess something. Instead he asked her a question. 'Do you find this distasteful?'

'Not at all.'

Eliot smiled and stopped before a glass case in which a pink negligée, fringed with white lace, had been shaped around a busty female torso made from clear perspex. At the base of the case, a brass plaque read 'Jayne Mansfield'.

'My tastes are rather eclectic, but I'm pleased you approve.' Eliot turned to face her, taking both of her hands. 'I always knew you were special, Poppy. That you'd understand me. I knew the moment I saw your eyes in the photograph.'

'Thank you,' she said, sweetly. 'And my own tastes are hardly conventional.'

'Quite,' he said, smiling. 'But I still have so much to show you. Your journey has only just begun.'

Poppy lowered her face. 'Of course, but can I see my clothes? It was hard to let them go. They became a part of me, a second skin.' She raised her face and stared into his eyes. 'They allowed me to be another woman. Can I see them again, now?'

233

'Right away? But what about dinner?'

'Dinner can wait. Curiosity forced me to smuggle myself into your apartment, locked inside a sculpture. A sculpture I made for my old clothes, a beautiful home for them. I have to see where my underwear has gone. I want to see my old friends, and then, maybe, I can tell you about where they took me, and whom they took me to.'

He swallowed hard, and his fingers trembled against her hands. He pulled her against his body and kissed her mouth, fiercely. 'This is why I need you here. If you hadn't come willingly, I would have taken you.'

'I know,' she whispered. 'You need me to tell you the stories. So much of my journey is etched on the clothing – rips, tears, stains, and scents. But you need more – names, dates, times, places. This is why I came, because I owe you so much. I want to repay the debt with the stories behind my sculptures. Your experiment worked. The clothes gave me the inspiration to create something fresh and to be corrupt, deliciously corrupt as only a woman could be in those clothes. And now you have the clothes, and have outbid everyone for the sculptures, you want the artist to tell you her secrets.'

Eliot was trembling, stunned at how much she had intuited.

'Come,' he said, and whisked her through the apartment. She followed him, clutching his cold hand, and glanced about her in amazement at the artefacts in his collection. There were gowns on headless manikins, slips on marble hips, corsets laced around wooden busts, and marble legs coated in famous stockings. These were the rags he collected, discarded by the beautiful and the adored. She saw how they had been straightened and presented, brought back from the dead and allowed to flirt again under soft lights.

'They're ghosts,' he said, panting. 'Like me. I gave them a home. This is the only place they'll be looked after and loved.'

'You're mad,' she said, laughing.

'We're the same, Poppy. It's why you belong here.'

234

But you collect the dead, she wanted to say, and hide in the dark like a spider surrounded by the husks of your beautiful, helpless victims.

'Beside my bed. All your clothes are there,' Eliot said, as they entered his dour, book-lined bedchamber. 'In here,' he said excitedly, and pointed at a large alloy trunk. It was wide enough for two people and topped with a heavy lid to keep them there. 'I've stored them here and waited for the last set – the furs you wore for me today. When they were all here with me, I planned to go down in the dark and surround myself with you and your lovers. I would have used my imagination as a beacon to light me through your passions. All of your passions, from the loving to the savage. But now you're here, I have a narrator.'

'But it must be christened first,' Poppy said, and smiled at him – the smile she gave her lovers when she wanted them to realise they would make love with her. 'Put them all in the sarcophagus. That's why I made it. For you and the tokens that were peeled from my body, by so many people after they had loved me.'

'You beautiful slut,' he whispered, and hugged her until she had difficulty breathing. 'A man could never forget you. Never let you go. Do you hear?'

Poppy closed her eyes. Without answering Eliot, she freed an arm and fished the last set of garments from her bag. 'This is the last story, right here,' she said, and held them under her chin. 'A story about two people who knew so much about each other without ever having met. Two people who communicated in dreams. Let's take all the undergarments to my sculpture and put them together.'

Eliot smiled. 'It'll be easy. They're nearly all still sealed in plastic. Little of your freshness has escaped. I wouldn't allow myself to tamper with them until the end.'

'Your a genius,' she said, in all sincerity.

'And your sculpture is as beautiful and sinister as the whole venture. I could sleep in it for ever.'

Standing across from Eliot, Poppy watched him empty the plastic bags containing her Sheen Couture cast-offs into the black sarcophagus. First, he emptied it of those garments she had arrived with – the cheap imitations she'd used to conceal herself. Then, he poured the Sheen Couture treasures inside. She could see the passion of a zealot in his eyes as he tore the seals and scattered the fluttering garments into the tomb she had made for him. When his ritual was complete, every stocking, brassière, corset, shoe, slip and pair of French knickers was inside the casket.

Poppy raised her face to him. Without a word or a smile, she unhooked her fur coat and let it fall to the floor. Next, she slipped the thin straps of her gown off her shoulders so it fell from her pale, goose-pimpled flesh to join the coat on the marble tiles. She stood before the master wearing nothing besides her high heels, stockings and a thin suspender belt. She pushed her breasts forward and then stepped to the side of the casket. Slowly, she extended her hand towards him. 'Will you lie with me?'

The master's lips moved but no words were forthcoming. Poppy smiled and carefully placed a leg inside the casket, so her heel sank through the sea of crumpled lingerie.

'Together?' he said, his voice no more than a rasp.

She nodded and wet her lips.

At first, his fingers fumbled with the buttons of his shirt, but then the movement of his hands sped up and in a fit of impatience he ripped his shirt open to reveal the bird-egg blue of his skin beneath. Her smile broadened. Eliot yanked his shoes from his feet, wrenched the jacket off his back and kicked his trousers across the floor.

'You first,' she said, narrowing her eyes. 'My behind is a little tender after your welcome.'

Slowly, he climbed over the side of the sarcophagus and curled his body around her leg, placing both hands on her slippery ankle. His long body settled into the softness of the soiled lingerie and a sigh escaped from his lips. Between his sinewy thighs, his long erection quivered in expectation.

'Lie on your back,' she whispered, and Eliot obeyed.

Poppy swung her other leg over the side and eased her body down into a crouch. With her glinting heels gripping either side of his hips, she moved her body up and down above the purple tip of his phallus, touching it with her lips before withdrawing it. His hands shot out and grasped her legs where they began an insistent tugging and pawing at her stockings. 'Now,' he hissed at her, moving his head from side to side in the casket and inhaling deeply.

She smiled and seized her tongue between her front teeth.

'Now,' he pleaded.

She reached for one of his hands and removed it from her leg to slip two of his fingers inside her mouth. Below her, she watched him writhe. With her eyes closed she sucked the length of his fingers slowly, drawing them in and out of her soft lips. His hips began to gyrate beneath her and she rubbed her dewy labia across the tip of his phallus and watched the muscles tense across his stomach.

'Now,' he repeated, his voice becoming urgent.

Poppy scooped a pair of French knickers from the base of the casket and held them up to the light where they shone. After slipping her hand inside the weightless shorts, she placed the hand over the master's face. He coughed and tried to move his head to one side. Poppy pressed her hand down hard and felt his nose, snug in her palm. Eliot stopped struggling and clutched her nylon-encased hand to his face. When she saw his chest inflate, she sat down and let his erection fill her.

One hand pressed into his face, she clawed his broad, hairless chest with her free hand and used the strength in her thighs to rise and fall on his cock. It stretched her wide and reached further inside her than before, because now gravity aided its tight passage through her.

Closing her eyes, Poppy pumped her body up and down on the master's penis, taking her pleasure, her final pleasure in Darkling Town. She hated him for playing god, but desired him for being a devil. 'Make me come, you cold-hearted fuck,' she swore at him. In response, he held her hand tighter across his face.

'Use me,' she said, and then gritted her teeth as he raised his buttocks and skewered her to the hilt.

'That's it,' she said with a groan. Slowly, she disentangled her hand from his face and left him clutching the panties across his nose and mouth. A sense of victory passed through her, complemented by the action of the thick cock inside her. Bouncing up and down, Poppy tore at her nipples and thought of her lovers in Darkling Town. She saw every face from her corrupt history and felt every sensation on her body: the heat and cold, the pain and delight. There had been so much experience, but now she would seek love.

'Were there many?' he asked, without uncovering his face.

'More than you know,' she replied. 'From the baroness –' she paused to watch him flinch '– who took my arse, to the strangers I just picked up.'

'Were they hard with you?'

'Brutal.'

Eliot released a sigh and began throwing his pelvis into her so hard her quick breaths were turned into yelps. His breathing grew hoarse and he seized her hips to hold her down while he ground himself against her sex.

'I want to know about them all,' he whispered.

'You will, when you're lying in the dark with the silks that have hugged my pussy, and the nylons from my legs, and satin from my bruised nipples. You'll have all the time in the world to taste my passion and breathe in my lovers.'

Leaning forward, she knocked his hands from her hips to take control. She seized his waist and tailored his penetration to suit her need for satisfaction. Now she could take him deeply and move her hips in little jerking motions so the friction spread from the base of his pillar to antagonise her clitoris. She bumped and squashed the little pip against him, moving and angling her body until she felt herself coming. 'I'll leave you with my ghosts, Eliot. I'll let you keep the souvenirs, but I won't let you keep me.'

As he groaned and the muscles in his shaft pumped against the walls of her sex, Poppy climaxed and gripped the sides of the sarcophagus to prevent herself from collapsing. After the last spasm in his shaft registered against the walls of her sex, and she felt the final cool splash of his seed inside, Poppy stood up. She looked at him briefly and then leapt from the casket. Eliot opened his eyes and said, 'No.' But it was too late. Before he could move, she shut him inside the seventh sculpture.

Epilogue

'Dana, is that a man in there?' Tina asked.

'Yes, he just moved,' Dana replied, unable to break her gaze from the sculpture. Apparently, it was the last one in the bizarre collection that had caused such a stir in the morning papers. The final piece was called *Oubliette*.

Dana and Tina had queued with hundreds of people outside the Daemonic to see the final addition to the notorious work of the still unknown artist. And everyone had been shocked the moment they saw the tall man, half-concealed beneath a layer of lingerie, inside the strange coffin.

At first, the girls had thought it to be another of the lifelike manikins featured in the other sculptures, but then people claimed to have seen the figure move.

'Did he really move? Damn, I missed it,' Tina said. 'If he is real I suppose he can breathe. Oh yes, look, he just moved his arm. That's amazing. I think he's trying to cover his face. Look, with his hand, he just pulled that . . . what is that?'

'A bra, I think,' Dana whispered, leaning over the sarcophagus, but then the red lights above the casket went out. 'Damn' she said. 'We'll have to wait for them to come on again. It takes about ten minutes.'

'I don't think he wants to be recognised,' Tina muttered.

'Nonsense, it's all part of the show. It's not as if he's trapped in there. It's all part of the artist's plan. I think it's a wonderful idea to combine sculpture with performance art. I mean, even though he's just lying there, he's made the exhibit come to life.'

'Still, I wouldn't fancy it myself. Imagine lying in there, covered in women's underwear while hundreds of people troop past and stare at you.'

'But it challenges our expectations and that's a good thing.'

'Oh don't be so highbrow; you're starting to sound like that critic over there, the French guy giving the tour.'

'Let's get a quick drink from the cafe,' Dana said, shrugging off her friend's teasing. 'I'm sick of all these people pushing. They're so rude, especially that prick in the overcoat. Look, he just shoved that guy. You'd think he was trying to save his friend or something. We can come back later when the lights have reset.'

'OK,' Tina agreed, and followed her friend through the crowd to the gallery restaurant. Immediately, other people shuffled forward to take their places and wait for the lights. Everyone wanted to look at the man inside the *Oubliette*.

NEXUS NEW BOOKS

To be published in May 2006

WHAT HAPPENS TO BAD GIRLS
Penny Birch

Natasha has escaped the troubles and pressures of modern life by retreating to the Channel Isles, where she plans a life of uninterrupted debauchery. A dream come true: to be liberated in a place where nobody can curtail her many pleasures. But, she hasn't reckoned with the locals, who are more assertive than she bargained for. Nor did she count on the possibility of her past catching up with her in the shape of the obsessively perverse Aaron Pensler.

£6.99   ISBN 0 352 34031 2

DOMINANT
Felix Baron

When he was still a teen, Cole met Vanessa: a girl with a voracious appetite for correctional punishment. Confused by his own dark desires, Cole suppressed his sadistic impulses and led an unfulfilling vanilla life. Until Kate. A ravenous redhead who craved discipline and yearned to be restrained. It seemed he'd found his perfect mate, until she demanded more than he was willing to inflict.

Female desire, he decided, could never be underestimated. Whether a girl was naïve, like Nurse Margaret, or a cynical sophisticate, like Melinda, if a man discovered their dark side and indulged it to satisfaction, they belonged to him thereafter. But Cole's oath – to never feel for any woman – is threatened the moment he is asked to mentor Lana. A girl who wields the ultimate feminine weapon – absolute undemanding surrender.

£6.99   ISBN 0 352 34044 4

BUSTY
Tom King

Busty is a collection of original short stories and confessions from both women and men, collected specially for those in love with women's breasts. This salacious body of work has been edited by a genuine enthusiast, drawing on extensive experience and an unashamed obsession with full breasts, from the pleasingly womanly to the down right gigantic.

This is not only an epic journey to the heights of breast worship, but the third book in the new Nexus Enthusiast imprint: an original series that will explore and tantalise the reader with the most highly detailed fetish literature actually written by genuine enthusiasts for genuine enthusiasts. It's as kinky as fiction can get!

£6.99   ISBN 0 352 34032 0

If you would like more information about Nexus titles, please visit our website at www.nexus-books.co.uk, or send a stamped addressed envelope to:

Nexus, Thames Wharf Studios,
Rainville Road, London W6 9HA

NEXUS BACKLIST

This information is correct at time of printing. For up-to-date information, please visit our website at www.nexus-books.co.uk

All books are priced at £6.99 unless another price is given.

ABANDONED ALICE	Adriana Arden 0 352 33969 1	☐
ALICE IN CHAINS	Adriana Arden 0 352 33908 X	☐
AMAZON SLAVE	Lisette Ashton 0 352 33916 0	☐
ANGEL	Lindsay Gordon 0 352 34009 6	☐
AQUA DOMINATION	William Doughty 0 352 34020 7	☐
THE ART OF CORRECTION	Tara Black 0 352 33895 4	☐
THE ART OF SURRENDER	Madeline Bastinado 0 352 34013 4	☐
AT THE END OF HER TETHER	G.C. Scott 0 352 33857 1	☐
BELINDA BARES UP	Yolanda Celbridge 0 352 33926 8	☐
BENCH MARKS	Tara Black 0 352 33797 4	☐
BINDING PROMISES	G.C. Scott 0 352 34014 2	☐
THE BLACK GARTER	Lisette Ashton 0 352 33919 5	☐
THE BLACK MASQUE	Lisette Ashton 0 352 33977 2	☐
THE BLACK ROOM	Lisette Ashton 0 352 33914 4	☐
THE BLACK WIDOW	Lisette Ashton 0 352 33973 X	☐

------ ✂ -----------------------------

Please send me the books I have ticked above.

Name   ....

Address   ....

  ....

  ....

  .... Post code ....

Send to: **Virgin Books Cash Sales, Thames Wharf Studios, Rainville Road, London W6 9HA**

US customers: for prices and details of how to order books for delivery by mail, call 1-800-343-4499.

Please enclose a cheque or postal order, made payable to **Nexus Books Ltd**, to the value of the books you have ordered plus postage and packing costs as follows:
  UK and BFPO – £1.00 for the first book, 50p for each subsequent book.
  Overseas (including Republic of Ireland) – £2.00 for the first book, £1.00 for each subsequent book.

If you would prefer to pay by VISA, ACCESS/MASTERCARD, AMEX, DINERS CLUB or SWITCH, please write your card number and expiry date here:

....

Please allow up to 28 days for delivery.

Signature   ....

Our privacy policy

We will not disclose information you supply us to any other parties. We will not disclose any information which identifies you personally to any person without your express consent.

From time to time we may send out information about Nexus books and special offers. Please tick here if you do *not* wish to receive Nexus information.   ☐

------ ✂ -----------------------------